In honour of my dominant yet gracious Master,
who taught me to know myself and granted me permission
to tell my story of self discovery as a testament to His teaching.

NEED

By
Francesca Anderssen

A powerful story of love and romance,
interwoven with domination and submission

Don't break the rules, leave them behind where they will be safe
H.G.Wells

My story is told in three linked books, compiled here into a single volume.
Every chapter is a short story in itself,
recounting a stage in my progress towards the
ultimate destiny of ownership by my Master.
In the interests of concise narration, the timeline has been condensed

****

I hope you enjoy this Romantic Bondage novel; I've tried to write something a little different. Comments to tell me whether you like it (or not) would be appreciated; that helps me to tailor my writing to fit the inclinations of my readers.
Permission is given to quote from my work, provided due reference is made to source.

You might also like my book of BDSM verse, also available on Amazon http://www.amazon.co.uk/dp/B00VU4CPCG/
A few poems from that book are included at the end of this book

WARNING
BDSM activity can be dangerous. It is a skill that must be learned, like any other.
Lack of experience can be rectified
But volatility or discourtesy cannot and reflect a dangerous personality. Avoid.
BDSM is about giving, not selfish taking.
Activities described in this book are written for entertainment purposes only,
do not attempt to replicate them.
Remember, Safe Sane and Consensual, always.

****

Table of Contents
Introduction

A few poems from my book of BDSM Verse:

Introduction

"Why do I write? I write because I have to, because it is all I know, because it is my truth, because I am compelled, because I am driven to make theworld acknowledge that women like me exist, and we possess a dangerous wisdom."
— *Pat Califia*

Sexual arousal and pleasure inextricably entwined with a need of erotic torture and suffering is the eternal paradox of a submissive masochist like me. But I had known only thoughtless abuse and ineptitude from men, who did not understand that my need to suffer must be counterbalanced by the gift of care and an awareness of what I am.

I sought a dominant man who could feed the vortex of my emotions, but despaired of finding someone who not only had a power I could fear and could deliver the measured cruelty demanded by my alter ego, but who knew how to love me with the tenderness I needed. Seeking to yield everything to a man masterful enough to command my obedience, I had only found the extremes: men too weak to deal with my submission and frightened of my intense sexuality; or overwhelmingly self obsessed control freaks, wanting to crush every aspect of my life, mind body and soul.

This is the story of my voyage of self awareness, where I found that my concept of bondage and submission was not what I thought it was, and how I discovered real love where I least expected it.

My mind and body have become enthralled by restraint and discipline at the hands of a true Master, who gives me a certainty of my own desirability by tempering his strength with infinite sensitivity, and His dominance with caring love. He drives my need for the taste of the whip and the bite of rope then shows me that submission and suffering also bring the gift of strength and a freedom to become the woman I had always wanted to be. I have come to know joy with Him on a pendulum of mutual passion, safe in each other's trust. Enthralled by an all-consuming rapture, we each bring the gift of self to one another

Part One: Desire

Where my direction is made clear

Chapter One

Frustration

*"So sweet and delicious do I become,
when I am in bed with a man
who, I sense, loves and enjoys me,
that the pleasure I bring excels all delight,
so the knot of love, however tight
it seemed before, is tied tighter still."*
— *Veronica Franco, Poems and Selected Letters*

'Fitz, I'm giving up on sex and men altogether.'

My lifetime best friend, confidante and crying shoulder looks up over his Sunday newspaper, fakes an expression of shocked amazement then laughs at me.

'Anna Kelhorn is giving up sex? Ah, to be sure and I will alert the media, it should make the six o'clock news.'

The silliness of my outburst is neatly summed up by Fitz, deliberately reverting to his native Irish accent to defuse my mood into giggles at his humourous one liner in response to my frustration. He makes me laugh at myself, but in a nice comforting sort of way. Despite that, my exasperation with the opposite sex cannot be altogether suppressed, after yet another encounter with a moron trying to pass himself off as a master.

'I mean it, men are useless, I've had enough.'

'And is it myself that's included in this assessment Anna?' Says Fitz.

'Not you—you know exactly what I mean, don't be difficult; and lay off the Irish blarney—you only talk like that when you want to wind me up.'

He smiles again indulgently, and lays his newspaper to one side on the couch.

'Well if you're serious, it will be a relief to most of the guys we know, you have one hell of a reputation for eating men alive, --and I don't just mean in that way either.'

That brings on a blush that can't be disguised. Jason Fitzhearne might be the CEO of the Fitzhearne Construction and Engineering conglomerate, but to me he is just Fitz, in part the big brother I never had, and part the father who had died before I was old enough to be alone in the world without him. He is at that nice age between the two and the one man in the world I can talk to about anything. Since we were kids he has always been around to look out for me, no matter what scrapes I got myself into; and I have been in a lot of scrapes. Despite running a multi million pound business I'm flattered that he still finds time to call in for a coffee and a chat to make sure I'm OK, and haven't done anything stupid with my life again.

I love him dearly, and though it is a love that has been too precious to risk on a physical relationship, lately it has been a struggle to ignore the power of the man behind that easy Irish charm and gentle humour. But there are no signals that he wants anything other than a lasting friendship, so I content myself with that. I find that there is a certain freedom in the warm security of never having to prove anything to each other, and knowing that Fitz will always be there to keep me safe with no agenda of his own.

That is the sensible me, talking to the idiotic me who cannot deny the need of the closeness of a man in the dark hours of the night, preferably one who has me tied to his bed with a gag shoved into my mouth and a whip hanging on the bedpost as a permanent reminder of what he's capable of.

'Can I help my sexdrive? Or that I haven't found a man yet who can deal with it?'

'Maybe you're looking in the wrong places Anna, and in any case everybody's sexdrive manifests itself in different ways, that's where a lot of incompatibility comes from.'

'How so Fitz? Men are all the same, at least the men I've met are; a ten minute grind and its all over, for them anyway. I'm just left with my fingers and my fantasies while my man of the moment is snoring his stupid head off. Why do I feel that sex has only ever been something that's done to me?'

'Hey, like I said before, I'm a man too remember?'

I lean across and give him a playful punch on the arm, then suppress a wince at the hardness of the muscle I connect with.

'You know I don't mean you Fitz, you crazy Irishman. I told you, you're not like other men, you're the best mate I've ever had, or am likely to have.'

He laughs again at my back handed compliment.

Fitz and I have always been in and out of each other's lives; our parents were close friends, and although being ten years older than me he was always there and never seemed to mind being followed around and worshipped as a god by a gawky little girl. Our age gap meant that he was always big enough and tough enough to protect me, and it meant a lot. But life for each of us took its usual twists and turns; we grew up and our lives inevitably went in different directions.

He was always destined to take over Fitzhearne Construction, but to prove his aptitude for the business his father made sure he worked on the toughest sites in university vacations, both in the UK and back home in Ireland, forcing him to absorb the basics of the construction industry at the business end of a shovel. Boss's son or not, he had to prove himself with hard men who suffered fools not at all.

Having got a first class civil engineering degree he was eventually able to take over the company after the death of his father, and expand it into a major player in the industry.

Despite that I know he still likes nothing better than to get out and graft, even though he could relax and run the business from a comfortable office in the City. A few days working on site tells him more about what's going on than any balance sheet, and being outdoors in all weathers is better than the gym for keeping his body hard and tough. It also gets him respect from his men, who know that he can do any job better than they can.

For a man in his mid forties, he hasn't let himself get soft, losing no muscle tone or youthful vigour. His six foot frame, work-honed physique, the shock of thick black hair that curls so sexily back to the nape of his neck, piercing blue eyes and easy relaxed manner are all aspects of him that are difficult to remain oblivious to. His looks and physique draw me to him, but deciding if he's conventionally handsome is difficult; growing up with someone involves watching a lifetime of constant change, from boy to man, while unaware of change happening.

In any event such thoughts must be kept under control, because there is still the air of tragedy about him that reflects the trauma of his wife being killed in a car accident within a year of getting married. He has never shown any inclination to talk about that, so I never bring the subject up, or try to penetrate the emotional wall that surrounds him because of it. I know that it has left a hole in his life that has not been filled by anyone and I've never sought to fill it; it's his space, which will no doubt be filled when the time is right. I find him a very attractive man but I respect his need to isolate himself emotionally if he chooses to do so.

There is also a nagging fear that if he remarried, or even found a new girlfriend, our level of friendship might somehow alter. New wives can have peculiar attitudes to old female friends, no matter how innocent; I don't want to contemplate the thought of losing his friendship. Without Fitz I really would be on my own. I have lots of friends but none like him. Most of the time I can keep that shut out of my mind, I know if I became possessive I would almost certainly lose him anyway.

Fitz is a man who wears his affluence lightly, without ostentation or the slightest arrogance, preferring people to work alongside him rather than under him. I also know from other sources that he is the main support for at least two charitable foundations. Another subject which is off limits to conversation.

My own life seemed to move along ten years behind his: university, a successful career in public relations, then married and divorced a moron; an episode that all but destroyed me. I detested that aspect of my life so much that I changed my name by deed poll back to Kelhorn, I wanted no part of my ex hanging over me.

Losing touch for several years after we both married and our parents died, we met again by chance at a party a couple of years ago. I was at rock bottom emotionally after my traumatic relationship had ended, but despite the sadness of his own life, Fitz held out the same unconditional hand to me that he had always offered years before.

I took it gratefully; somehow we managed to separate ourselves from our friends that night and he let me talk into the small hours. With Fitz I knew that there would be no hidden agenda to worry about, no price to pay for his support and understanding. He gave of himself with no strings attached and listened as I poured out the misadventures of my life in the years we hadn't seen each other, and held me while I shed a lot of fresh tears. There were no recriminations or judgements about right or wrong or just plain stupidity.

Holding me didn't go further than that; neither of us wanted it to.

Out of the devastation that was my life I was looking for a secure friendship uncomplicated by physical involvement; Fitz sensed that and gave it unstintingly just as he always had. He needed much the same thing. He was always there for me, and no other man has given me that certainty since my father died. In him I have the rock that will never move no matter how much of my life's wreckage I throw against him; I still see him as my tough protector. He carries the kind of edgy authority that I like, the kind that has no need of loud boorishness to assert itself.

****

'So tell me about these fantasies---what kind of fantasies?'

'What you said a moment ago, about incompatibility; I think that's my problem, not just fantasies. My difficulty is that I can't find anyone who is compatible with me, or vice versa. Maybe nobody is.' Most women have a girl chum they can exchange sexual gossip with, but somehow Fitz has taken on that role with me; I can tell him everything with the certainty that my trust will never be betrayed. Girls gossip, he doesn't. 'and my fantasies are a bit extreme, even to tell you.'

'Well try, I doubt if you can shock me, unless you're a closet axe murderer.'

'No I don't suppose I could. And no axes, I promise.'

'I'll take that as a compliment, I think. So tell me.'

I hesitate for a moment, then open up to him in a way that I never have before: 'Fitz, I am a sexual submissive.'

His reaction is typically Fitz, that of complete calm: 'That's not unusual, so where's the problem Anna?'

I had expected some kind of shock, instead I'm left with the impression that women tell him stuff like that every day. What I find difficult to put into words is that I have never been able to find a man who can deal with it. Either they think I want to be brutalized in some mindless fashion, maybe reenacting BDSM porn they've watched on the internet, or they are literally terrified of the idea. Submission, to me, is a form of subverted demand, constant, urgent, needy, a desire to be controlled but not demeaned. Men cannot understand that there is a difference, or grasp the idea that being tied up is a form of freedom to someone like me.

'I can't find a man who can handle it. Every man I meet seems to think I just want to be hurt, and nothing else; or thinks I'm weird and doesn't know what to do with me. They are the ones who just run. I haven't told you till now in case you did too.'

He looks slightly pained. 'Now why would I do that?'

'I'm sorry, that was a stupid thing to say, this must be one of my really mixed up days Fitz.'

How can I tell him that I want to be used for hours and then recover to want more? And that I don't want to be asked politely like most of the jerks I've been to bed with. I want to be tied down and forced, but more than that I want a man with the skill and understanding to make me want it that way. Can a man be all that and care for me as well? Can he be brutal and tender at the same time? I certainly don't want to find another abuser like my ex was, and even as I think it, I'm not even sure that line of thought is making any sense.

'How can I be used the way I want to be without feeling abused? Is such a combination possible?'

'To do that you need the right man to do the using, someone who has enough confidence in himself to spare some for you.'

'That's it exactly Fitz, but when I've tried to get into that mindset, I'm the one left feeling used but there's nothing more than that. I keep thinking it's my lack of experience as a lover that makes men prefer watching football on TV to making love to me. You can see why I feel so frustrated.'

'You mustn't think of it as your fault.'

'I do think that, I don't think men find me attractive.'

'You are a very attractive woman, but until you believe it, nobody else will.'

Fitz has never said anything like that to me before, but he says it as a matter of fact, with no sexual overtones. I want to believe him.

'Maybe that's why my relationships go nowhere.'

'It's more likely because all men have the delusion that they can satisfy a woman, when they meet one they can't they tend to run scared.'

'Why should they do that?'

'Bad for the old male ego I'm afraid. Some guys make an excuse to watch TV or whatever, some react to it by becoming abusive. Some just leave. Male arousal is a tender plant, it needs constant nurturing to keep it growing the way you want it, otherwise it runs amok or dies on you.'

'That's very deep Fitz.' He always seems to have the knack of reducing seemingly complicated problems into simple terms that make sense. 'But it still makes me feel inadequate between the sheets.'

'A man will often try to cover up his own inadequacies by making you feel that way. Men won't let themselves be shown what a woman wants, they like to think they know everything.'

'For a man, you seem to know a lot about men Fitz.'

'I like to think I'm a good observer, in a casual sort of way.'

'Well I'm tired of male egos, why can't I get what I want for once? I want a man whose attention is focused on me, no matter what that involves. Or am I being selfish?' Suddenly I pick up a subtle change in Fitz's voice, something almost imperceptible that would go unnoticed with someone who didn't know him well. There is a different edge to it.

'No I don't think you're being selfish, but are you sure that's what you really need Anna? Be very careful about getting involved with anyone on the level I think you're seeking, I wouldn't want you to get hurt again you know, mentally or physically. You've been through some bad times.'

He reaches out and touches my hand lightly, something he never does unless he is trying to make a point in the strongest terms and he's concerned about me. We seem to have a closeness that somehow goes deeper than the physical. The gentlest touch from him seems to transmit a kind of power that I find scary, yet it is not something that is unpleasant; quite the opposite. Perhaps that is why we keep ourselves at the friendship level, there are things about Fitz that I sense are best left out of our personal equation. Yet they continue to intrigue me at those fleeting moments when I let myself think about him in ways other than as a friend.

****

'Fitz, I..I'm sorry, I shouldn't have blurted all that out, you really don't want to know about that side of me. You must think I'm nuts or something.'

'No I don't think you're nuts Anna, but some men are just idiots, you've already discovered that men misconstrue your need as wanting something that might cause you real physical harm. You might get hurt worse than last time, you really don't want to go through all that again do you?'

'That's what I meant by wanting all that but not from an abuser, do men like that exist?'

'I'm sure they do, but be very careful; you know what they say about getting what you wish for.'

'I think the problem is in me Fitz, I have these inclinations, needs if you like, and I find them difficult to express in words.'

'I thought you expressed yourself rather well a moment ago.'

'To you yes, but it's easy to talk to you about anything and everything.'

'Well I suppose that's what I'm here for.'

With difficulty I squash the thought that I'd like him here for more than that. 'But it still leaves me dissatisfied with the inadequacies in the men I meet. The one I married confused my need to submit sexually with the weird idea that I was a docile doormat.'

'I know you're not that Anna.'

'Well he turned out to be an abusive, weak, possessive moron who thought he could control my entire life. He was also useless in bed, even though he was convinced he was god's gift. He also had a drink problem which didn't help matters.'

'A lot of men make that mistake, thinking that submission means docility and some kind of blind obedience, and that domination is all about trying to control someone else's life. And booze is an absolute no-no if you're fooling around with domination and submission.'

'That describes my ex perfectly.'

Fitz laughs softly, sometimes I think his insight is just too insightful.

'Domination should be all about giving you the freedom to be yourself, not trying to change you. But talk about your needs if you want to Anna; like I said, maybe you're looking in the wrong places.'

'How so?'

'Well you said you like to be taken, and men can't cope with you.'

'Yes.'

'Well maybe that's where your problem lies; they're not strong enough to just take you. Or they think taking you just means forcing you to have sex as part of some kind of rape fantasy and nothing else. But that isn't what you want I assume?'

'No it isn't, there has to be more to it than that. I know there's more to sex than just well, sex; but that's all most men seem to be capable of thinking of.'

'I think it's time you let all this out Anna, it might relieve some frustration to at least talk about it.'

'Oh, there's still the biggie to come Fitz.'

'You'd better tell me.'

'I've never climaxed while having sex, I fake it and do it myself later.' At least he seems genuinely surprised by that. 'and you're the first man I've told that to; my ex was too dim to be aware of it. I would get an Oscar for orgasmic acting if that category existed.'

He smiles sympathetically at my revelation, and accepts it with equanimity: 'You seem to have got mixed up with some hopeless lovers, I can understand why you must be going out of your mind with frustration.'

'Why can't I find something different in a man, someone who knows instinctively what I want, rather than concentrating on what he wants? Maybe then I wouldn't be the way I am.'

'You'll always be the way you are Anna, nobody can change that.'

Again, Fitz's logic is pin sharp, hitting me with a directness that makes me stop and think hard.

'You mean I'll always have these submissive inclinations Fitz?'

''Fraid so, and they will get more bizarre if you don't make them real. But tell me more about your fantasies, there's obviously a lot missing from your current sexlife.'

My sexlife. What a joke that has been for years. Sex death would be more accurate.

'What sexlife? Ten minutes of fumbling around followed by an hour of zeds then two hours of football on TV is not a sexlife. I think I'll become a nun, that'll solve the problem.'

Fitz laughs. 'No it won't hon., and anyway you'd get expelled after a week in any convent; you'd fail the novitiate test, or whatever it is they do in there. Now what about these fantasies?'

'Oh I dunno---it's all a bit embarrassing Fitz, I sometimes wonder if I'm just weird.'

'Everybody's weird one way or another Anna, I've known you for long enough to deal with your version of it.'

Fitz's gentle humour calms me down; after another night of frustration with some guy I want to forget I need calming down.

'So what exactly do you want Anna?'

'Promise you won't laugh if I tell you one of the things that really gets me off?'

'Of course I won't Anna, this is serious.'

'Well.....'

Fitz prompts me with an encouraging smile: 'Go on.'

I take a deep breath. 'You're going to think I'm really odd Fitz.'

He laughs: 'I remember seeing you in a baby buggy, I thought you looked odd then, nothing much has changed, so carry on.'

I make to punch him again, but he picks up a protective cushion and hides behind it, laughing, before I can.

'Just tell me Anna. I haven't failed to notice you've grown up a lot since.'

During all the years that our lives have been entwined, we have never ventured this far into emotional territory, even with light conversation; now we seem to be plunging into it in a rush, and he seems to sense that I want to talk more.

Chapter Two

Fantasy

"Erotic longing is really a longing to merge with something greater than oneself.
For every kind of love is a force that holds the promise of taking us
beyond the limitations of our individual lives."
— Charlotte Featherstone, Lust

'I fantasise about being kidnapped and used as somebody's sex object.' I pause and our eyes meet, but he says nothing and his expression doesn't change; he waits for me to carry on: 'even the thought of being kept tied up, blindfolded, gagged and unable to resist anything my kidnappers want to do to me makes me hot and wet. I can bring myself off over and over again just by thinking about myself in that situation.'

Blurting out something I've always kept to myself brings a sudden relief, and I find myself wanting to tell him more about the 'big thing' in my life. Fitz looks at me calmly for a few moments before replying. Even though I've known him all my life, I have never seen his composure ruffled in the slightest.

'Fantasy is one thing, reality might turn out to be quite different Anna, are you sure about all that? You've already been hurt a lot you know.'

'I've tried dropping hints, but asking takes the real excitement out of it, not that anyone I know would be any good at it anyway. Guys don't seem to have a clue about sex that's a bit out of the ordinary. I've had a few boyfriends who actually tried to tie me up, to give me what I want, but I've wriggled free in seconds; where's the fun in that? They were basically nice guys but ultimately bloody useless.'

Fitz isn't at all fazed by my pervy thinking, but then nothing seems to disturb his equanimity. By now, every other man I know would be hitting on me or making excuses to leave. Fitz does neither, that's what makes him different.

'Tell me more.' He says, smiling in encouragement.

At least Fitz isn't laughing at what I'm saying, so I pour out my frustrations to him.

'I want the whole works, including the kidnapped part. I don't want to know who's kidnapped me, or anything about where I am or for how long. It's something I've always fantasised over since I knew what sex was about. Now you can call me weird and I'll believe you Fitz.'

He moves to my end of the couch and slips a friendly arm around my shoulder. 'Hey now, c'mon, it's not weird at all, lots of women want to be dominated, as long as it's done in a way that doesn't cause any lasting harm.'

His gentle squeeze feels nice. 'They do?' It is difficult to ignore the hardness of the bicep in the arm that holds me, and the awareness that the white tee shirt he's wearing for this casual Sunday visit leaves none of his delicious muscle tone to the imagination. But I know this is just a reassurance hug from a friend, so I put such thoughts from my mind, and as if sensing them he eases from me before they can coalesce into something more positive. It is impossible to ignore that little pang of regret as he moves away.

'Sure they do, women have a far higher sexdrive than most men, problem is men don't like admitting to that. Women usually have a more creative imagination too when it's encouraged to take flight.'

'But I'm thirty two years old, surely I should have found the right man by now, but they all seem so useless in bed. I won't break; I want it rough and hard and often. And then I want to come back at a man who can match me, just as rough, hard and often, why can't guys see that Fitz?'

'They don't want to. Most men don't believe that a woman has the ability to climax repeatedly just by thinking herself into it, or know what happens to her mind when she does that, or anything about subspace. I guess they are so inept that they're only used to girls who have to fake it just the once.'

'Tell me about it.'

It crosses my mind that Fitz has never touched on this subject before, particularly subspace or the self induced multi-orgasm thing. I thought only girls knew about stuff like that because men never took the trouble to find out.

'I take it you're talking about full on BDSM here, not casual tie up games? There's a world of difference you know; you might run across some characters involved in that who are weirder than the ones you've met already.'

Again I get the impression that Fitz knows more about my thought processes than he is letting on. He can be pretty deep when he wants to be despite his laid back approach to life.

'Well, yes I suppose I am, I seem to need that sensation of being controlled by someone who knows what he's doing, someone who knows what I want without me having to spell it out, and where I don't freeze up because of clumsy ineptitude. Maybe I just don't have enough experience.'

'I'm sure that's not so Anna, I think most women are naturally endowed with experience, the problem lies with men who don't know how to tap into it; that means it can often lie dormant.'

'Would you categorise me that way?'

'I'm guessing that you are, but I can only offer you general observations, nothing more; but there are ways that you can find out if you want those needs to be fulfilled.'

Fitz's reply is quiet, yet carries authority, it has none of the flippant humour of our earlier conversation. I know him well enough to realise that he would never say something like that in any casual sense.

'I..I don't understand, how?'

'Well it's bit unconventional, but a woman who works for me confided that she had much the same difficulty that you've got, only with her it was a dozy husband who was more interested in golf than sex. She was going frantic with frustration too.'

****

It should be no surprise that other women open up to Fitz, he has that manner about him. I can't keep him exclusively to myself as a friend.

'So what happened with her? I'm glad it's not just me with this problem.'

'Well now it's your turn not to laugh, but you can actually arrange to be kidnapped, abducted, burgled, whatever sexual fantasy matches your inclination. She heard about it from another friend who went through with it. and apparently her experience was amazing, it seems she was left glowing in every respect.'

'Awww c'mon Fitz, you're kidding me; no matter how much I wanted it, I think I'd be scared silly if strangers really tried to turn my fantasy into reality.' Even as I say it my insides give a lurch because I know that while Fitz kids around sometimes, he would never wind me up about anything like this.

'No, I'm serious. Like you she had no self confidence with men, thought of herself as unattractive and somehow lacking in experience yet driven nuts by unfulfilled fantasies.'

Letting his words sink in for a few moments, I try to reject the idea and deny that I want it to happen.

'I'm still not sure about bringing my fantasy to life.'

'Well it's up to you of course, but as I understand it, that's all taken care of. An informal meeting is arranged to judge whether you are really serious about it; they obviously don't want a victim who will scream for the local militia after she's set free. You have to be right for them too.'

Suddenly I'm getting cold feet, thinking that maybe my bluff is being called, that my fantasy might be made real. I've known Fitz long enough to know that he always means what he says, and always does what he says he's going to do, despite his jokey manner.

'Anyway she was your typical golf widow—you know, left alone while hubby was away with his buddies weekend after weekend; she was frustrated as hell, so she finally plucked up the courage to find out about it.'

'And she really was OK after her experience with being kidnapped for real?'

'I can vouch for that, she's full of bounce now, a real asset to Fitzhearne Construction.'

'Wow…. so exactly what happened Fitz?'

I can feel myself getting hot just through the images conjured up by this casual conversation, I had no idea that Fitz knew anything about this sort of stuff. It's opening up a whole new aspect of him that I don't know about.

'Well Anna, I don't think it's quite as straightforward as just getting snatched off the street or anything like that, the people doing it need to safeguard themselves too; it would be easy for misunderstandings to arise.'

'Yes of course, that's putting it mildly.'

The thought that my fantasies might be brought to life is still leaving me steamy. I try to appear a little offhand about it, but I don't think I'm convincing him. Luckily our years of real friendship have removed any kind of shyness on my part.

'But tell me more Fitz.'

'Well just as a lot of women love the idea of getting abducted, it follows that there are lots of people who enjoy doing it, it's just a matter of bringing them together in an atmosphere of common consent and safety.'

'But if I consent, isn't that defeating the object of it all?'

'Oh, as I understand things you just agree to it in basic terms, then leave the details to them; you won't know the time or the place or the circumstance, only that it will happen. Apparently they snatch you in a very real sense, they don't send a taxi.'

I laugh nervously at the image that conjures up, and it helps to defuse the nervous tension rising in me. Fitz gives me a reassuring smile before going on:

'There has to be a formal agreement, otherwise you might change your mind as it is being carried out and start screaming blue murder.'

'Yes I see that.'

'As I understand it, once you've been kidnapped, your agreement remains in force until you formally revoke it; so you will find it happening again and again. Each time will become less 'expected' so to speak, and thus better for you. Those involved are very good at what they do apparently.'

'And the agreement, what does that consist of?'

'It is a properly signed and witnessed contract between all concerned, it guarantees their safety and yours.'

'And would I really be safe?'

'Well Anna, my colleague said she'd never been so cruelly treated or so well looked after in her life.'

'Sounds an odd combination Fitz?'

'I agree, it does, but apparently everything is created around mutual desire and need. And I wouldn't suggest that you get involved in anything where you would be in any real danger. Also it's not in their interest to leave someone physically harmed is it?'

'No I suppose it isn't, but what exactly happened to her?'

'Well she didn't go into too much detail, but it seems the initial discussion was by telephone, and she received a contract by email. Then she had to meet two of the people involved, and after the contract was signed they agreed a time window for the kidnapping. When it happened, she was bundled into the back of a van, forced to the floor, tied up, gagged and hooded.'

Fitz is telling me about this as casually as if he's suggesting a church picnic. I find my mouth going dry with a mixture of fear and anticipation, knowing full well that I need to take that same step into the unknown, while wondering if I dare.

'Then she guessed she was driven about twenty miles to an isolated house in the country, she didn't have a clue where it was. She was kept there, hooded the entire time and used however her kidnappers wanted, whenever they wanted, and punished if she failed to please them.'

'But wasn't she left with a few marks and bruises?'

Fitz laughs softly. 'Well yes, but nothing serious; in any case hubby isn't very attentive, and long sleeved blouses and nighties cover those until they fade.'

'They seem to have every angle covered.'

'I believe they are very good at what they do Anna.'

'I'm beginning to wonder just what it is they do Fitz.'

'She said the contract allowed her to set out any limits she had, and they respected those; it also gave her a safeword if she wanted one. If she wasn't being used, she was kept tied up in ways that maximized their cruelty and drove her orgasmically crazy.' Fitz's words may seem casual and practical to him, but they are making me decidedly twitchy in certain areas. 'To repeat her words, they were very imaginative in the ways they kept her in bondage and they made her climax till she passed out. Now she can't wait to wave hubby off on a golfing weekend so she can have her kidnapped weekend.'

I've never mentioned anything to do with bondage and domination to Fitz, but now he seems to be a mine of information on everything about it. He is totally frank and open without a shred of embarrassment.

****

'Good God Fitz...you do seem to know a lot about this sort of thing. You've never discussed anything like this before, it seems an odd subject to bring up in office conversation.'

'Women seem to want to talk to me about anything and everything. I suppose I'm just a good listener, and you did ask.'

'Yes I did didn't I?' I'm beginning to wonder just how Fitz knows as much as he does. 'and just supposing I was interested in anything like that, just how would I go about it?' I am finding it difficult to keep this at the level of casual interest.

'Well like I said, they check you out. They have to judge if you're as sane and normal as you want them to be. There are a lot of lunatics on both sides of this particular fence you know. It's a word of mouth thing, not something you can exactly advertise is it?'

'No I guess not.'

'In any case they don't want the tabloids sniffing around, I heard they get the occasional minor celeb in need of their services from time to time, so they have to be very discreet.' Says Fitz.

'They also seem very well organized.'

'I can pass on your phone number to my colleague if you like, then she can pass it on to the people who were responsible for her abduction, and you can take it from there—or not, as you wish. As I understand it they call you but they never try to persuade anyone.'

'I can see they wouldn't need to.' It is a struggle to keep my manner as offhand as his.

'No that's true.' He laughs. 'In broad terms the initiative for all this would have to come from you.'

'Oh pass on my number, it can't do any harm to have a chat about it.'

'If you're sure Anna? It's important to me that this is something you really want, not another passing daydream. If it's nothing more than a fantasy you should probably forget about it.'

Fitz knows all about my daydreams and flights of fancy, he's listened to enough moans when life hasn't added up to the reality I expected. I've gone through life never quite finding what I want, I know he's only looking out for my best interests.

'I don't know Fitz, it seems scary and crazy at the same time. But do it, I'll go nuts if I don't at least find out about it. And thank you for caring about me as you do.'

He takes my fingers lightly in his and looks at me silently for a few moments. I feel that unusual power of him again and try to quell the stirrings it puts into me.

'Anna, please be sure it really is what you want, because you're playing with dynamite. You may find yourself slipping into an alternative reality rather than mere fantasy, so you must be certain about it.'

There is a pause between us as I look into his eyes and he sees the certainty of my wanting, and perhaps more than wanting. Once again he diverts himself to make sure our emotions do not collide explosively.

****

'But we've talked enough about all this; it's a perfect evening, why don't I take you out to dinner? That will let you think about it for a while.'

'Oh Fitz, that would be so good, I can feel my stomach tying itself in knots with all I'm trying to put into words. Maybe I need food.'

'Is that little Italian place near the river still there?'

'Yes it is, and they now put the tables out in the street on summer evenings like this, trying to recreate some Italian atmosphere I guess.'

'Let's do that then, I sense there's a lot more you want to say, and having dinner and people watching might let you think a while before you tell me any more.'

Fitz is doing the right thing, why can't other men sense what I need like he does? I quickly dash up to my bedroom, lose my tatty jeans and find a pretty blouse and match it with a shortish skirt and pretty heels, whizz a brush through my hair, put some lippy on and am back in moments. He cannot fail to notice the spring in my step that has been put there by his suggestion.

'You look lovely Anna, we can talk more about all this over dinner.'

I don't see myself as lovely, but his saying it makes me want to believe it. Now I've opened up to Fitz, I find I want to go on talking as long as he has the patience to listen to me.

Chapter Three

Protected

I, with a deeper instinct, choose a man who compels my strength,
who makes enormous demands on me,
who does not doubt my courage or my toughness,
who does not believe me naive or innocent,
who has the courage to treat me like a woman. -- *Anais Nin*

'Haven't been here for years Anna.'

We've settled down to an Italian meal, dining alfresco down a little cobbled side street on a perfect June evening. Despite people walking past our table, there is a peace about this place, especially with Fitz as a companion. Warm evening sun, making small talk over a glass of wine is as perfect as it gets. He has that way about him that puts problems into perspective. Fitz laughs gently: 'But I think the tables are too close to discuss what we came to discuss.'

'That doesn't matter, it was a relief to tell you about it, that's enough for the moment. We haven't done anything like this for such a long time. We can just enjoy being here, people watching.'

I should have known such perfection was too good to last. Loud voices fifty yards down the street make me turn my head. My ex, Liam, obviously the worse for drink and with a bunch of equally rowdy companions is reeling towards us. I try to sink into my chair, and hide behind a menu as Fitz looks at me quizzically, sensing something is wrong. Before I have a chance to explain, Liam is looming at our table, swaying stupidly.

'Well well Anna, I see you've found yourself a new boyfriend.' He says, jerking a thumb dismissively back towards Fitz, who says nothing.

'Liam, please leave us alone, there is nothing here for you, I don't want you near me.'

Fitz sits quietly for a few more moments, allowing Liam to assert himself in front of me before interrupting his drunken tirade with softly spoken words: 'Ye wouldn't be for spoilin' a man's dinner now surely? 'Tis too nice a day for bein' angry with the world.'

Liam stops his rant and turns to Fitz, who has switched back to a thick Irish brogue while leaning back and smiling up at him disarmingly. I can only cringe and watch as Liam is lured into the verbal trap that I know is being set for him.

Their eyes meet, challengingly: 'Do I know you, Irishman?'

Liam is obviously too drunk to remember Fitz, who neatly sidesteps their having met at my wedding years ago, as he responds with a harder tone that still has a deceptive calmness: 'Sure an' I'm not somebody you would want to know, trust me.'

'Well what I have to say is between me and Anna, so make yourself scarce, or I will get to know you.' His voice is loud and threatening, and already other diners around us are beginning to turn their heads.

At that Liam tries to enforce his point with an aggressive poke at Fitz's chest. What happens next is so fast I barely see it. In the split second that Liam's finger makes contact, Fitz grabs his right wrist with his left hand, and the offending finger with his right, bending it sharply back at right angles. I hear the crack as Liam's face turns white with agony as he lets out a scream that echoes along the length of the street. As the diners around us stop eating and look round, Fitz has already turned back to his plate to pick up a forkful of lasagna as though nothing had happened.

'You broke my fucking finger you Irish bastard.' Liam's voice is loud and his agony is obvious to everyone within earshot as Fitz looks up again. He is doubled forward, clutching his hand, searing pain letting him speak only between short gasping breaths.

Fitz's reply is as lightning fast as his reaction had been to Liam poking him: 'Ah to be sure now, is that what ye use it for? I guess ye won't be doing that with it for a while. Maybe ye could use somethin' else?' I hear several barely suppressed sounds of choking laughter and spluttered drinks from nearby tables as Fitz skillfully turns an unpleasant situation into one where Liam is being laughed at. Then in a quiet voice, audible only to the three of us: ''Tis not broken now, I just hurt ye a little as a warnin' not to touch me again.' But it also carries a well defined menace. 'but if you insist on making a nuisance of yourself you have my promise that I will break more than a finger. Now please go away, you are disturbing these other good people here.'

Fitz's voice isn't raised and his calm is unruffled. But I can tell he means what he says. Liam makes a raised fist with his undamaged hand, but Fitz's response is merely to put down his fork and look up with a warning shake of his head and an intake of breath between clenched teeth: 'You're in enough pain already man, 'tis not good to look for more.'

Liam lowers his hand and backs away, suddenly aware of what he is facing and humiliated by other diners nearby turning and laughing at him. I look up and see the tears of agony in his eyes and he recognizes my dismissive scorn. 'Please Liam, just leave us alone, you know you have a restraining order not to come near me.' Even now, I have no desire to see him badly hurt, I just want him away from me.

Now the manager is at our table, apologizing profusely for the fracas. Fitz reassures him: 'It is quite alright, I think he had had a little too much to drink, everything is fine now.'

'But sir, your evening has been ruined, you must accept the meal with my compliments, it is the least I can do by way of an apology.'

'It really is OK, it wasn't your fault, the food was perfect and there's no harm done. I wouldn't dream of not paying for our meal.' Insists Fitz.

The diners around us settle down again, and we watch Liam meander off down the street, still clutching his hand and shouting back something about getting even. He looks back at us then rejoins the group he was with before making such a fool of himself.

'I'm sorry Fitz, I should have told you more about Liam. It was a pure coincidence passing in the street like that. He had obviously been drinking heavily, I had no idea something like that would happen.'

'Do you want to talk about it Anna? I always got the impression that there was something about you and Liam that you hadn't told me, the bit about the restraining order?'

An awkward silence betrays all that is on my mind. 'Fitz, I can't expect you to deal with everything in my life that goes wrong.'

'You must tell me Anna, I won't have you worried about something like that.'

I open up and tell him all of it, that even though we're divorced, and my name has been changed by deed poll back to Kelhorn, Liam has never got over my rejection of him. I tell him that my divorce had been acrimonious, and my ex is unable to accept that he is no longer wanted in my life, and that he is still a constant pest that I can't rid myself of and that I had to have a restraining order put on him to keep him away from me.

'But Fitz, I can't dump all that on you, I can deal with it myself. It was pure coincidence Liam showing up like that; there's a big music festival on near here, I'm guessing that's where he's been.'

'What happened with Liam just now tells me you can't deal with it on your own.' His hand reaches across the table and touches mine while his piercing blue eyes seem to hold me for a heart stopping moment in the space between us. 'You should have told me all this, I could have helped before things got to this stage.'

'Thank you, but I think I'll be OK now.' Fitz continues to look at me, the tears that I am fighting back telling him that things are not OK.

We finish our meal as quickly as possible, wanting to escape the embarrassing glances from the other diners. Fitz signals for the bill, but the head waiter smiles politely with a shake of the head.

'Lets get away from here, this is getting silly.' I say.

'Agreed.' Replies Fitz. As we get up, he takes some notes from his wallet, slides them under a plate and smiles at me. 'that should cover it, we don't want any more arguments this evening.'

'No we don't, everything was perfect until that happened.'

'I'm only sorry that fool spoiled things for you, at least I can begin to understand why your marriage broke up.' Says Fitz. 'let's walk a little while until you've calmed down a bit, I can see you're very upset.'

He offers me his arm and I take it, grateful for the steadiness that contrasts to my churning insides, and bringing my thinking back to a level of normality. I have to subdue the slight tremor within me as my hand touches his hard muscle.

Somehow the glory of a warm June evening, and the physical touch of Fitz starts to bring my life back into focus as we take the meandering path down towards the Thames.

****

'Still trying to get inside her pants Irishman? You'll never satisfy her.'

My hand tightens on Fitz's arm: 'It's Liam and the two men he was with, they must have followed us; let's get away from here.'

Fitz gently separates my arm from his, and moves away a little. 'Don't do this boys, I've hurt enough people for today. Liam there has only one hand left to fight with, so I guess he's persuaded you two morons to share his pain.' He seems totally unconcerned that he's now facing three antagonists.

'Please Fitz, you can't take on three at once.'

Liam sneers: 'Anna will always belong to me Irishman, don't try getting smart now.' Backed up by two others, he's obviously got some bravado back.

The three of them are facing us on the narrow alleyway, this time Fitz is really going to have to fight, and all because of me.

'Anna, get away from me now.'

I hesitate for a moment, and Fitz barks an order I can't ignore: 'I said NOW Kelhorn, I don't want you close to me while I'm handling this.' His odd use of my surname makes me jump, and I run back up the footpath, leaving Fitz between me and his attackers.

'I'm coming for you Anna, just as soon as we've finished with your Irish friend. I'm going to show him what you really need.' Getting badly hurt by Fitz has made Liam mad, and booze has made him irrational. I also know that seeing Liam here like this makes me aware of his weakness, that he needs others to fight his battles for him. Even the sight of him makes my skin crawl.

I can only scream at him: 'Liam, don't do this, you're drunk. Can't you understand how I detest you?' I'm scared, and a loud voice is the only weapon I have to help Fitz, but I realize I'm giving him vital seconds to pick his fight, while I'm frantically dialing the police on my mobile. Pointless, because if they get here in only ten minutes, Fitz could be badly injured or dead, but I call them anyway, and have the presence of mind to surreptitiously take a couple of photos of Fitz's attackers. We're on a secluded footpath, a police car can't get within a hundred yards of us.

'You still belong to me bitch, and I intend to show you how when we're done with Irish boy here.'

Luckily the footpath is narrow, making it difficult for them to come at Fitz all at once. I glance down at my phone, only to look up to see the side of Fitz's hand connect with a throat. Clutching a damaged windpipe, his would be attacker falls in a crumpled heap, retching violently.

'That's one of ye down, come on, who's next? Fitz's work toughened fists are already lunging for Liam's other companion, who tries to turn and run, only to have his collar grabbed and hauled back and his body swung round as a shield between himself and Liam to stop him getting close enough to do damage.

'Oh no sunshine, ye came here to fight, so fight ye will.' Fitz raises a fist to smash into his face, then draws back in disgust at the look of terror in his eyes, his hands dropping to his sides in a gesture of submission: 'ye're not worth skinning my knuckles on.' Fitz throws him to one side, allowing him to scramble to his feet and get away, leaving Liam to face Fitz on his own.

'Haven't you had enough? Clear off and sober up or I will hurt you some more.'

'Look out Fitz—Liam's got a knife.' There is a bright flash of steel, but Liam is disadvantaged by having to use his left hand, and too drunk to coordinate his movements properly. Fitz reacts quickly, swerves his body and the knife thrust misses its intended target, throwing Liam off balance. He stumbles forward and Fitz twists around again with the grace of a dancer and crashes a fist down on the back of his neck. Liam no sooner hits dirt face down than Fitz picks his head up and smashes it down a second time. His face is a mess of blood and gravel. Liam's left hand is still holding the knife, and Fitz stamps down on it hard, crushing his fingers around the handle.

Liam screams.

'Fight dirty would you, even when there's three of you? I tried to warn you, now both hands are busted.' Fitz is down on one knee, snarling in his ear, lifting his head up again ready for it to be smacked into the ground a third time. 'and your friends seem to have deserted you.'

I have never seen any anger in Fitz, let alone something on this level. And the speed of his reaction, from laid back easy going Fitz to this streetfighter is frightening. Though knowing him all my life, I suddenly realise he's capable of killing a man with his bare hands.

'Please Fitz, no!'

Fitz looks up at me, the anger fading from his eyes, his voice under control again. Liam is limp on the ground, barely coherent.

'It's your lucky day little man, I think Miss Kelhorn just saved your life.'

I am shaking, not so much with fear for myself, but with what Fitz has inadvertently revealed about himself. 'Thank you Fitz, he isn't worth it.'

He drags Liam out of the dirt, holding him at the back of the neck, fingers twisted in his collar to form a choking grip. 'But you will apologise for the trouble you've caused.'

Liam is pulled up into a kneeling position, and he tries to get to his feet. But Fitz keeps him on his knees in front of me.

'I said apologise you lowlife; to do that to a lady, you kneel.' Fitz is making sure that his humiliation is complete.

Liam wipes dirt from his bloodied mouth, his lips so swollen he is barely able to speak.

'Anna, I'm s...'

His voice trails off as he feels Fitz's fingers tighten at the back of his neck. 'Her name is Miss Kelhorn, kindly address her as such.' He is driving home the point that I no longer bear his name. 'now say it and mean it; don't make me do anything more to persuade you.'

'Miss Kelhorn, I am very sorry to have caused you so much trouble.'

Fitz prods him with the toe of his boot: 'And promise you will never come near her again, ...say it.'

'And I promise that I will never come near you again.'

Fitz drops on one knee close to his ear and whispers: 'And if you do, I give you my word that our next meeting won't have her to stop me making a real mess of you. I don't rely on restraining orders to deal with people like you. Do I make myself clear?'

I can see Liam has been badly frightened and is visibly shaking.

'Yes, I won't come near her again.'

'Remember me now? I was at your wedding. I thought you were a little creep then, now I know you are.'

Recognition dawns on Liam's face just as two of Thames Valley's finest appear round a bend in the path.

'We had a call to this location, what seems to be the problem?'

'Three muggers officer, two got away, but this one had a bad fall and hurt himself.' Says Fitz. 'he also had a knife, it's still where he dropped it.'

One of the policemen carefully retrieves the knife, and they glance at Liam's bloodied face and hand, and then at each other. 'A bad fall you say, and you were attacked by three men?'

'Yes officer.' Replies Fitz. 'they weren't very good at it though.'

'Is this correct miss?'

'Yes, we were walking down to the riverside. I ran back up the path and called the police, but I managed to take some pictures on my phone while Mr. Fitzhearne fought them off.'

I show the constable the pictures of three men attacking Fitz.

'That showed great presence of mind miss. The use of the knife makes this a far more serious matter. It means he will be our guest for a little while.'

Fitz gives the policeman his business card. 'Thank you Mr. Fitzhearne, we can take over now. I think he might need medical attention before we take him to the station.' There is a look of relief on Liam's face as he is taken into custody and away from the threat of any more damage from Fitz.

'You will be required to come into the station in the morning to make a statement sir, and if you could bring copies of those pictures as evidence?'

'Of course officer.'

I lean against Fitz. 'Take me home, please, I feel I'm going to throw up.' Our lovely summer evening has ended in a fiasco.

I feel the strength of Fitz's steadying arm around me and he gently touches my hair. 'You're going to be OK Anna, it's all over now. Liam isn't going to bother you any more.'

'You stupid Irishman, you could've got yourself killed back there because of me.' But even as I say that, I know it was Liam who could have been killed if I hadn't begged Fitz to stop.

'Ah no, they were drunk and clumsy. I know a couple of pubs in Limerick where one of the barmaids could have sorted out those three clowns, and anyway I think I'm getting too old for that kind of stuff.'

He makes light of the incident, but I know his self deprecating manner is hiding a harder tougher man. And there's something welling up inside me that is becoming impossible to suppress. I may be an idiot where men are concerned, but I dare not risk my friendship with Fitz, no matter what. Why do men have the ability to tear me up inside, even good guys like him?

'I'm still frightened Fitz.' His hold around me tightens, is he really unaware of what his touch is doing to me?

'I know you are Anna, but you can be certain Liam won't try to hurt you again; anyway, weren't you the cool one, taking pictures?'

'I was the only thing I could do.'

'Not many would have done it in that situation. It's good that you're able to think straight under pressure.' He still holds me tight, and I don't want that to end just yet.

'I wish you'd told me about your problem with Liam, I have a couple of seriously scary friends who would have had a quiet word.'

'What you just showed me was terrifying enough Fitz. I don't think I would want to meet them; I didn't know you could be like that.'

'Only when necessary Anna, I prefer not to be; it would have been better if you hadn't seen it. I try to avoid that sort of thing if I possibly can.'

I turn and look up at him, seeing a man I had not known until now. Avoiding violence or not, in dealing with those three attackers it was obvious his moves had been too slick and fast not to have been honed by a great deal of experience. His encounter with Liam outside the restaurant showed a lot of skill too. Which Fitz is he, the gentle man I've always known or someone capable of murderous violence?

'I thought I could fight that battle on my own, I'm useless at everything.'

He calms me with his usual reassuring laugh: 'No you're not, and no one is going to cause you any more harm.'

I want him to see that protecting me like that has increased my ache for him. 'Is that a promise Fitz?'

'It is, and when have I ever let you down on a promise?'

I can only tell him the truth: 'Never.'

'Then hold on to that Anna, always.'

The man can be so maddening at times, I want to scream at him to take me home and hold me in his arms all night, nothing physical, just keep me safe.

'Just get me away from here Fitz, I feel sick.'

****

After what started out as a perfect day, I'm throwing up in my bathroom while Fitz waits patiently for me to recover some kind of equilibrium. My insides gradually settle down to allow coherent conversation of sorts.

'I'm so sorry Fitz, today shouldn't have been like this, I didn't know I would react that way.'

'It's OK Anna, it's just a normal way of dealing with stress and fear when you're not used to it, don't worry about it.'

'I think I was frightened for you too you know, the thought of you getting hurt. I'm still scared, Liam is so unpredictable.'

'He won't trouble you again, but if it would reassure you I can stay here tonight, if you can make up the bed in your spare room.'

The leap in my heart at his suggestion of staying the night is instantly crushed by him not wanting to share my bed. Instead we slob out on my couch, each with a glass of wine and our private thoughts, making idle conversation. Watching a stupid cookery programme on TV, neither of us is inclined to change channels or switch the damned thing off. He offers me an arm, just like he always does when I've got real problems, and I accept it gratefully. I slide up to feel the close warmth of him; the heat of his body is tantalizingly real, but common sense tells me that he is offering no more than reassuring comfort.

'You really do care about me don't you Fitz?'

'Yes I do.'

Just those three words make my eyes moisten, He keeps his arm around my shoulder as I make a fuss of blowing my nose to hide my real feelings, desperate not to lose it altogether.

Though wanting to hold onto these precious minutes of physical contact, heavy eyelids tell us both that it is bedtime. Falling asleep on his shoulder would be a delicious first, but instead we disengage ourselves, making small talk before showering and heading for our separate rooms. I want to kiss him goodnight, but there is no sign from him that he would welcome that. We have never kissed, at least not the all-consuming tongue locking variety, so I don't. Even the lightest kiss now would be unbearable, if it brought no more than a dispassionate response in kind. Being made cruelly aware that the fire is not mutual might destroy me after the trauma of today.

Filled with such a mixture of emotions my mind will not calm itself, if Fitz has any self contained thoughts about me they are well hidden. We offer each other no more than a polite 'goodnight' as our respective doors close.

Fitz is sleeping in my spare room, just yards from me. Only a few hours ago I had been content to respect the wall that he had built around himself, not wanting to intrude on his space, valuing his friendship. Now all that has changed. He had put himself in harms way for me again, only we weren't kids in pretend games, this time he might have died for me. I cannot proof my emotions against that.

I want to crawl into bed beside him and lie there, pressed close and safe. No sex, I just want to be where he is; only the thought of being crushed by a rejection stops me from going to him. If kneeling in supplication at his bedside would let him see how I feel, I would do that. I would even sleep on the floor in there if he asked me to. All he has to do is come and find me, or call out to me, but he doesn't; so I cry into my pillow, my face buried so that he will not hear the sobbing that precedes a night of fitful slumber.

When I wake, my house is silent, I want Fitz to be here but there is no sound of him. A note propped against my kettle tells me that Fitz has gone without so much as a goodbye.

I peeked in and you were sleeping soundly, I have an early meeting I can't avoid so thought it best to leave you to rest after yesterday. I promise you are going to be safe now. Will see to the police problem and catch up soon. X Fitz.

PS follow that dream!

After the trauma of our encounter with Liam, I want to hate him for leaving me, yesterday showed me a very different man to the one I have always known. Which is he? He has left me with only the certainty of a lifetime of solid trust.

Chapter Four

The Contract

A sub shouldn't be terrified, but a little anxiety was good.
— Cherise Sinclair, Breaking Free

The days have drifted slowly since Fitz spent the night here after the incident with Liam. I would have liked more than to have him sleeping in my spare room, but it didn't happen, so I have to accept that. All the things he said, or rather inferred have stirred me in unusual ways. I've known him all my life, yet perhaps I don't know him after all.

The only certainty I have is that he's never broken any promise he's made to me or done anything that would cause me harm or to doubt his word, despite having a weird sense of humour sometimes.

I've only had one call from him, just to check I was ok and that the problem with Liam had been taken care of and I had no need to worry. We have had no other contact, but that doesn't mean anything; we are best friends, but with no call on each other beyond that. He runs an international business, I don't expect him to be looking after me all the time. Today is Thursday, and the thoughts he planted in me still won't go away. His suggestion that I might find what I was looking for hasn't faded from my mind, but has rather grown in intensity; so much so that every night I've found myself alone with fantasies that grow more bizarre with each imagining. Instead of lying here by myself, I want to be held safe and close to someone who not only owns me but cares for me, preferably in some form of physical restraint.

I've long given up trying to rid myself of such vivid mind pictures, I can't. I need that sensation of loss of freedom. It has led me furtively into fetish shops to buy a ballgag, blindfold and handcuffs to add something to my immediate reality. But it is not enough; such toys can feed my imagination, but no matter how I put myself in bondage or gag myself into silence it cannot substitute for the tender sadism of the man I need to control me. To me they are not real, they are still only toys. I want someone else to do it, not put myself in restraints I know can get out of. Handcuffs are too easy, I want ropes to make tight deep furrows in my skin, and a whip that leaves marks on me as an assertion of ownership and as a statement of what I am.

Always the same need: the desire for tightness and constriction, the unyielding pressure of rope closing me in on myself, of being unable to move; an exquisite helplessness followed by a sensation of inevitable violation of my body by a man who I know is going to use me to the fullest extent of my need as well as his, keeping me on a knife edge of constant demand. My mind draws the imagery I want, I provide the desperate reality of my own body, my fingers finding the slick moisture of arousal. I climax over and over again until I send myself into a sleep that is profound and dreamlessly black where nothing intrudes on that self created private space. It is a scenario played out so often, that I can lie on my bed and just think myself into whatever scene I desire, and make myself climax through the power of my intimate thoughts.

Yet my mindspace is not always inviolate.

Somewhere there is a phone disturbing my post orgasmic serenity. I do not want reality. My day has been reality, I want this time to lose myself in my own private world for an hour or two.

The phone is insistent.

If this is another call selling something there's going to be obscenity screamed at whoever it is.

'Hello?'

'Miss Kelhorn?'

'Er-yes?' It is a man's voice I don't recognize.

'Your name has been passed to us, with the suggestion that you might have a need of our - shall we say - services?'

'Services?'

There is no response at the other end, only silence; no barely intelligible voice trying to sell me double glazing or some internet investment scam.

'That is as much as I can say, until you think back, and recall why you might be getting a call of this nature.'

'Oh, god, I'm so sorry, this isn't something I was expecting.'

'I hope I haven't called at an inconvenient time?'

'No, not at all.' I lie; feeling a rather foolish holding the phone with my wrists in handcuffs, breathing still a little short from pulling a ballgag out of my mouth after my recent excursion into erotic fantasy. 'I didn't know that my name had been passed on to you, even though I said it could be.' I try not to sound flustered, but find myself stumbling for words. It seems silly to ask if he's from Kidnappers R Us.

He has a nice voice and is very polite, whoever he is. He laughs softly. 'Don't worry, most people have your reaction first time, they don't really believe that we exist.'

His voice is soft, gentle, non insistent, yet authoritative.

'I..I really don't know what to say, I feel as if my bluff has been called, and now I'm a bit scared to be honest.' My stomach knots up, common sense starts to kick in to make me stop this nonsense right now.

'Well, we needn't take this further, it's really up to you Miss Kelhorn, or you can have a few days to think things over. We realize that this sort of thing might need a little thought on your part, but at the same time we don't enter into prolonged discussions about it.'

I go silent for a few moments. I know that if I quietly end the call, I will hear no more about it and I can go back to my session in self-bondage, and occasionally even more boring men. For once a man is talking to me without an agenda or trying to persuade me into anything. Apart from Fitz, that in itself is a revelation.

'No, it's OK, I was just catching up with my own thoughts, this isn't your average sort of phone call is it?'

'No it isn't, I can understand your initial reaction, but you must be absolutely certain of what you are looking for in this, there is no place for real fear even though what might happen to you might be seen as terrifying to an outsider.'

This man certainly gets to the point very quickly.

'I rather gathered that when someone discussed your enterprise with me the other day.'

'Well we do value our reputation Miss Kelhorn.'

I can't repress a nervous giggle at that concept.

'A little humour is a good safety valve too, life shouldn't be entirely serious.'

'Thank you, I appreciate that. There's something about a contract?'

'Yes that's right, to safeguard you and ourselves, we have to have your consent in writing first. Actual kidnapping is illegal of course, but once you've agreed to everything, we make it absolutely real for you. I assure you we don't indulge in play acting just to give you a cheap thrill.'

I realize he is deadly serious, and obviously knows what he is talking about. What has Fitz let me in for? I know he would never allow me to come to any harm, but sometimes he can be so inscrutable. Can I trust myself to a total stranger just on Fitz's word alone?

'Am I allowed to know anything that will happen to me if I go through with this?'

'Certainly not, once you have entered into an agreement with us, you won't be told anything else. We only respect your safeword, and any limits that you tell us about beforehand. There is an agreed time window, and we don't do anything that would infringe upon your personal or business life at all.'

His voice has the sort of authority I need.

****

'You seem to have arrived at the point of all this very quickly?'

'I didn't call you to discuss the weather or the state of the economy; your fantasy is about getting kidnapped. If we entered into days of discussion about it, I can assure you that you would get bored with the whole idea and never quite make the decision to go through with it. Only you know if your need of it is greater than your fear of it.'

He is perfectly correct of course.

'I believe there's something about other girls being kidnapped too, at the same time?' I ask.

'Let's just say that there is rather a heavy demand on our services from submissive girls with such needs, we get a lot of repeat business so to speak; to be with someone else in your predicament might excite you. If it doesn't then you'll just have to accept it or drop the whole idea.'

I'd never thought of myself as attracted to other women, but when my imagination makes me browse the internet, and I find thousands of pictures and videos of women in bondage, I cannot deny myself the feelings they bring on. There is a subtle gentleness when one woman ties another; they know every intimate nuance of touch and emotion. Now the thought of seeing my predicament mirrored by someone else equally helpless has become arousing.

'No, I'm OK with that.'

'Good, you will find that it is better to be in similar company, rather than just feeling isolated and alone, particularly for the first time.'

'So what happens next?' I ask.

'I email a contract to you, you read it and make sure you understand what it entails. You then print off two copies and bring them with you to a meeting that will be arranged with a colleague and myself.'

'A meeting? Where?'

'Oh, it will be a quiet country pub, a few miles from you, where we can discuss this without being disturbed. The owner is a friend of mine, we can use a little back room there to talk things over in privacy. You will be perfectly safe.'

I pause for a moment, and ask myself if I'm getting in too deep in this. It is as if my caller senses my hesitation at every step, and counters it with gentle encouragement.

'If we arrange to meet, I would suggest you tell a friend where you are going and when you will be back, as a safeguard for yourself. You still want to go on Miss Kelhorn?'

'Y...yes I do, but it will depend on the chemistry between us when we actually do meet of course.'

'Oh I agree entirely, if either of us finds the other too repulsive, there's not much point in moving to the next stage. I have to be sure that you really want all this, and you are not just fantasizing about it or thinking it might be just a bit of fun.'

'No no, not at all, it's the real thing with me I can assure you.'

'I'm glad to hear that Miss Kelhorn, we just don't do pretend. Our reality starts where your imagination leaves off, please bear that in mind. But whatever we do to you, there will be no lasting harm because it will essentially be a response to your own need.'

I suddenly realize this man can do all the things to me that I have been fantasizing about. My entire being is crying out for it.

'Yes I've been told something about what happens, you seem to have a profound effect on women who are inclined towards what you have to offer.'

He laughs softly again and casually drops one of my trigger words into the conversation.

'I find women so....responsive to a mixture of tenderness and discipline.'

My voice lowers in reply to his words: 'Yes, that is something I need.' The catch in my throat confirms that he has what I'm looking for. I think what a beautiful bastard to say something like that, knowing what it would do to me. 'I don't think it has been put to me like that before, expressed as tenderness and discipline.'

'I'm glad we think alike Miss Kelhorn, it will help to create the right ambience if you take the next step in all this.' He knows full well that I have taken the bait he has thrown me, and eagerly too.

'You'd better let me have your email.'

'Yes, of course.'

Suddenly I realize that my mind is falling into an obedient mode as I dictate my email address.

'I'll send the contract over immediately. Take your time digesting it and all that it means. Every word has been chosen with careful thought, with both the dominant and submissive in mind.'

'Thank you, I will.'

'Good bye Miss Kelhorn, I hope you want us to meet up soon.'

And he is gone. Was that a dream or a nightmare? He had thrown in the word 'discipline'; is that what I am really looking for? Now that the word has been planted in my mind, it has a nice shivery scary connotation that I cannot deny: a man who might offer the control I seek. I can't get the words tenderness and discipline out of my head. Can there be someone who can give me both in the combination I need?

****

Then my inbox pings, and a single item just says: 'Contract'. It snaps me out of my daydream and back to reality again. I look at the word. It is a challenge, an invitation, a command rolled into one; but my finger refuses to press 'open'. And it refuses to press delete. My finger hovers, so I do what I always do, chicken out and dash to the kitchen and make tea. I find my hand shaking as I pour the boiling water in the mug, thinking of what has just been said to me. His words were so calm, with no more emotion than offering me a theatre ticket. Perhaps that is how they want me in all this, as theatre with me as the star turn.

Or maybe the contract is a ticket to a new way of life. I haven't thought of it like that before. It is impossible to deny the stirrings in my nether regions that his voice has created. And that's before we've even met.

I sit and look at the screen for minutes, clutching my mug with both hands as if it is some kind of final hold on my past reality and maybe even sanity. I know I cannot put off the inevitable. I open the email, and begin to realize just what I will be letting myself in for; like he said, this is no casual bit of playacting. If I sign it, I surrender myself to him totally, reading through it confirms as much.

Contract

This contract is to confirm that I
ATTACH PASSPORT
SIZE PHOTOGRAPH
HERE
AND SIGN ACROSS IT

Wish to be kidnapped, and by virtue of this document do hereby grant
....
such access to my person and property in order to carry out aforesaid kidnapping without further recourse and discussion with myself after the date and time on the foot of this document
I also affirm that there are no limits or boundaries set, other than the safeword agreed between us beforehand and the limits prescribed by the necessary time window given by myself. It also affirms that the use of the safeword, in any situation whatsoever will automatically cancel any and all conditions of this contract until I choose to restore it.

Conditions:

I accept that my kidnapping will require me to be kept under strict restraint and discipline as thought necessary by my kidnappers without time limit other than my overall time window.
I grant my kidnappers complete sexual use and abuse of my body while held by them
I accept that my kidnapping will involve punishment meted out to me while under discipline if my behavior warrants it.
It is understood that my life and career outside the time window of my kidnapping will not be infringed upon and in that respect my life remains as unchanged as I wish it to be.
I accept any form of restraint without time limit.
I accept any form of chastisement, administered in any way.

I accept actual imprisonment, including additional physical restraints which may be necessary to use on my body during such imprisonment, and without limit of time.

I accept that I remain under the disciplinary code imposed by this contract at all times and am bound by its terms and conditions in all situations, whether closely supervised or not.

I _____,

do set my signature to this document of my own free will,

in full understanding that I may be used for any sexual or disciplinary purpose whatsoever, but within certain prior limits as set out in this contract. Non consensual consent has been given through my signature being applied to this document without duress and has been duly witnessed.

SIGNED: _____date_____ time_____

SIGNED: _____ on behalf of kidnappers

PASSWORD: _____ ACCEPTED [ ] REFUSED [ ]

Witnessed by _____

Once this document is signed by the above, she becomes a supplicant, and may only address those she has submitted herself to by respectful prefixes, Sir or Master, Madame or Ma'am and she may only refer to herself in the third person singular.

And there's a note on the end.

```
Dear Miss Kelhorn,
   please read this contract carefully and be in no
doubt that it means what it says. Take your time, and
email me back when and if you're happy with it. I trust
you understand why we have to word the contract as we do,
and have your photo on it, one can't be too careful in all
this.
   If I don't hear from you, we can forget the whole
thing. You will not be pursued further.
   If you do get back to me, I'll send you details of
where you are to meet me.
   Print off 2 copies and bring them with you.
   Best wishes
   Jon
```

I read the contract through, and then read it again. They seem to have covered every angle to protect me and themselves. If I give myself too much time for rational thought, I'm going to chicken out, so I allow myself a decency gap of an hour then email back:

```
Jon
I want go through with this.
Please start moving to make it happen
Respectfully
Anna Kelhorn
```

Brief and to the point I think, no sense in wasting time on waffle.

And he emails me back:

```
miss kelhorn
Very well
We will meet tomorrow evening.
Be at the Oak Inn, Fareton at 8 .30, tell the
landlord that you are there to meet me.
Please confirm this by return.

Jon
```

This man really doesn't mess around, but I'm glad, doing it is one thing, indecisive waiting isn't something I want, at least not at this stage. I need to know if he can do what he is promising to do. It doesn't escape my notice that my name has been changed to a lower case 'k'

```
Jon
I will be there
respectfully
anna kelhorn
```

There is a further email:

```
miss kelhorn.

One further detail. At our meeting you will dress
formally,
We do not expect you to wear casual clothes or shoes
etc.

Jon
```

They obviously intend that my submission and obedience should be at a fundamental level.

Suddenly tomorrow evening seems forever away. All that has been implied has begun to awaken my sexuality in a different way, and I feel myself getting rather moist in anticipation of what Jon seems to be promising. And do I want what he is promising.

Jon didn't sound like a daydreamer or a wannabe, much too down to earth about it all. But can he live up to that contract---or can I live up to it? I don't want to let myself or my fantasies down. I don't want to let him down either, or Fitz, who prodded me in this direction in the first place, not now I've committed myself.

Jeez, I need to stop reminding myself of all the thoughts Jon just fed into my brain, as I squirm myself backwards across the couch, my fingers working overtime with my eyes closed willing tomorrow night to come faster than I can.

My mind has already been kidnapped by him; I'm mentally begging him to be real and not another wannabe. I feel myself rising and squirming in hot anticipation as my fingers work themselves precisely on the spot where I want to feel him touching me while he has me tied, helpless and unable to resist him. My cuffs reinforce my mood a little, but I don't want to be in control of my own body, I want someone to take that away from me and just use me as a sex object for their own pleasure. But my mind won't focus properly.

In desperation I phone Fitz, so he can tell me I haven't done something stupid. Let him be home.

He finally answers.

'Fitz, I've...' He interrupts me.

He laughs: 'Don't tell me, you've had the call.'

'How the hell did you know?'

'Oh I think there's something different in your voice.'

'What have you talked me into?'

He laughs even more. 'Me? You talked yourself into it, I only gave you a helping hand, just like I always do.'

'Tell me I'm not an idiot.'

'You're not an idiot.'

'Shut up, I'm not convinced.'

'Have you been sent a contract Anna?'

'Yes I have.'

'How have you reacted to it?'

'It blew my mind....somehow I think you know that.'

'Yes I've heard about that contract.'

'And I've said I'll meet the guy who sent it, I must be losing my mind Fitz.'

'You really will be OK Anna, trust me, go ahead, the meeting doesn't force you into anything. As I understand it, they let you react at your own pace. When are you seeing him?'

'Tomorrow night. And the guy who rang me suggested I tell someone where I will be, so that's you I guess.'

'That's very sensible, give me the address and just go ahead with the meeting, you don't have to follow it through. I promise you'll be perfectly safe.'

'Sorry Fitz, I'm a bit calmer now I've talked to you about it. I'm only going through with this because I trust you.'

I give Fitz the address I'm going to.

'Good, now go for it girl.' Fitz always has a way of putting over good sense when I most need it. 'You're going to be fine, I know it.'

'Thanks Fitz love, you're a real mate. But I still can't stop shaking inside.' Hearing his voice is making me more than shake all over; I've got to stop that; he doesn't want me other than as a friend.

'That's OK Anna, get on with it, and ring me afterwards if you haven't climaxed yourself to death while you're thinking about it.'

'Har bloody har, very funny. OK, I'll phone you to let you know if I survive.'

Now all I have to do is wait until tomorrow night to see where my crazy desires take me. It's going to be an interesting twenty four hours.

Chapter Five

Awareness

"Woman, especially her sexuality, provides the object of endless commentary description, supposition. But the result of all the telling only deepens the enigma and makes woman's erotic force something that male storytelling can never quite explain or contain."
— Cherise Sinclair, Breaking Free

Thinking my satnav is infallible is my first big mistake. I find myself driving down country lanes that seem to get narrower with every turn and I'm directed and misdirected by every straw chewing yokel I come across. First one then another points me in seemingly opposite directions. I begin to wonder if my kidnapping fantasies are worth all this hassle. Maybe he invites all his kidnap victims down here, no one would ever find them, even though it is only thirty miles from London. I didn't know places like this still existed, a timewarp where nothing much seems to happen. Even if I don't get kidnapped I doubt if I could find my way out of this labyrinth of lanes. Just as well I allowed plenty of time to get here, I'm just glad it's not dark or I'd really be in trouble.

A church steeple and a few cottage rooftops visible through a gap in a hedge seem to suggest human habitation. I hope they can speak an intelligible version of English; I've already decided I should be using Google translate for the local dialect. And there's actually a pub, the Oak, just coming into view as my satnav is about to give up on me. I pull up in front of it and walk up to a low oak door that creaks ominously as I push it open, the eyes that follow me as I approach the bar seem to suggest I might be a rare treat. The Oak Inn is just an old fashioned boozy pub, with no pretentious restaurant attached to it; just a few leery locals who look at me over half empty beer glasses thinking neanderthal thoughts of their own. Choosing what to wear for this meeting had been difficult enough, so I had decided on something unfussy, just a plain and simple button through dress and some pretty heels. It should have been longer, I don't think female legs are on view much in these parts.

At least the landlord guesses who I am, what a relief not to have to ask.

He looks at me without pausing his polishing of beer glasses. 'You'd be the young lady that Jon is expectin' I daresay?'

'Er, yes I am.'

'Come through miss, if you please?' He lifts up the counter flap, and I follow him through a door behind the bar.

'Your lady guest Jon, the one you are expectin'?'

'Ah yes, thank you George.'

Jon gets up to greet me and comes around the table to shake my hand in welcome. I feel reassured that the image I got from our telephone conversation somehow matches the man: tallish, attractive without being storybook handsome, about six-two, dark hair, older than me, about forty five I guess, with an educated voice. Then I realize that he is not alone, a woman is sitting in another chair, to my right. She is smartly dressed in a well cut formal black business suit with a crisp white blouse, and unfussy black court shoes. Her black hair is swept back in a style that serves to accentuate her features, giving her a somewhat severe, yet not unattractive appearance. This has the look and feel of a formal business meeting, and it does not escape my notice that the table has a riding crop lying on it. Its significance is obvious, and there is a tightening in my stomach at the sight of it. No comment is made on the fact of it being there, and I pretend not to notice.

'Allow me to introduce you Miss Kelhorn, this is Miss Cory Littleton, who is also involved in our little venture.'

She doesn't get up, or offer to shake my hand, but sits there taking in all my physical characteristics. I sense that it is best to maintain formalities here. 'Pleased to meet you Miss Littleton.'

'Good evening Miss Kelhorn'. Her greeting is friendly enough but somehow distant. Something in her eyes tells me that she has the kind of cruel streak that I might not be able to deal with.

'You found us OK then? Not too far off the beaten track I hope?' Says Jon.

'Well I did take a few wrong turns, this is the first time I've been out here. So close to London yet surprisingly remote.'

'No matter, you're here now, please sit down and we can discuss what made you seek us out. You must be perfectly frank if we are to match your needs with what we have in mind.'

I take a deep breath. 'I feel a bit awkward, just discussing things coldly like this in front of strangers.'

'We quite understand, take your time, the first encounter like this isn't easy for anyone. We know roughly what you want, and to have plucked up enough courage be here at all must mean you are pretty serious about exploring your desires. Nevertheless we do need to know something about you, in some depth.' Says Cory.

'Yes I can understand that.'

I have an awareness that Cory is holding my eyes steadily with hers. She looks at me and speaks with pointed insistence: 'Although we have not yet entered into a formal arrangement with you Miss Kelhorn, we do not expect interviewees to sit crossed legged in our presence.'

Crossing my legs as as I sat down had been a reflexive action, I uncross them quickly, to continue the meeting with my knees held primly together. I am being left in no doubt that my behavior here is going to be closely monitored. Having my legs crossed brought a subconscious protection, disallowing that is the first physical manifestation of the power these people will have over me if I go ahead with this.

Cory waves a hand with a dismissive sideways gesture: 'No, your knees should not be together, but an inch or two apart will suffice for the moment, later you will be required to place them wider than that at all times.'

Common sense is screaming at me to get up and walk out of here, but instead I obey her and move my knees to open my legs a little. It makes me realize that I have never sat in front of anyone with my legs slightly parted in this way; such a subtle thing, but the gap now between them seems to reveal myself with an invitation more blatant than if I was sitting here stark naked. I make another protective action without thinking, and try to pull my skirt down. At that I receive a frown: 'You must rid yourself of such reflexes Miss Kelhorn, they are unnecessary and unbecoming.' The reprimand is a mild one, but with the inference that it could be much harsher if need be.

****

'Very good, we find that it's best to start as we mean to go on.' Says Jon. 'please do not cross your legs again. You must to get used to the way we expect things to be.'

It is a stern order thinly veiled by soft words of polite convention, which make them more compelling. I realize the symbolic meaning of not being allowed have my legs crossed, but their matter-of-fact approach to it all makes me feel easier in their company, and hopefully they in mine. It is being made clear that here there must be obedience, nothing less will be acceptable.

Cory paints a more vivid picture: 'If you are to have a future with us, no part of your body may be obscured or denied to anyone who wishes to see or use it, keeping your legs apart at all times sustains the message to yourself that it no longer belongs to you. Unless your legs are bound together, your knees must never touch. If any area of your body has been exposed, you may not cover yourself without express permission.'

I keep my hand away from the hem of my dress; my pulse is racing in response to her words. Already the concept of bondage has been brought into our discussion as a form of normality.

Cory's brusque way of setting out basic rules and taking command leaves me in no doubt as to her capabilities if this should go any further.

'To get to the point, you are aware of what BDSM means, in its real sense?' Jon continues.

'Bondage, Discipline, Sadism and Masochism.' I reply without hesitation.

'Very good; we hope you tick all those boxes Miss Kelhorn, if you can't it's best to say so now, before we go on. What made you take the brave step of coming here tonight?'

It is obvious that there is going to be no small talk here. Focusing my brain in response takes effort, not wanting to appear clumsy or foolish, the absolute truth seems the best way of dealing with this.

'The thought of being dominated; forced in a sexual context has always been in the forefront of my imagination. Since I became sexually active, thoughts like that have been all pervasive, but it was something I kept to myself for a long time because I thought I was weird.'

'Have you had experience in that respect, or is this just a fantasy that you hope to bring to life? It is important that you know we are not interested in dealing with fantasists who only daydream about submission without understanding what it really means on our terms.'

My reply is truthful, yet somehow cannot hide a truth I would prefer to keep to myself. The hesitancy in my words reveals more than a signed confession: 'Yes I have had some experience; and no, I'm not a daydreamer.'

'That doesn't sound as if you enjoyed it very much, it was not what you wanted or expected?'

'Before I had any real experience, I married a man who told me he was a dominant, I believed him then found out he was nothing of the kind; he turned out to be an idiot. When I said that I liked being tied up and dominated, he took that as license to become an abuser.' Cory nods her head, with an expression that is sympathetic despite her outward appearance of severity. 'He became very possessive and controlling.'

'And you resisted that?'

'I wasn't really experienced in BDSM, but I sensed that the way he was treating me was somehow wrong. He wanted the kind of docility from me that I was unwilling to give, because I was getting nothing in return. He ultimately showed himself as weak.'

'Dominant men in this context will never say they are.' Says Cory. 'Only the submissive can decide if a man is dominant within the parameters that she desires; that can take many forms of course.'

'I was young and naïve. I wanted someone to control me, but I won't make a mistake again with someone like that. I have tried BDSM with other men since, but haven't found anyone capable of giving me what I need.'

'Please go on Miss Kelhorn, your positive attitude is the right one.' says Jon.

'At first I thought something was wrong with me.'

'A lot of submissives think they have to accommodate stupidity, it really isn't like that.' Says Jon.

'The more he became aware that he couldn't really give me what I wanted, the more he abused me mentally and physically. I gave it a couple of years then left, it wasn't a pleasant time, and I've tried to put it behind me as one of life's mistakes; I know there's something better out there. I feel that there is more to bondage and domination or even ordinary sex than boorish behavior and mindless brutality at the hands of a moron, I just haven't found it yet.'

'At least it didn't put you off the idea altogether Miss Kelhorn, though it's a pity your experiences haven't been good up to now; but what you have told us is not uncommon.' Says Cory.

'I think it almost destroyed my confidence in any sexual involvement with men, I know what I want, but I but I sometimes think it's my fault for being unable to find it, as if I am somehow unworthy.' Jon looks at me, smiling sympathetically. 'My sexual experiences have left me with the feeling that any inadequacies are my problem, now clumsy sex just makes me freeze up.'

'I'm sure that's not the case Miss Kelhorn, you have had the confidence to come here tonight, most women wouldn't have the nerve to do that.' Says Jon.

'Perhaps. I know where my sexuality lies, I've just had difficulty getting there I think. I've always wanted sex that removes control from me, I want no say in what happens to me, but that doesn't mean I want to be damaged or brutalized in some way, or to repeat the mistakes of my marriage. I figured some sort of abduction would fulfill my needs provided I could rely on the safety angle.'

'And you heard about us?' Says Cory.

'Yes a friend of mine knows a couple of people who have, er, passed through your hands; they came away exhilarated to say the least. I wouldn't be here if I didn't trust him implicitly.'

Cory allows herself a brief smile at my compliment. 'This person is not sexually involved with you?' She seems to have the uncanny knack asking questions with seeming innocence, yet which probe my inner self. I hesitate momentarily, finding it difficult to keep Fitz as my personal secret.

Chapter Six

Revealed

*"Sometimes our balance has to be upset and our course reset
in order to help us navigate to our final destination."*
— Ella Dominguez, Becoming Sir

'N..no, I do not have any emotional commitment to anyone.' Cory looks at me for an eternity of seconds, but lets my answer rest for the moment. I am the world's worst liar. 'I find any kind of physical involvement frustrating to say the least, so right now I'm deluding myself that I can do without it, but of course I can't; that is why I'm here.

'We can understand that.' Says Jon.

'But at least I can rely on my friend's advice in all this, he would never try to coerce me into anything where I might get hurt in ways I didn't want to.'

'You seem to know your own mind, and what you want Miss Kelhorn; that is good. What you are entering into isn't for the faint hearted.' Says Cory.

'I have a successful career that demands a strong personality, I'm not getting into all this on some kind of whim.'

'We are very good at what we do, so it's important that you are aware that if we accept you into our world of sensuality, you can never go back to your own. If you go through with this you will become a true submissive, yet it will empower you and give you a new kind of strength.' Says Cory.

'I don't quite understand.'

'You will be dominated and controlled by people who know how, that will make you intolerant of those who don't. You will be able to tell doms from idiots; it will not weaken you, instead you will be given a power you cannot yet imagine.'

Her words turn me over inside, and I know I can still run from all this. But somehow I'm aware that this is my last chance at fulfillment on my terms, and I hold my nerve.

****

'We will change you into someone you perhaps didn't know existed, but in any event your old self will be gone for good; we will give you a new one, if that is what you really want.'

'I..I don't think I like this self very much, I would prefer to find something better if such a thing is possible.'

'That is the best approach to all this, as long as you know what that involves Miss Kelhorn?'

'Yes I am fully aware of everything I think, at least in general terms.'

'You must be certain; the change I speak of will not be transient or casual, but immediately fundamental and permanent Miss Kelhorn. Does your confidence in us allow you to leap that far into the unknown?'

'But I am not to know what these changes will be?'

'No; other than knowing you will not be scarred mentally or physically. In any event, every submissive is different, so her pathway into BDSM must follow a different course. All we ask is your trust before you step into our world.'

I take a deep breath, then speak before I have time to think about what I'm saying: 'Then change me.'

'Good. And you have thoroughly read and understood the contract that was sent to you?'

'Yes I have, I fully accept its terms and conditions to the letter. It fits my way of thinking pretty much exactly.'

'That's excellent.' Cory says. 'And you have brought two copies of the contract?'

'I have them in my bag.'

She holds out her hand and I take out the contract papers and hand them to her. I get the impression that she might be running this show.

'You do realize that by signing this document, and within the timespan set out, your mind and body belong to us?' Says Jon.

'Yes I do, I want that.'

'Have you decided on a safeword?' Says Cory.

'I think a safeword might be counter productive, if you abduct me, the power of it might be somehow subverted if I know there is a getout if I don't like it.'

'That's a very brave step to take Miss Kelhorn, you must be certain about it.' Knowing myself well enough to be aware that my arousal in thoughts of enforced sex is interlocked with the situation of having no control over it, I need it to be as real as possible, and they have the experience to make it so. Too much time has been wasted in the past explaining what's wanted. This time it must happen.

"I've thought about it a lot since you sent me the contract, I am sure.'

'So you wish to enter into an arrangement with us which would be consensual non-consent, if you can understand the meaning of that?'

'I take it to mean that once I have given my initial consent, I am assumed to have consented to everything that happens after that, with no further recourse to me?'

Cory looks at me intently and pauses before replying: 'That is exactly what we mean.'

I take a deep breath and a moment to consider the implications of what is being asked of me. Jon and Cory wait for my reaction to what they have offered.

'Then that is what I want.'

'Do you think that being kidnapped will satisfy your needs Miss Kelhorn? Says Jon.

'I..I'm sorry? I thought that was the point of all this.'

'It is, but your experience in all this so far, your confident certainty and refusal to have a safeword leads me to think that you need to take things far deeper than that if you are to reach a point of ultimate satisfaction.'

'I'm not sure I understand.'

'Something with perhaps more meaning and emotional depth long term?' Says Cory.

'Can you explain a little further?'

'We think if would be better for you if you became objectified, reduced to nothing and then emotionally remodeled.'

'What makes you think that?'

'You are undoubtedly a dedicated submissive, and in my experience real submissives never really find contentment until they come under the control of a dominant, a real one that is, not the wannabes you've met so far.' Says Cory.

Cory's observations penetrate me to the core, telling me that I need to learn more about myself. Perhaps kidnapping won't give me what I'm looking for, that it is only a fantasy that will ultimately not bring me the reality I need. I have difficulty finding the right words to express what I do want. The concept of objectification thrills me and scares me at the same time. Yet I know they have revealed myself to me in ways that I didn't think possible.

'In your case I think that control should be taken to a more fundamental level than being kidnapped.' Says Cory.

'Is that why I'm here?' It is as if my mind is being opened, thoughts that I was sure belonged exclusively to me are being extracted from my most secret heart.

'Jon and I think it is.'

'But how would that happen?'

'At this stage it is impossible to say, things have a habit of unfolding in unforeseen ways if your mind is open to accept them.' I feel my chest tightening, not with fear but with choking emotion at being opened up like this. 'We think you are ready for a deeper commitment than has been discussed so far Miss Kelhorn.'

'Objectification does sound very different to what I was expecting.' I reply. 'I'm not entirely sure what it means, in this context.'

'Can you bring yourself to trust us and step into the unknown, way beyond the kidnapping fantasy, and be prepared to leave your old self behind? You might find a power inside you that you were unaware of.' Says Jon.

Having never thought of myself as powerful in this context, Jon is offering me something that I'm not sure I can handle.

'As a submissive on our terms, you will not be a docile doormat; quite the opposite, once we show you how strong you really are.'

'You don't think I'm wasting your time?'

'Not at all, you are here because you are driven by your own need; submission is part of what you are, but so is the strength of will that forces you to be here at this moment. You do not appear to be a mere thrillseeker who will fold when you start to suffer.'

'And will I suffer?'

Cory looks straight at me, and I know that she is using trigger words to judge my reaction. 'Yes, you will most certainly suffer.'

****

She sees that I do not back down at her direct words, despite knowing that they are intended to test me. Although frightening, I find her directness of manner somehow reassuring. 'We may illtreat you, but we will always support your self confidence and allow you to build on that.'

'The man who suggested I come here said I was looking in the wrong places, perhaps I've been looking at all this in the wrong way too.'

'That's very likely. Without knowing just what you're looking for, finding it is likely to be almost impossible. But if you leave yourself open to it, it may find you.'

'I hadn't thought of it in quite that way.'

'Let's just say we will be happy to point you in the right direction.' Says Jon, with a knowing smile.

'You seem to know what I want better than I do.'

'That may well be so Miss Kelhorn, at least in this first stage. We may be sadistic, but we have no desire to crush your spirit, that would be counter productive.'

'I think I would resist that for real.'

'You are a very brave woman, and we do appreciate your trust in us.' Cory says. 'With a safeword, your limits would be precisely defined and we would never exceed them. Without a safeword and having your non-consensual agreement we will take you to what we judge to be your limits, then push you harder in the direction we think you want to go whether you like it or not.'

'In one sense I don't want to enjoy it, at least not in a conventional way, but I need it...if that seems right to you?'

'Reduced to an object, you can have no say in what happens to you. That seems be what you want?'

'It is.'

'And the more you resist what we do to you, the better we like it, and the more you will get out of it. In any event, a woman cannot easily disguise what she is enjoying can she?' Says Jon, smiling.

'No, I suppose she can't.' I find myself blushing like a schoolgirl at his inference. 'But by the same measure she it's difficult to pretend to enjoy something if she isn't.' Jon laughs at the comeback I fire at him.

'We always make sure of that part; saying you want something here, as you are now, is very different to saying it in the sort of situations you will find yourself in later. But if you do freeze up and just lie there, curled up in a submissive frightened heap, we will just give you a big hug, a cup of tea and send you home. We won't need a safeword to recognize that it isn't working out for you.'

'Oh, I would hate that. I don't even want to think about it. But thank you for saying it.'

'We're not thoughtless lunatics, we accept that for some people it just doesn't work, no matter how much they say they want it.' Jon laughs. 'The reality can be scary...we know that some girls have a sudden change of mind when things start to happen; we just put it down to experience. There would be no recriminations, but it's important to be aware of that side of things as well.'

'Thank you, I appreciate that, I'm a bit nervous but I'm sure I'll be OK.'

'BDSM isn't a sexual panacea for everyone, there are no guarantees in all this.' Says Jon.

'I know that, but I know what I want.'

'Your certainty is reassuring.' Says Cory.

I try not to reveal that I am shaking like a leaf inside, knowing that I'm being led into the unknown by two people I met just ten minutes ago. I want Fitz to be here with his arms around me, telling me I'm going to be OK, but he isn't here. I have to do this on my own, supported by the certainty that he has never once let me down.

She picks up my contract and looks at it. 'So Miss Kelhorn, are you ready to sign on the dotted line?'

Chapter Seven

Controlled

And painful pleasure turns to pleasing pain. –

Edmund Spenser

'Yes I am.'

Cory looks at me searchingly. 'One final word Miss Kelhorn, once you put your signature on that paper, your life is going to change. I don't mean in a few days or weeks, I mean immediately.'

My heart skips a beat at that inference, but I know that I cannot turn back now. Suddenly there is a new certainty about my future even though it is unknown; something inside is saying that perhaps it is better that I do not know. Their instructions when I arrived on the way I must sit is an indication of how specific their control is going to be.

'I want my life to change, that's why I'm here. I've had an abusive marriage, I've tried vanilla relationships that bored me rigid, I've dated wannabe doms who turned out to be nothing of the kind; there has to be another way.'

'If you can stand the pace we set for you, I'm sure you will find that with us.' says Jon, who pushes both copies of the contract across the table, and hands me a pen. 'You will sign both copies, we keep a copy, and you retain a copy.'

With a final glance over the words that give my life away, I sign my name across my photograph at top of each document. Then I add my signature at the bottom, and confirm that no safeword is wanted. Jon signs it, and Cory witnesses it.

'I must ask you about this contract just once more Miss Kelhorn, you can still tear it up and walk away. You have signed it as 'no limits', are you fully aware of the power that gives us over you?'

'Yes, I think so.'

Cory's voice has a harder edge to it. 'Thinking so isn't quite good enough, it's important that you know.' There is a lurching sensation at the realisation that my signature has altered the dynamic between us, and that my first impression of Cory was the right one.

'If I make limits, then I'm still in control. I don't want to be in control. We discussed objectification, that's the whole point isn't it?' I realize that I feel a bit scared, but I'm pretty sure they are not going to cause me any lasting harm, not with everything arranged like this. 'The suggestion I come here was made by someone with whom I would trust my life. I feel I would be letting him down if I backed out now.' Though I know Fitz well enough to be certain that he would never mention it again, it is important that I go on.

'We prefer that attitude.' Jon smiles, 'It allows our thinking to be much more creative with you.'

Cory relaxes into a smile. 'That really is the best approach to all this, we have to be very careful about who we involve ourselves with, because we don't treat people with kid gloves.'

'I wouldn't want you to.'

Now that the contract is completed, they keep a copy, and I put the other copy back in my bag.

'Now we must arrange a time period to abduct you; once we've fixed that, our possession of you takes on a more physical aspect, is that clear Miss Kelhorn?'

'Yes Cory, I understand that.'

Her eyes flash towards me with a new hardness. 'You assured us that you had read your contract Miss Kelhorn.'

'I.. I'm sorry, I did, or I thought I had.' My stumbling words reveal my confusion.

Cory passes the contract back to me and orders me to read it again. 'Miss Kelhorn, I shall tell you this once and once only. Signing that contract has changed what you were into something different, you may now only address me as Madame, or Ma'am, and Jon as Sir. Do you understand that the contract has given us ownership of you, irrespective of whether you have been kidnapped or not?'

'Y..yes, Ma'am.' Somehow my mind finds it easy to slip into a submissive mode, perhaps this is what I truly am; a total submissive.

Cory stabs a manicured finger down on the contract as it is pushed back across the table. 'That contract document is not a trivial matter, it means what it says. Please read it again.'

Her sudden harsh words cause me to lurch inside as I read the last paragraph: *may only address those she has submitted to by respectful prefixes, Sir, Madame or Ma'am and she may only refer to herself in the third person singular.*

'From now on, you also lose your concept of self in our presence, or in the presence of anyone we so delegate. When we take you into our custody, your emotional and physical identity will be totally subverted. Anna Kelhorn will effectively cease to exist in a personal sense.'

'Ma'am?'

Jon explains, in a slightly gentler tone: 'You refer to yourself only in the third person. You become unworthy to regard yourself in the first person singular. To us you become an object to be used, nothing more. You'll get used to it.'

'I..I think I understand Sir, I... this girl didn't really take it all in.'

Jon frowns at me.

'Er.. this girl understands your meaning Sir.'

Jon smiles. 'You learn quickly Miss Kelhorn.'

'This girl thanks you sir.'

They have a clever way of objectifying me, reducing me to nothing in their presence. I should feel demeaned, but I do not. Instead I feel a strange elation, that such a seemingly trivial thing has lifted what I was from me, and set me on a path to new existence where my submissive status can be formalized and where I no longer need to concern myself about it. I can just be accepted for what I am and taken to a place where I know I shall be used in the manner I desire.

Jon looks hard across at me, breaking into my thoughts: 'But I hope you do remember that, because if you forget it you will be punished severely. It applies in any dealings you have with us from now on, no matter what the circumstances. You will be free to lead a normal life in conventional respects, when our ownership of you will not manifest itself in any obvious sense. That doesn't alter the fact that you belong to us. We will know your movements, and will snatch you when we feel like it and will use you in whatever way we want. You have refused a safeword so will have no say in the matter. Are you prepared for everything that that entails?'

'Yes, Sir, this girl will try to remember that.'

'Trying isn't good enough Miss Kelhorn, trying will only get you welts across your backside, we demand more than mere trying. We insist on perfection; you are now in bondage to us wherever you are and whatever you are doing.'

'I....I'm sorry...sir, of course I meant I will do that, and I know that I am bound to you now that I have signed my contract.'

Cory's eyes narrow towards me.

"I..I mean.. this girl will obey you sir, she knows that she is bound to you now that she has signed her contract.' I am stumbling nervously with my tenses, this isn't the best place for remembering the rules of elementary English, while still trying to come to terms with the effect their undeniable aura of control is having on me.

'That's better---you will not get another chance to correct yourself girl, transgressions mean punishment, swift and hard.'

'No Ma'am. This girl understands and thanks you Ma'am.'

'That's much better. In your day to day life, our ownership of you will of course be low key, you need have no concerns that we will intrude on your every day existence in the slightest degree.'

I try to pay attention, but her words are conjuring mindpictures that refuse to go away.

'Am I making myself clear to you Miss Kelhorn?' Cory snaps, jolting me back to here and now.

'Er yes Ma'am, this girl wants to be aware of everything that is to be done to her.' I have no doubt that Cory knows I am finding it difficult to concentrate.

'If the first encounter with us is successful, you will find that the need for it will grow stronger. If it doesn't work out, then we will just let the whole thing drop.'

Finding myself slipping under someone's total control is making me wet and horny as hell, the threat of the whip making me even hornier. Their initial order that I should face them with my knees apart has resulted in an involuntary movement that puts them, unbidden, even wider now in an invitation that is beyond my control. I realize that it wasn't a conscious act on my part, but a reaction to their words and domination of me. And all this at our first interview; my mind struggles to imagine what more they are capable of. The invitation of my parted thighs cannot be hidden, to them or to myself. The thought of stopping at this stage makes me want to go down on my knees at their feet and beg them not to.

Madame ignores my flustered state: 'I take it you have an online diary, showing your general movements week by week?'

'Yes   Ma'am.'
'Good, you will be required to email us the basic times and dates, on a weekly basis, and notify us of any unforeseen changes. That is essential so that we can avoid your normal day to day work and established social commitments, we want no part in any of that.'

Jon explains it further in a slightly kinder tone: 'It is a difficult concept to put over Miss Kelhorn, but we won't be breathing down your neck all the time, the awareness of what you are will become integral to your being without constant monitoring from us. You will come to crave for what we have to give you, and only through that can we own you in the fullest sense.'

'I think I understand....Sir.'

****

As I say that Cory picks up the riding crop, it has obviously been put there in anticipation of my transgression. 'You will stand up and unbutton your dress.'

My fingers fiddle nervously with the tiny buttons. Why the hell didn't I think of a dress with a zip.

'Neck to hem if you please.' Orders are given with an edgy politeness, and I find myself standing with my dress fully open, facing them in my black bra, thong, seamed stockings and heels.

'Across the edge of the table.'

The polished oak surface feels cool against my already hot skin as I place my hips against the table edge and force myself into a prostrated bend, in full knowledge of what Cory intends to do with the whip. I had spoken of myself using first person singular, something expressly forbidden and which I had been warned never to do. I sense the pain that is coming, I fear it, yet I need it. Inside me there is a need to prove to myself that I can take it. I need to know within myself that I can hold to my no limits intention. It is an initiation to which I must submit myself to prove that I am willing to enter their sadistic world of my own accord.

'You will lift the hem of your dress.'

Common sense is screaming no, but need is screaming yes. I must submit to myself, which is exactly what Jon said I would do if the need was powerful enough. They could force me, but make no move to do so; the force must come from within me and I must show that I cannot resist it. No one is going to hold me across the table, or tie me down. The choice is entirely my own. Bent across this table I am in submission to my inner self, Jon and Cory are the instruments of my chastisement, not enforcement.

'Yes Ma'am.'

My hands reach behind and lift my dress clear of my bottom and drape the folds of it carefully across my waist. For some reason an instinct had told me to wear stockings and suspenders tonight, I have no idea why I did that, but it obviously meets with their approval.

'Panties down.'

I obediently hook my thumbs in the waistband and push down, though they are so flimsy they could not possibly offer me any protection. They fall as far as my knees in a tightening circle of silky nothingness, somehow accentuating the availability of my body as it bends across the table top, arms outstretched in front of me. I find that my fingers can just grip the far side of it.

Madame Cory gives a sharp order: 'Legs spread.'

I move my feet apart at the insistent prodding of the tip of the riding crop, feeling the elastic of my panties tension itself into tight muscle. The whip touches me with an intimacy that might not be strictly necessary to administer a whipping, and causes an involuntary tremor. The fact that I am not tied down reinforces the truth about myself, that I am here because I want to be. Being tied across the table would make it easier. These people do not intend to make things easy.

'Miss Kelhorn, kindly tell us why you are now bent over the table in this fashion?'

Words stumble from my lips, betraying fear of what is to come. 'I' ..then stop just in time I collect my thoughts: 'This girl referred to herself in the first person Ma'am, this girl is very sorry Ma'am.'

'Exactly.'

'And what did we say a few minutes ago about such transgressions?'

'That this girl would be punished Ma'am.'

'And is this punishment deserved?'

Bent over in this obscene manner, there seems little choice, but she is intimating that the options are still open, that any pain must be drawn onto myself, willingly. I still have the option to say no.

'Yes Ma'am this girl deserves to be punished for such an infraction of discipline.'

'Now girl, you are going to count the whipstrokes, but in advance. They are going to be hard and real, and will hurt you and mark you. If you don't count what I deem to be sufficient punishment for your transgression, then you will receive double what I think it should be...is that clear?'

I clench my teeth in anticipation, forcing the words out: 'Y..this girl understands Ma'am.'

'Very well, you will begin counting, and you will also thank me for each stroke. If you do not, the stroke will be repeated.'

This is doubling my torture. Forcing me to make myself suffer, maybe more than I need to, then having to humiliate myself by thanking her for it, all without knowing what she has in mind to dole out. She intends to test my resolve to be what I want to be. I feel the riding crop being casually rested across the waiting flesh of my backside.

Chapter Eight

Chastised

"It's like an itch, isn't it? You can feel it in your throat. You want to scream for me."
— *Nenia Campbell, Bound to Accept*

'Please begin.' Cory's words sound like polite request, but I know they are not. Unable to push myself over the edge of imminent agony, I make the mistake of hesitating for a few seconds. The force of the whipstroke drives my thighs against the table edge as the pain explodes with a blinding light in my brain.

'When you are instructed to do something, an instant obedience to that instruction is expected.'

I scream, because nothing can keep that reflex from exploding out of my mouth. And as I scream, I realize I can be heard out in the bar, and I don't care. My backside is on fire.

'And that's one extra already girl, and it doesn't count in the total due. I would advise you to start counting immediately.'

Despite Cory's accentuated politeness, I know that I can cry halt now and all this will stop; yet I do not want that. It must go on. Being forced to accept what my masochism really means is revealing what is within myself. There is an undeniable urge to find out just how deep this need is, both for myself and to discover what my tormentors are prepared to give me.

The pain is already all consuming, but I force out the words I know must be said, they are dragged out of me as part of a gasp for air: 'This girl thanks you Ma'am.' The pain has an intensity like nothing I have ever known.

Then somehow the next word is forced out: 'One.' Briefly hearing the sound of the whip cutting down, there is another scream as the blinding flash of pain engulfs me once more, fingers digging into the table top so hard I feel my fingernails must be tearing into the wood itself. I fight to keep hold of what shreds of self composure I have left.

Air hisses out between clenched teeth, hair already plastered across a sweating brow, struggling to suck in enough air to let me speak... 'Ttt... thank you Ma'am.'

'Two.'

The leather of the crop cuts across my bare flesh again, and the pain consumes me, the scream is unrestrained. Fighting back tears, I thank her again. The torture is refined to subtle perfection, humiliating me completely. I turn my head sideways to look at Jon, who is sitting back to my left and absorbing my determination to take it, silently telling me that if I want it I must beg. For an instant Jon's face somehow becomes Fitz's, I want him here, watching me take my punishment and helping me through it, but he is not. Jon's face comes back into focus through my haze of suffering, but our silent exchange somehow strengthens my resolve.

'This girl thanks you Ma'am.'

'Ttthhhreeee...'

Even as the pain explodes on my body, I feel a growing moisture betraying me, insisting that I want this, expect it, and need it; lightly caressing fingers confirming my wet excitement at being whipped despite the screams of protest which by now have lost any vestige of inhibition. Jon is still watching calmly, no doubt enjoying the sight of me stretched out this way, and all the turmoil this is causing.

Again the pain sears across me, driving my thighs into the edge of the table and forcing out yet another scream. A gag would make it easier, they are not interested in making it easier.

Coherent thought is becoming difficult, let alone speech. I struggle to say what I have to say: 'This girl thanks you Ma'am.' Words seem to come in a succession of short gasps again. I can barely speak at all.

Somehow I find the resolve to go on to six, counting ahead and thanking my tormentor for every stroke, unable to rid myself of the thought that I'm going to have walk out the way I came in, past all the leering locals who have heard my punishment being administered.

Each stroke is taken until my backside feels like one enormous flame, and my fingers still gripping the table edge as I hang on during the punishment. As Madame had warned, each cut is being delivered with full force, making sure I know that she will always do to me what she says she will do. The flogging having forced sweat to pour from my tortured body, I can feel a wet impression of myself on the polished surface.

I stop at six hoping that I've judged her intentions correctly. In any case, I have been given seven stripes. I wait expectantly, breathing hard and gulping in air in tortured gasps in a pointless effort to counteract the pain. Madame draws the tip of the whip across my weals, then slips it gently between my legs. Not daring to move, there comes a soft probing to arouse me still more, making me even wetter. Rising up on my toes, there is a desperate urge to clasp my thighs together and writhe on it, to hold it in and use it shamelessly, but with that thought comes the certainty that it would invite further punishment. Instead the tip of it is flexed upward and drawn out across my most tender flesh with excruciating slowness, then brought up to lips that open to accept it; I suck on it with blatant eagerness as searing pain transforms itself to a flood of ecstasy that engulfs my abused body. It is obvious that they both want to see me stimulated and wet like this, humiliated by undeniable need, discovering just how far my libido will drive me. The change of breathing cannot be suppressed as the teasing leather of the whip inflames a new and different desire.

'Taste what you have become girl.'

The whip has forced a self debasement as I lie across the table, spread, open and available. My eagerness to have the leather tip in my mouth becomes an obscene act in itself. I am sucking my own juices while Jon sits back and watches humiliation transform itself into an even more rampant need.

Cory puts one hand on my violated bottom and withdraws the whip from my mouth. I feel it being intimately moistened once more between my legs then she leans across my stretched body to put the whip to my lips again. I draw it in eagerly, unable to suck enough of my liquid desire from the leather that has just caused so much pain. Feeling the cool texture of gloved fingers on the weals rising on outraged skin, the slightest extra stimulation would create an earth shattering climax. I force myself to hold on to what little sanity I have left.

Under her touch, I can only manage short gasps of response: 'This girl thanks you for her flogging Ma'am.' The words of thanks are not the same as those used while the flogging was in progress, this time they are given with meaningful sincerity, looking imploringly at Jon while they are said. Bent like this, another overwhelming need arises; that he should come round to this side of the table and take full advantage of either or both holes on offer. Both are wet with desperation; he recognizes the unspoken invitation, but does not accept.

'If I ordered you to climax right now, you would obey me wouldn't you? Says Cory with a whispered softness. With fingers teasing me into raging arousal, such obedience can be in no doubt.

Barely able to speak, my reply is effectively pleading: 'Yes Ma'am, this girl would obey you if that would please you Ma'am.'

I do not know how she could order me to climax, but I know that I would do it to gain the slightest shred of approval from her. I find myself wanting her to tell me to do that, to show my ultimate submission. I had been barely able to stop myself climaxing while the whip was cutting into me.

'Then you must also obey me when I tell you not to. The whip confirms that you belong to us now. This is where you begin to leave your old self behind.'

Madame Cory smiles at my admission and seems to recognize the depth of my emotion. Fingers stroke tenderly and her voice is a little kinder: 'It is too soon for that my dear, there will be time enough to submit yourself in that respect when you are my prisoner.' Somehow a word of endearment penetrates me and fires an intensity of response. 'I want you to leave here and think about what the future holds for you. You may stand now, you understand why you were beaten?'

Standing, it almost impossible to keep fingers away from burning flesh, to try to find some way to soothe the seven stripes that Cory has doled out. There is an instinctive awareness that there may be no attempt to ease the pain, only by standing still and staring rigidly ahead is it possible to deal with it. Varying degrees of cruelty and hints of tenderness are taking me to a different level of mindgames. Effectively naked, such an aroused state cannot be disguised.

'Yes Ma'am, this girl understands now and will not repeat her mistakes.' I realize that my panties have slipped down around my ankles, and without permission, stooping to pull them up is out of the question.

'Good, because even with your contract, you still have the ultimate freedom to walk away, no-one will raise a hand to prevent that. Flogging you like that was to make you aware of what your future holds with us. Being taken and used in the way we have in mind isn't going to be easy.'

'No Ma'am. This girl understands that.'

'It's important that you know it Miss Kelhorn, I did not allow you to climax because you are going to learn discipline.'

'This girl appreciates that Ma'am and doesn't want it to be easy and is aware that she lacks discipline.'

'And I did not use you for the same reason.' Says Jon.

'Thank you sir.' In this instance gratitude is certainly not sincere, the wanting of him had been so overwhelming. As if reading my mind, he winks, with a light smile in my direction. It is a seemingly trivial gesture, but it defuses the imminent explosion of my emotions just a little.

****

'Now, about your timeslot for abduction.'

Madame's conversation has reverted to an even normality again as if nothing untoward has happened as I stand in front of them, my dress still fully open.

Trying to assume the same attitude to all this as Cory and Jon is difficult while resisting the urge to massage soreness and absorb the still throbbing pain. 'Well, starting on Friday the twenty first, this girl has two weeks holiday booked, and hadn't planned to go anywhere in particular, maybe something could be fitted in around that time Ma'am?'

'That seems very convenient, I think you should make yourself available from that date onwards, it could happen any time after that.' Says Jon.

'Thank you Sir.'

'We don't expect you to alter your normal life in any way, we will take care of things from this point on, but during those two weeks you have no other commitments, no one will want to know where you are or think it's odd that you are missing?' Cory asks.

'No Ma'am.'

'You should also know that while you are our prisoner, you will be allowed no contact with anyone other than those who hold you. No TV radio or newspapers, you may see other captives, but you and they will normally be gagged and under some form of restraint, and no talking will be possible other than at our discretion. Gags are removed only when you need to use your mouth, or when one of us feels like using it, or if you are directed to use it in some other respect or while you sleep. You will of course be fed and watered and allowed normal bathroom facilities, but only under close supervision.'

'Yes Ma'am, all that is understood.' I can feel my heart pounding as my future predicaments are described to me. The flogging has left no doubt as to its reality. She looks me up and down as I stand there.

'One more thing, I notice you are shaven and have ringed labia.'

'Yes Ma'am.'

'When was that done?'

It is a question that can only be answered with an honest confession, the flogging has stripped away all reticence. 'Some time ago Ma'am; in this girl's private moments, she likes to see herself in a submissive context, even though she is not owned at present. The rings are a permanent reminder of what this girl truly is. Being shaven makes them visible. They are there to be locked by my rightful owner, when he makes himself known.'

'And your nipples?' Says Jon.

'They are ringed too sir.'

'Show me.'

With my dress pulled aside so blatantly, I have no inhibitions about drawing down the filmy gauze of my bra as ordered. Jon comes close and lifts each ring with a light pull. No words are exchanged, they are not necessary; nipples harden involuntarily at his touch, forcing a barely withheld gasp as my eyes offer my body to him in unspoken supplication. The pain from the whip has somehow reflected itself in their sensitivity, and without need to check, there is a certainty of a flooding arousal that would welcome fingers or anything else that might be put there. But frustration is not to be relieved, and rings are left hanging, wet with the proof of desperate need. I have to hold myself rigid to prevent myself falling to my knees and begging him to use me. What I want has become so desperate, the whipping has driven me to the point where I don't care that it has become so obvious.

'We like your approach to all this, it lets us think of different ways in which to use you. Eventually we would have had you ringed, the fact that it's already done saves time.'

'Thank you Ma'am, I...this girl appreciates that.'

Madame raises an eyebrow, but accepts my quickly corrected error.

'Very well, now you are free to go, please bear in mind everything we have told you tonight, and be under no illusion that it will not become reality. You may remove your panties altogether and leave them here.'

'Yes Ma'am, and thank you.'

'Don't thank me until you've experienced what is going to happen to you; remember you are still free to back out of all this.'

'Oh no Ma'am, this girl has no intention of backing out now.'

Cory responds with a light smile and a hint of tenderness: 'No, somehow I don't think you will; you may now leave, you will be hearing from us in due course.'

Fingers search for the buttons to do up my dress, but Jon frowns with a shake of his head. It is an order that requires no words; the brief time here has taught me that I may only do what I am told to do, so I leave my dress open and my bra pulled down with my breasts exposed as Jon left them because I have been refused permission to do otherwise. I have been told that I may not use my hands to cover myself, so I do not. They are still testing my nerve to see if I have the determination to go through with it. The inference is clear, that I must leave here exposed as I am. I want Cory and Jon to recognize this as part of my submission as I kick off my panties, and in doing so finally leave my old self behind.

****

This is the unsaid part of the deal that has been created here: whipped, and exposed in a way that hides nothing of an already shredded modesty. But in return for that I carry their gift of empowerment, the strength of will needed to walk out of the door with an intact and increased pride.

I came here unsure of what I was, now Jon opens the door leading back into the bar with an air of gentlemanly courtesy and respect. George, the innkeeper, opens the counter flap for me with a nod and a grin, and I pass through the bar making no attempt to cover myself. I find my head lifting; as my walk becomes strong and purposeful, my dress falls open as I stride towards the door.

Moving proudly past all those leering men who have just heard me screaming while being beaten I realize that I am challenging them to look. I know what I am, and boldly meet the gaze of each one of them with what I suddenly realize is anything but submissiveness. I have that certainty of being able to endure what they could not.

Such is the real empowerment of submission. I leave them to the obscenities of their thoughts as the inn door creaks shut behind me, while the cool dusk of the evening seems to offer its own particular embrace to my body. The sound of girls being flogged is obviously part of village entertainment, but now I know I need be afraid of nothing, least of all myself, the people around me or my strange desires.

There is an elation in knowing that my punishment was my initiation, and that it has cemented my resolve to carve out my emotional destiny, even though I do not yet know how that is to come about.

Somehow what I've just been through has made me realize that I am no longer the woman who came here an hour earlier. The contract is not only with my kidnappers, but with me; it has given me a feeling of superiority, a different kind of freedom. I get into my car and lift my dress to let burning skin make contact with cool leather as I slide behind the wheel; the sensation of it excites me.

My dress remains unbuttoned, there is a normality in my parted legs as I drive away. I want to feel exposed to the night air and take my time getting home, my naked body is yet another aspect of both submission and freedom, allowing me to absorb the implications of this new life I have chosen for myself.

The lanes that lead me back the way I came now offer a comforting anonymity in the growing darkness, but my mind cannot concentrate on driving; I find a quiet spot to pull over and take a moment to think myself back to what Madame's whip did to me. I have been sensually flogged for the first time, and by someone with an awareness of how to put meaning into it; my body leaves me in no doubt that I want more of the same.

My thighs spread, knowing what I want; I am still dripping with a desire driven by the throbbing pain across my abused flesh. Fingers and thoughts meld into an erotic unity as I mentally will myself back across that table, taking my flogging with unconcealed need while trying to drive myself into a state of orgasmic excitement within the confines of the car. But my mindset has been changed, I can no longer do it to myself, they have altered me.

Having to wait to be kidnapped is going to be hell; I want to drive back to the pub and beg them to take me now. Or at least offer me some release from what I can sense is their enveloping bondage.

Aware of nothing but my own thoughts I get home in a haze of frustration and ecstasy; my mind so full of anticipation of the future. Wanting no distractions before bed, I shower, towel myself down then allow myself a long look back in my full length mirror at the seven neatly spaced weals Madame has put on me. I find myself admiring them, indulging in the ultimate perversion that I should take such pride in having sought out such intense suffering.

They are vivid and red, a finger traces along each one, the pain of them still there but subsiding into dullness now. There is that certainty that I could have stopped the whip from abusing me, or that I could have counted on and absorbed still more pain to satisfy my longing for it. I did neither, even though Jon and Cory had made it obvious that the choice was mine and mine alone. Am I thus a freak for needing pain so much? Each mark is showing me what I am and the raised welts will be with me for days as a reminder. But I received only what I needed and expressed a desire for.

Re reading the contract, seeing it as a document that changes who I am into someone I want to become, reinforces what I know of myself. As Madame Cory said, I am a dedicated submissive as well as an outright masochist. Do I want to take the ultimate step and be rendered into a sex object? The ache within gives me the answer.

My body has never known anything like this, but I recognize my stripes as a true mark of the submissive, because they were put there with care and understanding, rather than the thoughtless stupidity I have known in the past. Suddenly I realize that I want my body to remain marked in this manner from now on; I want to keep them on me, and earn more. A glow of pleasured pain consumes me again, reliving my blissful beating; my need no longer in any denial because it is an integral part of my being. Tonight has been an awakening to what submission can really mean.

Finally falling into bed, I still attempt to make my fingers relive what I have learned about myself. Though moistened with toying with the rings on my nipples and labia, and with the searing pain from Madame's whip still fresh in my consciousness, self pleasure no longer works. They had given a clear warning that they owned me, and I would be changed. The immediacy and reality of it has been a shock to my system; by belonging to them I can now only get what I want from them, a subtle form of enthrallment that I had not anticipated. The thought that they now hold the key to any form of sexual release makes me their prisoner far more effectively than any dungeon. The awareness of myself has been brought sharply into focus, but my understanding of Fitz less so. I try to shut out the futile thoughts of wanting Fitz to imprison me and concentrate instead on what Jon an Cory have done to me.

I went to Jon and Cory at his instigation; after putting himself in harms way for me, was he so blind that he could not see my need of him beyond our friendship? Maybe he had recognized my growing desire for him and just passed me over to them to get me out of his hair.

Perhaps I must accept that his wall of emotional trauma is just too strong for me to penetrate and so I must continue in my search for the man who will come to own my body and control my inner sexuality. But right now it still seems difficult to conceive of sexual solace without him.

What Jon and Cory did tonight has left me without the potency or ability to pleasure myself, and though I fight to keep my mind away from thoughts of Fitz, he is the one missing piece of this unfolding exotic jigsaw. Could he really have been so unaware of what tonight's encounter would do to me, or that I would be left in such a state of denied arousal and mental turmoil? Sleep finally claims me with thoughts that Fitz would never play such games with my mind. Or would he?

Part Two: Ordeal

Where suffering becomes reality

Chapter Nine

Abducted

"Right on the edge of fear was where trust could grow."
— *Cherise Sinclair, Breaking Free*

It has been one helluva week, my boss has finally flipped, no one is doing anything right, clients complaining about missed deadlines, and he's trying to blame everyone but himself for his own stupidity. Thank god it's Friday, as they say, and I can get the idiot out of my hair, at least for a couple of weeks. Two weeks of blank---wonderful. Let somebody else deal with him. I've had enough for the moment.

I collapse on my sofa, not wanting to think about anything, except maybe tea. Tea is always a good idea, calm me down; I've been hyper the last few days thinking about that kidnapping caper, was I stupid to say I'd go through with it? Plagued with doubt and second thoughts I have convinced myself it was daft idea. No matter, I can always call it off when it happens; if it happens. I'm still trying to figure out how Fitz seemed to know so much about it all. He's been a bit odd lately, since he told me his uncle had died and left him a bit of money, as if he needed any more.

I turn on the tap to fill my kettle, no damn water. Bugger. I keep turning it on and off, still nothing. This is too much, water cut off without warning. I've paid my water bill, or I think I have.

I glance through the window. Typical, a big water company van, with two guys in yellow jackets standing looking at the stoptap cover outside my house, with the usual head scratching.

'What's the problem?'

'Oh sorry miss, we've had reports of water interruptions all day in this area, we're having to check each house to find out what's wrong.'

'Will it take long?' I yell at them through an open window.

'Hard to say miss, we have to check everything, including your kitchen mains tap in a few minutes, will that be OK?'

'Oh very well, I suppose you have to, the quicker you get it fixed the sooner I can make my tea.' Soon there's a knock on my door. I open it, the two water fixers are there. They present ID cards and I show them through to the kitchen and leave them to get on with whatever it is they need to do.

Then everything goes black.

My screams are stifled by a hood dragged over my head as I am thrown to the floor. My wrists are jerked roughly behind my back and lashed tightly together. I feel my elbows drawn back until they touch, and rough rope passed around them. I feel it bite into my skin. I want to scream, but a hand clamps my mouth shut through the hood. The hood is lifted a little, just enough for a ballgag to be shoved into my mouth, and its strap tightened at the back of my neck. I feel the ball depressing my tongue into silence. I know this is something I've asked for, but it still hurts like hell and I want to scream.

I instinctively fight and struggle against the ropes that are tightening around my body so brutally. I feel groping hands begin to strip my clothes off; I hear my blouse being torn and my skirt pulled off me, then I feel my bra and panties being yanked tight then casually cut away and discarded. I sense my nakedness, but the ball distending my mouth stops any word of protest as unknown fingers find my wet excitement at being bound like this.

It is impossible to hide myself, I am open to whatever they want to do to me. They remain silent, but I feel fingers probing deep as my body reacts to their violation, making me wet with the need of more. God, what a total slut!

Then I feel ropes around my waist, tight, then jerked tighter still until I gasp for breath. Rough hands trail a doubled cord down between my legs so that it buries itself deep into me then back up to my wrists. The slightest struggle causes the rope to bury itself deeper, the suffering made more exquisite by my clit being trapped between two strands of rope. I want to scream, but the gag prevents it.

I feel my ankles, knees and thighs forced together, and expertly bound, then my ankles are brought up to my thighs and lashed tightly to them.

They shove my head forward and rope my shoulders down to my knees crushing my breasts against my thighs.

My captors have me roped into a tight little ball, and absolutely unable to move. I try to scream behind my gag but I can only gurgle. Then I get a hard slap on my exposed bottom. Through my hood, I hear a muffled voice making a phone call.

****

'Yes, there was no trouble, we have her here all nicely tied and gagged, the slut is eager and dripping. We will deliver her in about an hour. We have the other two bitches already in the van, this is the last one for today.'

My god! They've already kidnapped two other girls! I hear my door open and close, I sense one of my kidnappers is still here with me. They don't say anything to me, I just have to lie here, bound and gagged and aware that I am exposed to him. There is nothing I can do about it. There is the sound of my other kidnapper returning.

'I've backed the van up close to the door, that way nosey neighbours can't see what's going on. Anyway, slip her into this bag, if anybody does see anything, it won't look unusual. She'll be OK in there just till we get her into the van and away from here, best not to hang about. Don't forget to lock up the house and bring the keys with you.'

I feel myself being bodily lifted, then slid forward till I feel and smell leather begin to envelop me. They've obviously come well prepared, the leather encases me tightly, and I hear a zip fastener being closed. Now I can hear nothing, only feel myself being lifted and carried, obviously outside to the waiting van. I feel myself dumped on a hard surface, then there is a dull thump of the van doors being closed. The sensation of vehicle movement is transmitted through to me, and it is distinctly uncomfortable, the ropes have been tightened with devilish expertise, every bump in the road makes the cords cut deeper in. When these two sadists tied me up, they knew exactly how to do it for maximum arousal. I make myself squirm harder to tighten my ropes even more as my mind loses itself in a haze of exquisite suffering until I eventually sense the van coming to a halt.

I hear the zip fastener being pulled open, and a welcome draft of fresh cool air flows around me. Hands lift me clear of the leather bag I've been kept in and dump me on the unyielding cold steel floor of the van. I feel fingers grope me again, and I cannot prevent the ropes creating a flood of sensations through my mind and body. I make muffled squeals inside my hood, and hear other similar sounds close by. I know that the other two girls they spoke of must be lying close to me and suffering as I am.

The hood is suddenly pulled off my head, and I blink in the dim light in the back of the van. The other two prisoners are lying nearby, they are also ballgagged into silence like me. We stare at each other, none of us knowing quite what to make of the predicament we find ourselves in. We cannot communicate, only look. Each of us is bound into the same tight ball, to create the maximum sexual torture and wild arousal. I can see that they are going as crazy with it too.

'Now you horny bitches, we're going to release you from your ballties, so you don't get cramp lying there like that, but you're still going to stay tied and gagged—you'll just be able to stretch your legs a bit that's all. We want to deliver you in good condition.'

They untie the ropes that hold me into the ball, and do the same to my two captive companions. We take the opportunity to stretch out and I see the obvious relief on the other two girls' faces, as the three of us lie on the van floor as our captors set off again. We can only look at one another, seeing each other's suffering and arousal. I can see cord disappearing between both the other girls' legs, tight and deep, as mine is.

Our nakedness reveals what we are, what our captor called us: horny bitches, brought onto permanent heat by our situation. The van takes a sharp bend in the road and causes me to roll against the other captive closest to me, and I feel my senses aroused even more as our hot flesh comes into pressing contact. The bondage and exertion of the last thirty minutes has made us both sweat, we are hot in every sense imaginable as our bodies roll and almost fuse together.

I can smell the animal heat in her, and she feels the heat of me. Bound as she is, she moves her thrusting need towards me, to drain something from my body that she obviously needs. The girl is as worked up by all this as I am as our bodies come together, fighting to maintain some physical contact as the van sways at speed beneath us. The other bound victim senses our need and manages to prop herself up against the van side so she can watch. I can see her legs squirming together to bring herself off while she's looking at us.

We are all strangers to one another, and until this moment, I wasn't even aware that I had lesbian tendencies; now here I am grinding my naked breasts against another woman, both of us tied and gagged, doing everything short of actually screwing her while another helpless woman watches.

The cords are hurting me beyond the point of caring; the pain has become a drug, serving only to intensify it all. I manage to lift my bound legs up and across hers, to drag her closer to me, to feel her rising climax as it is about to burst simultaneously with my own. We press close as the excitement of each of us raises the other to fresh heights of animal ecstasy. Denial of what we both want is making us want it more. As we fight for what we need, so our arousal intensifies, multiplying on itself to make each of us explode against the other. Our gags can barely contain our screams as our orgasms cause our bonds to tighten. I have never known such sexual intensity, my whole body is on fire.

I glance up at the third girl, looking longingly at us. My eyes invite her to join us, as best she can, and I draw back a little to let her body roll against ours. I feel her excitement rising and know that she is as wet and dripping as me. Obviously watching us has driven her crazy, she wants the same and finds it impossible to stop herself from forcing herself against us and using our bodies as a lust focus for her insatiable appetite. The movement of the van thrusts the three of us together in a frenzy, each desperate to drive the other two insane with wanting.

We almost lose track of reality, only the here and now matters as we roll around on the dirty van floor and climax ourselves repeatedly against each other. There is only our common captivity and the straining ropes that are driving each of us into oblivion. Time itself seems to become an irrelevance.

****

We feel the van come to a halt and there is a silence as our captors get out and walk away. But we three prisoners are still consumed by the heat of one another. Each of us has the other two as a reflection of what she is and of what we need from this. Knowing that we are here willingly to bring fantasy into sharp reality gets rid of the last shred of inhibition; it forces us to use what little freedom we have to give and take pleasure to satisfy our mutual urges.

Our ropes are sadistically tight, yet the suffering becomes sweet when a soft hot body is pressed tight and close, and eyes plead silently for release of a very different kind. We are three strangers yet in the last hour have become fused with a blazing passion for one another, each of us squirming on the cutting cords. We are making them go deeper than is bearable, then using that pain to force orgasms that rise within each of us until each one becomes submerged by the breaking wave of the next. Muted screams of suffering from my two companions match my own, and I use my bound hands to pull my crotchrope further into me. I realize that my captors are sadists who know how to be creatively cruel. We have been tied and left here as a demonstration of what we are.

Suddenly the van doors are flung open, and our writhing bodies are on full display to three men who have obviously come to get us.

We stop, and look at them, our bodies hot and sweaty and dirty from rolling around on the floor of the van, hair streaked into a mess across our faces. We are beyond caring that we are naked and bound, it is why we are here.

Our captors stand at look at us. 'Well well ladies, it would appear that you have already been indulging in forbidden pleasures on the way here.' Says one of them, with a knowing laugh. 'I'm afraid that means a taste of the whip for all three of you later. You really will have to learn discipline and self control while you are with us.'

I have a good memory for faces, and I immediately recognize him as one of the leering locals in the bar of the Oak inn a few days ago. 'Nice to see you again miss.' He says, addressing me with with mocking deference as he catches my wide eyed look of recognition and takes in every squirming exposed inch of me lying in front of him. It would seem that he's well used to having naked women tied up in the back of his van, and that self control is going to be the one thing we will never learn here, wherever here is.

Each of us is grabbed by our bound ankles and unceremoniously dragged out of the back of the van, made to stand unsteadily for a few moments before being casually picked up and thrown over the shoulder of one of our captors like a side of meat.

Which as I am about to find out, is pretty much how I am going to be treated while I am held prisoner.

I am hanging across the shoulder of a total stranger, tightly bound, with a gag in my mouth. I've been kidnapped and I'm aching all over from a rough hour spent bouncing around on the floor of a van with two other women in the same predicament as myself.

My head is hanging downwards, but I try to twist it round a bit to get some idea of where I am. It's nearly dark, there are no streetlights anywhere. We are being carried openly, so we must be in secluded grounds somewhere. The man carrying me is obviously loving every moment of having me like this, the hand that holds me over his shoulder is probing me far more intimately than is strictly necessary to keep me in place. I try to squirm against his fingers, but that gets me a sharp slap on my naked bottom.

'Be still girl, behave yourself.'

I try to keep still, but those fingers are still arousing me like crazy. I try to protest, but that gets me another slap, harder this time. Problem is, that only makes things worse. The wet desire mixed with stinging pain is driving me nuts.

I try to look around some more. I see the other two girls behind me, being carried as unceremoniously as I am, obviously we are being taken to where we will be held captive. I can't see much, only the naked backsides and bound legs of the girls I was brought here with, and the two men carrying them laughing and making obscene comments about us. I twist around further, to become aware of a large house looming ahead of us in the fading light.

'Got a raunchy lot here boss.' I hear my captor say as the door opens ahead of us. 'These bitches were on heat and rolling around and bringing each other off while they were still tied up in the back of the van.'

'I might have expected as much, it's discipline they need, and they will get it here I can assure you.' It is Jon's voice, and I'm guessing Madame Cory won't be too far away.

'Take them upstairs and just dump them, there's another girl up there already who was delivered earlier, be sure to tie them tight so they can't get at each other this time. I'll send up some of the maids to make sure they're all right, I'll come up to deal with them myself later.'

'OK boss, no problem.'

Although I cannot know it, entering the house has become my portal into a new life. The previous days, the initiation interview at the Oak, being lashed by Cory, the kidnapping from my home, the insane ride to get here, have all led up to being incarcerated in this place. They obviously intend to find the limit of what my mind and body will take. At this moment I cannot know if there is a limit. I must find my true self, or I will never discover what I seek.

Chapter Ten

Delivered

"The exotic and the erotic ideals go hand in hand, and this fact also contributes another proof of a more or less obvious truth – that is, that a love of the exotic is usually an imaginative projection of a sexual desire."
— Mario Praz, The Romantic Agony

Christ, just how much demand is there for kidnapping and abuse? The thought runs through my mind as my captive companions and I are carried up a wide oak staircase, offering a chance for me to look down and around at the inside of the house itself. It is obviously big, palatial even. There is a certainty that these people have sufficient resources to indulge their predilections for sexual adventures such as I am now part of.

A woman scurrying across the hallway below doesn't even look up at us as we are being carried upstairs, suggesting that this is normal, not worth a second glance. Unfazed by the sight of three kidnap victims being brought into the house, bound and gagged, it is obviously a regular occurrence.

The way that she is dressed leaves no doubt that this house is run on very traditional lines, a quick glimpse is enough to see that she is wearing only the shortest of black dresses, black stockings, five inch high heels with a frilly white apron and white cap. There are no feminists' rights here. Not that I expect any.

A big door is pushed open, we are carried into vast room. It has oak paneled walls and a wooden floor made dark with age and use; it amplifies the sound of any activity and reinforces the predicament in which we find ourselves. The ceiling is high and vaulted with dark oak beams that are almost lost in shadows thrown by soft lights that give only a subdued illumination, set at intervals along the walls. The high roof beams are supported by wooden posts, set at intervals so that they are about six feet apart, each having a row of a dozen iron hooks positioned evenly spaced up the length of one side. A ringbolt is fixed in each post, about eight feet off the floor, the purpose of which is shudderingly obvious.

One of the posts is already occupied; a pretty redheaded girl is tied to it. She is naked, and her demeanour reveals that she is exhausted, but the ropes that hold her have been passed over the hooks screwed into the back of the pillar itself to keep her erect.

They are tensioned upwards against any tendency to sag down, the cords hold her permanently on her toes by a rope that passes between her legs to bury itself deep and back up to one of the hooks. Her legs are tied apart to the sides of the pillar and she wears a wide leather collar that allows her head to be strapped back to the post without constricting her throat.

Held in that fashion, it is not possible to do anything but stare straight ahead in an enforced attitude of obscenely open and upright attention. So rigid is such bondage that she might be part of the post itself. She gives a slight stir of anticipation at the new arrivals but a muted moan is all that such a posture of restrained suffering will allow.

The remaining unoccupied posts stand as a silent invitation to expected guests.

I try to take stock of where I am. At the far end of the room a long mirror covers the entire wall, and I make the bizarre connection that it is exactly the same as one sees in ballet schools. A mess of whirling emotion does not find an immediate meaning for that other than to have our incarceration constantly reflected; it is another dimension of eroticism that doubles the length of the room, surreally replicating everything within it.

Posts, walls, lights and in particular four bound, naked, squirming females. Nothing has prepared me for the visual onslaught that is my reflected self. The man tying me to the post is dressed entirely in black, which accentuates the white vulnerability of my naked body. There is no option but to watch as well as feel the rough handling from our captors, and to see my fellow prisoners being subjected to the cruelties of harsh restraint as I am.

Along one wall is a row of iron beds, each one having a bare mattress on it, but nothing else. The beds are empty, but there is no doubt that this room is where we are to be held captive, and those beds are where we will be sleeping, if sleep is possible here.

It is obvious that our captors know what is to be done, as each of us is stood against a pillar. I feel the chill of it against bare skin as my arms are untied; the flood of relief that brings is short lived, as they are dragged back behind the pillar and rebound as securely as before. With elbows being drawn tightly together, the roughness of the ropes as they are looped over a hook for maximum discomfort multiplies on itself. The other two girls are being tied in the same sadistic manner, their bound arms are not only drawn back, but up to maximize tension on their shoulders.

I can watch myself and the others being similarly bound, a cord is doubled tight around my waist, then passed between my legs and back up to another hook. Fingers twist and pull on it, forcing me up on my toes before I feel it being tied off behind me. Bound like this I have a choice of either staying on my toes or burying the ropes deep into my outraged sex. With legs spread apart and lashed to either side of the pillar in exactly the same way as the other girls, the ropes are tensioned upwards and over the hooks so that my bodyweight is taken by rope for maximum discomfort.

****

Can I take this? I must, my no limits contract says I must, or quit. But I have given consensual non consent. The decision not to have a safeword was

124

entirely my own. Even if I don't like it, I have to take it. But the heat burning inside me says I do like it.

The gag is removed from my mouth, and a wide leather collar is put around my neck. It is strapped back to the pillar to hold my head erect. I could protest, but know that it would be pointless. I can only moan as the ropes begin their deadly torment of my body.

The long mirror allows each of us to watch the others being treated in the same cruel fashion; each of us has been made as rigid as the post we are tied to, open and vulnerable to any excess our captors choose to inflict on us. Hands that twist the ropes for maximum discomfort find the most intimate spots to inflict aroused suffering on their victims, watching intently as fingers discover undeniable slicks of wet need and squirming response against bonds that should allow no movement at all.

We can only look at one another in the long mirror, reflecting pity and sympathy, while prevented from offering each other the mutual release that we were able to in the van. The three men who have delivered us do a few last checks to make sure our ropes are totally secure, with particular attention to the cords placed strategically to cause the most discomfort.

They allow their fingers to a final exploration of outraged flesh to create yet more arousal, then turn and leave the room.

****

Strangers, yet sisters in bondage, we can only look at each other for minutes. Our predicament is outrageous, yet has a powerful sensuality. It is obvious that all four of us feel that. We can see it in each other's eyes through the mirror that reflects us. We are alone and not gagged, so I venture a whisper: 'Are we allowed to talk?'

The redhead who was here when we arrived whispers back: 'If you must say anything, keep your voices down, Madame likes to use that whip.'

'I've noticed.' I reply. 'I'm Anna by the way.'

'I'm Alice, hello.'

'How long had you been there before we arrived Alice?'

'Two or three hours, you lose track of time in here.'

'Ouch.' I reply.

'Its OK.' Says Alice. 'you get used to being tied like this and relax into it, you have to with Madame Cory. If you don't like the pain, don't play the game, as you might say. I was grabbed first and brought here, this is my fourth time, they know what I want and how I want it.'

'I'm Maisie, this is my second time; after my first abduction I couldn't stop thinking about all this and wanted more of it.'

'Yes it is addictive.' Says Alice.

'And I'm Kerry, this is my first time.'

I try to glance sideways at my companions, but my collar will only allow me to exchange looks via the mirror. Rigidity of control is everything here. 'Good to introduce ourselves properly at last, even if it is only like this. It was wild coming here in the van, this is my first time too.'

'You've felt Madame's whip then Anna?'

'Yes at our introduction meeting.'

'How many strokes?'

'Seven.' I reply.

'That's about average, she always finds an excuse to use it at the first interview, it weeds out the fantasists. Daydreamers and wannabes cry off when the pain gets real. If you'd done that she wouldn't have let things go any further and had you brought here.'

'It still bloody hurt.'

'It was meant to.'

'So what's likely to happen while we're here Alice?' says Kerry.

'Well, Madame Cory does have some routines which you will find interesting, just to remind us of what we are, but the variety is endless. She never repeats any action, and keeps her submissives guessing that way. That's why I keep coming back. I can guarantee it's going to be painful though, and you're going to get used a lot.'

'It sounds exciting.'

'Anybody here signed a no safeword contract?'

'Me.' I reply.

'Me too.' says Maisie.

'Ouch.' says Alice, 'You two must be real painsluts, Madame will have special plans for you.'

Maisie giggles: 'Yes I remember from last time. Works much better that way though, if you've got the nerve for it.

'What time is it? I ask.

'That's another thing.' Says Alice. 'You won't see any clocks here. Time is an irrelevance in this establishment. Time for us is what Madame says it is.'

'Yes I noticed my watch is missing.'

'Don't worry, you'll get it back when you leave.' Replies Maisie.

'Is there anything she doesn't control?'

'Not really, nothing of any importance anyway. A few days in this place and you wont be able to think anything other than the doms here want you to. You will be made into nothing more than an object, to be used any way they want.'

'Does anyone chicken out of this?' Asks Kerry.

'Very rarely.' Says Alice. "Bondage like this becomes part of what you are, you'll find you can't do without it, because of the freedom and serenity it puts into your everyday life. Sex on the outside isn't the same once you enjoyed the attentions of Madame and her friends. An outsider wouldn't see it, but all this is very empowering.'

'So what happens now?' I ask.

'We wait; we can just enjoy looking at each other.' Says Alice. 'you like being tied up and tortured, it's why you're here.'

She's right of course, the ropes cut into me but in ways that make me want the insistent hurt of it. Watching each other brings it's own arousal, I am seeing myself reflected again and again in the bound sensuality of my fellow captives. I have had the guilty pleasure of watching online BDSN porn movies, but this is me, here, now; brought to life where I am in a leading role.

We cannot resist twisting and squirming to find some slack in the cords; there is a perverse excitement in knowing that there is none.

We look at the reflected images of each other. There can be no doubt that we have been tied and left in this fashion so we can watch each other's helplessness and growing stimulation. Even through this haze of suffering I find myself wanting to more about them, whether their desires are the same as mine in all this.

We are literally the mirror of one another, bound into a state of arousal, knowing the inner ecstasy of it. My mind focuses itself on them and I find myself driving down on the rope buried deep within my body. I force it even deeper in than my captors did. I want the hurt of it because I want the pleasure of it at the same time. The two have become inseparable in my blurred brain. The expression in the eyes of my captive companions tells the same story, they are using me as their pleasure focus just as I am using them.

****

Here time has no meaning, it is measured only by degrees of suffering and pleasure inextricably mingled in ways that I still cannot fully comprehend. After being left with only my companions in bondage to endure this haze of ecstatic suffering, eventually there comes a vague awareness of the door opening, a figure walking across the room and moving behind me. My cords are being checked by softer, gentler hands. Fingers that know where to probe and touch to make sure that I am still at a peak of arousal. I see that each of my companions is also being attended to by a maid in the same way, as Jon had instructed earlier. A glass of water with a drinking straw is offered to my lips, which I suck on greedily.

'T..Thank you, so much. This girl needed that.' Unconsciously my mind has switched itself into submissive mode, referring to myself in that manner.

The maid smiles with her eyes, but does not speak; then I see that she cannot. Her head is encased in a black leather hood. It is tightly laced down the back of her head but with a hole at the crown which has her long blonde hair pulled through it into a beautiful mane. There is also a high leather collar locked around her neck that holds her head in a rigidly upright posture; the hood leaves only her eyes to see and nose openings to breathe and it fits like a second skin. It has a rectangular leather panel covering her mouth with a narrow reinforced slot at either end of it that fits exactly over hasps rivetted into the hood itself. A tiny padlock is fitted into each hasp, which locks the mouth panel in place.

Having experienced a little of what happens here, I have no doubt that the panel carries a gag behind it which thrusts into her mouth to maintain silence. When locked on, the gag cannot be removed even though her hands are free. It is a deliciously cruel form of discipline that allows the maid to go about her duties while still under control. Prisoners can be attended but may be told nothing, held here in captivity with no way of communicating to anyone.

'You are not allowed to talk to us?' I ask. The maid responds with a shake of her head. So silent yet so close, the scent of her is intense and arouses such wanting. She wears only the shortest of black satin skirts, with a tightly laced black leather corset that pushes up to force her naked breasts up and outwards over the top of it into provocative promise. Her nipples have gold rings inserted into them, joined by a thin gold chain. They are dressed the same as the girl I saw downstairs: black stockings, five inch heels and a frilly white apron and cap to complete an ensemble that makes her irresistible. Everything here is designed to keep a woman on a knife edge of arousal at all times.

It is obvious that she is very content with the arrangement. Service in this establishment seems to suit her very well, and it is easy to see why. She is held here in bondage just as I am, and I get the impression that she is a part of the permanent staff. She unties me, and gives me an arm in support as I involuntarily sag forward. As she guides me to a chair and allows me to rest from my ordeal, I realise that she carries a set of cuffs.

She kneels in front of me and snicks a cuff around each ankle, reaffirming that here there will be no freedom of any kind, only an existence that will be punctuated by degrees of bondage. The long mirror lets me see that my captive companions are being similarly attended to, given a drink, helped down from their posts then locked into leg irons by a maid; each one of whom is sex personified, tall elegant, beautiful and self assured. The girl knows her own irresistibility as she attends to me, who has been brought to such a pitch of arousal that her need is constant.

No doubt aware that the journey here has released a latent bisexuality in me, she is using this opportunity to flaunt her irresistibility. The closeness of this exquisite creature is making me realize just how much that is part of what I am.

I try to get closer to her, but she playfully puts her finger against her leather mouthpanel, stands up then steps back a pace and lifts her tiny skirt.

She is confined into a chastity belt. Any thoughts I might have about her are excluded by tight leather and stainless steel. The woman is obviously owned, the locks on her gag and chastity belt make that abundantly clear. Her holes are sealed and locked up tight, and only her owner has access to them. These maids are kept in a state of constant stimulation counterbalanced by frustration; they cannot touch themselves or each other and obviously remain under the control of the Mistress and Master here.

The belt fits so tightly that she cannot even get her own fingers behind it to relieve herself even if she wants to. In a sense it is the ultimate bondage to put a woman into: she may exercise no bodily function without permission. I find myself wanting to be controlled in that way, envying her already for being under such subjection. The maid is fully aware of the power she has to arouse; it is impossible to deal with, yet somehow it has to be dealt with.

The mirrored wall reflects our mutual torment; like me the other girls are beginning to realize just what they have let themselves in for. Their attendants are exactly as mine is, dressed to provoke but locked to frustrate. It was made clear before I signed the contract that this wouldn't be play acting, and it isn't. There are now four of us incarcerated together, and we can each see the other's bondage in intimate detail; I get the feeling that we are going to get to know each other very well over the next few days.

Chapter Eleven

Initiated

Dominance and submission is an intimate binding. Those who submit must trust that those who dominate will never take more than they can give. Those who dominate must give those who submit everything they need but never more than they can endure."
— *Patricia A. Knight, Hers To Cherish*

Our attendant maids are silent, offering no communication other than gestures to convey necessary orders. A clear signal motions each of us to our feet, which we obey without hesitation. Already an awareness of what follows disobedience has been made obvious to us. We each see ourselves, naked except for leg irons, and already marked with weals of deep red from being kept bound for so many hours. Yet somehow our marks serve to reinforce what we have chosen to become. Within each of us there is a need to be held in this fashion, and an insatiable desire that it should continue.

There is a growing pride in such marks and an unashamed awareness that their renewal by fresh punishments will be welcomed, despite the screams of resistance to them at the times such discipline is being enforced.

We are each taken by an arm and led through into a large shower area; our silent captors indicate that we are meant to shower together, and under close supervision. No modesty or privacy is allowed, and we have learned that protests and resistance are pointless. The prospect of hot soothing water on our abused flesh is a wonderful invitation to remove the sweat and dirt picked up by rolling around on the floor of the van. Filing into the shower area, hot jets of water hit our naked bodies from all sides as our maids watch to see that we are thoroughly hosed down. There are scented soaps and shower gels for the choosing, and we need no second bidding to use them. The streams of water are powerful, pumping new life into each of us, seeming to wash away the old. Our naked vulnerability is accentuated by the chains upon our ankles, serving to remind us of the thralldom we have chosen to enter into. We have reached a new definition of normality, where servitude and submission are established facts, and freedom is anathema.

The water is controlled from outside, and it shuts off as suddenly as it started. The doors open and their silent maids motion us to file out to receive a big fluffy bathtowel each. No orders are necessary to dry ourselves off. A maid stands behind each of us, and there is no longer any self concern about our nakedness as we sit on stools in front of dressing mirrors. The use of hair dryers and combs allows precious minutes to make ourselves look almost presentable.

Brought back into the bedroom, our minders gesture again that we should form into line, and a maid measures each of us at neck and wrists and notes down the appropriate figures, before moving to a cupboard which contains an assortment of restraints in various sizes. They return with the correct size for each submissive and fit steel cuffs to wrists and a collar around each neck with a practiced efficiency.

They are finely wrought in stainless steel, with an inner lining of soft leather. Each ring of steel is formed of two half circles, hinged together, and closed by a tongue and socket joint crafted into the edge of the steel band. As the tongue slides into its socket, it is tightened in place by a small hexagonal screw, which beds itself within the body of each steel circle. When closed the effect is a smooth ring of polished metal with no ugly locks, with a joint so fine as to be almost invisible.

I can only watch as the metal is tightened around my wrists by the maid who focuses on her task with quiet concentration. The closing of the steel is not frightening, the tightening sensation of each cuff is a welcome thrill that stirs an undeniable excitement. It serves only to accentuate the woman I seek to become; there is nothing that can happen to me here that will not reaffirm the need of that. All that is unfolding here is beyond any imagining or emotional anticipation, it is like an unseen destination that has been awaiting my arrival.

I see that the maid's wrists and necks are imprisoned by similar rings of steel, worn in a manner that emanates an obvious pride and certainty of belonging. The rings give the clear inference that, although some freedom is allowed, an instant restraint can be applied should the need arise. Such confidence accentuates the beauty of the wearer and offers an affinity to the prisoners in their care.

The cuffs have links such that they might be brought together, or, I imagine, be used to stretch her arms above her head, or spread her arms and legs to secure them in any manner her captors choose. The thought that she can be restrained in any position makes my thoughts race ahead of my immediate situation; even as my wrists are drawn together and secured behind my back I feel an excitement in watching others being made equally helpless.

Hearing the soft click of steel closing on steel makes me aware of the practiced skill of the maid twisting the hexagon key to close them tight. Tensing wrists slightly confirms a delicious helplessness, as another chain is run between wrists and collar. The other captives are being similarly bound, secured like animals, yet with an undeniable sensuality heightened by knowing fingers straying over exposed flesh as the confining tightness is made certain. The thoroughness of my captors leaves no doubt that this is the intention.

Next, the collars are linked together with six foot lengths of chain. The maids walk around us, for what purpose can only be guessed at. Hands are thrust between our legs to make them move wide apart; though no immediate sexual intent is intended it is impossible to disguise the effect it has, as gloved fingers find a slick and desperate welcome. The maid's eyes widen in mock surprise, grinning mischievously at the blush this brings on. Legs thus spread make ankle chains taut as each prisoner is forced into the same exposed posture, making their collar chains tighten. It is obvious that they are being lined up for some kind of inspection. Ranged in that manner each captive is forced to hold the others rigidly to attention.

We have only to wait a few moments, before Madame Cory makes her entrance. No longer dressed in the smart streetclothes of their previous meeting. Now there is the sheen of menacing black leather outlining every curve, buckles that tighten a succession of straps into a corset that constricts a small waist, laces that hold thigh high black boots with needlepoint heels, that stop just short of a tight leather skirt.

The effect is to further accentuate a perfect body and reflect a dominant and sadistic personality, a woman totally in control of what she is doing and of herself. Her menace is all pervasive and the four maids react in unison to her entry with a low curtsey, eyes cast submissively downwards; the obvious power she has over them creates a frightened awe of her.

Yet they are there because they need what she can give them; in that they are no different to those of us newly brought into captivity. Madame carries a long thin wicked looking whip, and her manner indicates that she is accustomed to using it.

****

'Are the sluts ready?' she snaps, to no one in particular. They are words that expect no response, unsaid commands having already been carried out under implied threat of punishments if they had not.

The maids who are in attendance nod in assent. Madame Cory makes a casual sweep with her whip, and the maids immediately form themselves into a line facing the prisoners.

It is obviously a ritual well practiced.

Inspecting us, she carelessly drags the tip of the whip across any part of our bodies that she feels inclined to. I flinch slightly, immediately a swish and a sharp crack leaves a weal across my left breast.

'Girl you do not move unless given express permission to do so.'

I have the presence of mind to answer in the third person, thereby avoiding additional punishment. 'Y..y...yes Ma'am this girl is sorry Ma'am.' Is all I can mumble through a haze of searing agony. I hold myself rigidly to attention to avoid any further chastisement, with the certainty that every effort I make will not be enough to prevent my flesh being marked again, and often.

It is quite clear that Madame enjoys inflicting pain. She continues to inspect all four of us, and it becomes obvious why we have been made to stand with our legs so wide apart. She draws the tip of the whip across our most tender spots and inspects it for each of us as she does so. She naturally finds what she expects: a glistening of aroused moisture that we are powerless to hide or disguise. Each of us feels herself running wet with need and anticipation. The whip slides softly and suggestively across the exact spot where it creates the most excitement, and we each fight our own emotions in order to stand as rigidly as we have been ordered to do.

I hear muted whimpers as the whip discovers undisguised arousal, but keep my eyes fixed rigidly forward into inexpressive blankness as the whip is flexed upwards to slide slowly between my legs. Fighting against my need as it becomes lubricated with my juices, breaths become shortened gasps, muted in fear of the pain of the whip, yet unable to deny what is being done to me with it. Needing to plead to be allowed to climax but knowing that doing so would result in a refusal and a flogging for impertinence. Rigid control of sexual expression is the prime function of this place.

The whip is drawn out of me slowly and up to my lips. Our eyes meet and my mouth opens obediently in response to Madame's unspoken order, so that I must lick the flood of my own needs, just as I did stretched across the table at the Oak. My own desires are on the flexing leather, saying how much I want to feel its pain again despite my denial of it.

This woman is hell on heels, forcing me to acknowledge my inner self. She walks back along the line, repeating the slow tantalization of each of us in turn. Each woman is inflamed to a fever pitch that reinforces the certainty of why we are here, yet no-one dares to move in response to it. The whip is lubricated with the juices of all of us, and we are forced to acknowledge the taste of one another.

'Hmmm, from the look of this whip, I think all of you are going to feel it again one way or another during the coming days, but now it is late and close to your bedtime.' The four captives stand in apprehensive silence as she turns to address her maids. 'Slaves, see that these sluts are fed and watered and put to bed. It will not be necessary to keep them gagged for sleeping.'

Our silent captors nod in deferential obedience and I allow myself a sigh of inner relief at the thought of being allowed to sleep with at least some degree of normality.

But I am about to find out that normality takes on many forms here.

****

We stand still, chained, horrified yet fascinated by what is being done to us, the hellish twists and turns of Madame's mind, unaware of what is to come next. Their maids busy themselves around us and I am aware of shallow foodbowls being placed on the floor. I risk a glance down, and realize that we are to be fed as animals: one bowl each containing food, another holding water.

Our maids make a gesture for us to kneel in front of our bowls, and I lower myself awkwardly to my knees along with my captive companions. As we sink down, the maids fix short chains between our collars and floor rings, pulling our heads even lower until our faces are close to the food to make sure we stay in the feeding posture. We are chained to the floor like tethered cattle.

I feel fingers dragging my hair back to secure it with a band, obviously to stop it trailing into the food.

Cory stands in front of us. 'Get used to eating and drinking in this manner ladies, I suggest that you lick your foodbowls clean, I shall be happy to encourage you if you do not.'

With my head pushed down towards the bowl, and after such exertions, I need no second bidding to begin to eat and drink even though it is awkward to use just my mouth with wrists chained behind my back. Some kind of meat and vegetables, cut up small to allow us to take convenient mouthfuls. In my need for sustenance I become oblivious to the humiliating obscenity of my naked backside raised into the air, and the target it offers to Madame; it is only when I feel fingers caressing me while I eat my food do I realize that the duties of our handlers also allows certain privileges. Somehow I manage to eat everything in the bowl, and lap up some water to wash it down.

Then a hand twists in my hair to drag my head up and back while my face is washed clean of food mess with a soft wet cloth, then dried off. The degradation is studied and comprehensive, with no opportunity lost to remind us of what we are.

Led into the bathroom again, a toothbrush and toothpaste have been placed ready on each of the sinks, ready for use. Wrists are unchained to allow a few moments of blissful freedom as we ready ourselves for bed. The silent maids make hand gestures to chivvy us along to finish our preparations for the night, a prospect that fills me with a dread of hours of discomfort, having seen the bare mattresses on which we will be expected to sleep.

Held by the arm and taken back to the bedroom, the maid looking after me sweeps a hand towards the bed, motioning me to lie down on my back. Arms are stretched out to the top corners of the bed, and chains are attached to wrist cuffs. The routine here is anticipated well enough to realize that legs must be placed wide apart to meet the shackles waiting for my ankles. Stretched out but not uncomfortably so, it is possible to move a little; simply to be resting on a hard mattress is more of a luxury than expected discomfort.

Chapter Twelve

Taken

"Intimacy is based on shared vulnerability...nothing deepens intimacy like the experiences that we share when we feel flayed, with our skins off, scared and vulnerable, and our partner is there with us, willing to share in the scary stuff"

~ From The Ethical Slut by Catherine A. Liszt

Even stretched out as I am, there is a welcome relief in being horizontal.

Our maids look us over, then each of them stands to attention at the end of the bed to which we have been secured. I realise that this is part of the bedtime routine.

Within a minute or two, Madame sweeps in; the maids visibly stiffen at her approach, knowing that their charges are going to be inspected. We can only lie rigidly to attention, spread open for her examination.

She walks along the line of cots, letting the tip of her whip trail across prostrate naked bodies. There is a squirming as it reaches each of us, an inability to deny the effect of it. She checks wrist and ankle restraints and nods in approval, then leans over each captive in turn and lets her gloved middle finger find a wet arousal.

I cannot suppress tensioned excitement as she explores me with her hands.

'Good work girls, I think you deserve a little reward for attending to this new intake so well.' She beckons the maids to her in a little circle, I strain my head up a little to see what's happening and realize that Madame is unlocking their chastity belts and the locks that hold their gags in place.

She turns back to us: 'Now because my girls have worked so hard today, it's only reasonable to give them a little something in return, which happens to be you four sluts. I'm sure they are going to enjoy you.' With that Madame sweeps out of the room, leaving us to the tender mercies of the maids.

Mine moves to the side of my bed, and perches prettily on the edge of it. I am aware that my three submissive companions are also being attended to in a similar fashion. One on one. She is still hooded in soft black leather, totally anonymous, her face hidden except for her mouth and eyes that offer a gentle smile. It is obvious she has the skill to use both to devastating effect. Somehow I expect her to leap on me and inflict more punishment, but she doesn't. I can only look up at her expectantly.

'Hello Anna.' She says. 'I trust you're enjoying your stay here so far?'

The use of my name with such a gentleness of tone throws me into a different emotional perspective. Until now I have known only outright sadism, now the tempo changes, seeming to offer a gentle tenderness.

'Y..yes, thank you but it takes a bit of getting used to.'

'If you got used to it, it might be less arousing for you, that's why Madame keeps everybody guessing. I'm Chloe, you've been given to me to look after, I won't always be able to talk to you, but you can see how things are organized here. We all suffer the discipline of the house one way or another.'

'Yes I can see that.' It crosses my mind that it is a weird conversation to be having with a masked woman while spread-eagled naked. Fingers caress my body as we talk, but so lightly that there is barely any skin contact. Chloe explores all of me, with a softness that starts to create a suffering that is more exquisite than the whip in its infliction. I cannot understand how I can be raped without being touched. Yet this is what is happening to me.

'Please.' I hear myself beg. 'Please.'

'Please what?' Says my masked tormentor.

'Please use me, take me, do anything to me. I'm going insane like this.' Being kidnapped and held in bondage has aroused me beyond anything I thought possible, and my frantic desires force me to pull frantically at the restraints that hold me down.

'It only feels like you're losing your mind, while you are here someone will always keep it safe when it leaves you for a while.'

She takes one of my clenching hands, leans across, and our lips brush together softly. Chloe draws back as I strain upwards, shaking her head with a light smile.

'No.' She whispers softly. 'We do this my way. Everything that happens here is done by the ways of the house; your desires are of no consequence. You will do well to keep that in mind.'

Then my mouth is brushed lightly once more, just using gloved fingertips; it makes desire grow in intensity as I feel the lightest of caresses burning skin that is already alight with wanting. Chloe brings her lips close but they do not meet mine, instead we exchange no more than breath. It is a subtle intimacy where the body-warmed scent of leather adds to the electrifying sensation that passes between us.

****

My mind is a raging confusion. The carefully contrived suffering of being brought here, the arousing cruelty, and now equally unendurable tenderness. 'I have never been kissed like that before.' I murmur softly.

'You haven't known the tender loving that a woman can give you?'

'No, my first time was in the van on the way here and that wasn't like this; it is all so new, so different.'

'You need to be trained in such loving my eager pretty one, as well as the more violent kind. Having you tied down will let me show you how that can happen. Everything here is intended to make you control your wanting and use it to become all that you desire to be.'

Chloe's fingers glide so close that I can feel the warmth of them, but not their touch. By not being free to reach for her, thoughts are aroused with tantalizing possibilities. Chloe is making me want her tenderness in precisely the same way that Madame made me express my masochism.

'These are such pretty nipple rings Anna. Have you been told how beautiful your body is?' Chloe's head goes down to allow her tongue to circle first my right breast, then my left, with my rings taken softly between her teeth and gently teased upwards as each nipple is tormented with tender bites. A hand closes over my mouth to contain screams at a suffering more intense than even Madame's whip could deliver. It is torture that consumes from within, building and building on an altogether different scale of refinement.

'Shhhh, now.' Chloe whispers softly, as her hand tightens over my mouth to contain mewling sounds. 'I want you to be aware that mine is a different kind of torture Anna. Focus your mind on what I am doing to you, let it absorb your being.'

My psyche slowly loses any awareness of self and focuses instead on my captor and what is being done to me through hypnotic words that flow like endless caresses. The sound of the muted screaming of fellow captives being similarly used seems to fade into the background until it is lost in the interplay between Chloe and myself; suddenly it is if we are alone, aware of no sounds other than those created between us. Nothing is allowed to intrude on the tender joy that we are exchanging.

As Chloe slides her mouth down the length of my body, soft kid gloves, the satin of her dress and the chain between her nipple rings caress my skin with cleverly choreographed sensuality. One by one, knowing kisses seek me out, wordlessly telling where they are headed. Softly opened by leather clad fingers, obviously skilled in such pleasures, there is a flood of excitement as a tongue lightly plays with my rings to discover an uninhibited welcome.

The exploration of my need begins with a slowness that carries its own agony, a sweet penetration that is intent on discovering every nuance of my rampant sexuality. Spread thighs are opened further with pressure of gentle hands until deep probing kisses find every spot that awaits them. Chained down, I can do little except take all that I am being given, my flooding desire leaving no doubt as to the wanting of it. Chloe lifts her body and moves over me until thighs enclose my head and she slowly lowers herself to find an eager mouth. The satin of her short skirt almost acts as a discreet veil over what I want to do to her, as my rigid tongue forces itself up to respond to an insistent downward thrust.

The juices that flow from Chloe's excitement make me tease her to increase them, gently using teeth just enough to drive the need for more, feeling aroused pulsations on my wet upturned face. Stiffening my tongue again, I feel Chloe do likewise so that we can both take what we need from each other, creating soft moans that can be felt as well as heard.

Intimate attentions are reciprocated until we are both cresting a wave of mutual ecstasy. We hold one another on it for infinite minutes, until Chloe's scream of release precedes her mouth burying itself in me as I respond by driving my tongue up to draw her down with unrestrained greed, wanting this to go on into the night until we are consumed by the blackness of oblivion.

Chloe subsides, lying in a stupor as helpless as I am, chained beneath her. I tease little shuddering aftershocks from her body, bathed in her flowing sweetness. Neither of us moves; being absorbed in the joy of one another we do not want to break the spell of tender giving. There is a contentment in each having the other there until the need arises again, until tongues stiffen in response to renewed need and irresistible desire asserts itself. I want my arms and legs free to wrap tightly around her, but for the moment I must accept that I am denied that.

I feel myself cresting again, with an urgency that forces my eager tongue deeper in, deeper than I would have thought possible; until a screaming explosion consumes us as Chloe's grip tightens on my thighs. With hands bound out of reach, my tongue must work harder to keep Chloe where she can be penetrated deeply with it. With a writhing and squirming that takes on an increasing desperation, I feel teeth softly biting, tenderly hurting. My spread-eagling bonds are jerked tight in a frenzy, the chains tensioning against the corners of the bed, as screams of mutual orgasm are muted by moist depths that turn to floods of welcome.

We lie in soft exhaustion, our needs sated for a few seconds until the next mounting insistence. There is a mutual awareness that all that passes between us could be endless, until emotions are stripped bare and there is nothing left to give.

Chloe moves around to lie close, and slips an arm under my head and softly strokes my face while kissing me gently, tasting her sweet arousal that is still on my lips and tongue.

'You taste of me Anna.'

'Do I? You taste of me too. I want the taste of you on me Chloe, being loved this way.'

'This is part of your new self Anna, it's why you are here; accept it as our gift to you. It was beautiful, feeling you respond to me as you did.'

As a last act of gentle giving, Chloe strokes my body and kisses the juices from my upturned face. Again, exquisite kindness is measured out as a counterbalance to acts of outright sadism.

'Chloe, I've never known loving like this, you make it so beautiful, it drains everything from me, I feel that I have nothing left to give.'

'You have been brought here to reveal all your desires Anna. And you still have a great deal more to give. We intend to draw it out of you.'

'Chloe, can't you stay with me, just a little longer or even all night?'

Chloe smiles and shakes her head. 'Not now my pretty one. You are a no limits girl, Madame has special plans for you. But I promise there will be more.'

'But I...'

'No Anna.' Chloe's words are still gentle, but with a firmness behind them. She puts her hand across my mouth. 'I have pleasured you, now it is time to prepare you.' My thoughts are racing again; everything seems to be a preparation for a next step, all into unknown territory. 'Think of it as the next step in finding yourself.'

'Prepare me? You mean there is more to come?'

'Shh now, no limits, no questions Anna.' There is an enigma behind her smile.

****

Before I can protest further, she picks up the leather hood and puts it over my head, closing me off from the world again. I feel my head raised and the laces retightened, and a collar locked around my neck. A gag is put to my lips, and I dutifully open my mouth to have it inserted. It is an indication of control they now have over my mind, that in my dark isolation the contours of that which fills my mouth is now welcomed. There is the familiar sound of press studs locking it into me.

Chains are removed from my wrists and ankles, but my freedom is short lived; I feel my arms dragged roughly behind my back, rough hemp rope looped around my elbows, drawing them together until they meet, knots are brutally tightened on my arms and wrists that scream in protest at the tension. But only moans come from my throat as I am pushed to the floor while probing fingers check my constant arousal. My knees and thighs are roped tightly, and my ankles are tied and dragged back until they touch my wrists. My body is bent into a tight bow, and I feel myself being lifted by several hands.

'Good, you can take her like that.' I hear Madame Cory say.

Take me? Take me where? This is only my second day of captivity.

'Careful now, she is valuable property.'

There is a sensation of being carried; a door opens then I am aware of cool night air on my naked body. I hear car doors opening, then feel myself lifted up then let down carefully onto a hard surface, doors slam shut and there is a sensation of one closing over the top of me. There are no voices now, no sounds at all. Then I hear an engine start and movement transmitted into my body, I realize I am locked into the boot of a car and can only guess that I am being transported to another location. For what purpose I cannot yet imagine, but as I shall arrive there bound and gagged, there seems little doubt that it will be more of what has just happened to me at Madame Cory's.

I use the pain of my bondage to bring myself to orgasm after gagged orgasm until my body can take no more and shuts itself down; that finally allows me some grateful rest and soft black sleep despite the discomfort and movement of the vehicle transporting me. It is a sleep of oblivion, where I am aware of nothing, not even time, the relentless violation of my body or even any caring about where I am being taken.

A sudden waking makes me realize that the car has stopped, and everything is silent.

There is a sound of the boot lid being opened, and fresh air wafting around me. I feel a chill of steel against my skin as a knife carefully cuts the ropes that have been keeping me hogtied for so long, releasing the bonds around my legs and ankles. Hands are around my shoulders. They are strong male hands but not the rough lewdly probing hands of previous encounters. They offer a quiet strength that helps me to overcome unsteadiness as I lever my legs out of the boot and try to stand up. A soft covering is draped around my shoulders to keep off the chill of the evening air as a gentle arm leads me forward and supports my few tottering steps. Sensations under my feet tell me that I am being taken into a house. Guided forward a few paces, the same hands gently press down onto my shoulders, causing me to kneel on a carpeted floor; my covering is removed to leave me naked again.

The air around me is warm and somehow I recognize a welcome even though nothing is said. The ropes biting into me are cut away and the sudden rush of blood as restriction is lifted brings a tingling to my arms and hands, and an involuntary flexing to ease the pain of it. No move is made to take off my hood. So I have no choice but to remain kneeling in dark and silent isolation. I feel no threat in what is happening; what has happened during this whirlwind of timelessness has been an ordeal, but it has also been a journey of awakening where fear has had no place. I know now that this is yet another stage in that journey. Once again there is only waiting.

Even without sight or sound there is an awareness that this is a different environment, and I am alone now, with someone who is gradually freeing me. The gag is unsnicked from its press studs and withdrawn slowly from my mouth, but I dare not speak until I am granted permission to do so by whoever is holding me prisoner. The collar around my neck is unlocked, and the laces that hold my hood tight are loosened.

Gentle hands guide mine to the hood, as a wordless indication that I may remove it. Easing the laces loose and pulling it off my head takes maybe half a minute; I have been locked in disorientating darkness and silence for so many hours, it is difficult to focus on my surroundings. I am not bound, but having been subject to strict restraint for so long absolute freedom feels unnatural. I find myself in an otherwise darkened room facing a bright light which silhouettes the outline of a man.

'Good evening Anna.'

Part Three: Fulfillment

Where new self is revealed

Chapter Thirteen

Recognition

How blessed am I in this discovering thee. To enter in these bonds is to be free. -
John Donne

'Fitz!' I recognize Fitz's voice, scramble to my feet and run across the room into his waiting arms. I cannot contain my pent up feelings or hold myself in the required kneeling posture; the joy of my immediate happiness is out of control and the events that brought me here are beyond any emotion I have ever known. I find myself holding him tight until my thoughts settle into something that might pass for normal. Neither of us can find the right words so he keeps me close for silent minutes until I am ready to talk.

I look up at him. 'Fitz, what does all this mean?'

'It's what you wanted isn't it?'

'Yes it is but....'

Fitz cuts across my questions: 'And I made you a promise that you would be safe?'

'You did, but Fitz, how did you - why did you put me through all this, and where are we?' I am still confused, half laughing, half crying, unable to make my questions coherent. 'I..I'm sorry, but I seem to have passed through a whirlwind of emotion, so much in such a short space of time.' I cannot suppress the joy at finding myself where I have always wanted to be. 'And I still can't believe you organized all this, and just for me; why did you keep it a secret?'

'Because everything had to be exactly right for everything to work out as I hoped it would.'

'I don't understand, I told you what I wanted was full on BDSM.'

'I know that, and I wasn't being secretive Anna, I had to create all this in a way that I thought would work out for both of us. My kind of BDSM and your take on it might have been two different things, I had to be absolutely sure we were on the same wavelength; to do that everything had to be arranged this way.'

'But why have you brought me here, tied and gagged and stuff? If you'd asked me, I would have come anyway. Not that I'm complaining you understand - I'd just like to know what's going on.'

In my excitement I forget all about the third person thing, and Fitz doesn't seem to mind for the moment.

'I know you would Anna, but me asking you wasn't quite good enough.'

'I don't quite follow?'

'My style of BDSM is driven by the need of the submissive; I don't ask and I don't use crude force. You are here of your own volition without any influence from me whatsoever; what brought you was a need deep within yourself.'

'This is all very new to me, I still don't quite understand your thinking.'

'I was concerned that our lifetime of straight friendship would put a barrier of inhibitions between us, and prevent you from asking for what you wanted in the way I needed you to ask.' Fitz holds me close; I curl up across him wanting to be enveloped in his arms, feeling the heat of his beautiful hard body. I am warm and safe and want to stay pressed against him, feeling my nakedness thrust against his shirt. The fact that he is fully dressed in contrast somehow reinforces my sense of submission. 'I know all this seems rather odd, but you will come to understand. I needed to be sure you wanted things like this Anna; our friendship has been so important to me down the years, I wasn't prepared to risk that for anything.'

'That was my fear too, but all this still seems unreal.'

'It is most certainly real. I do know what you've been through, but I've brought you here like this because I must discuss a few things with you.'

I look around, and realize that we are not in Fitz's house in the suburbs. Instead this is somewhere quite different, built to serve a different era. The ordeal at Madame Cory's has not been a preparation for this.

'Discuss things? I don't quite follow; you've brought my every fantasy to life, I don't see how there's much to discuss, except that I want more of it.'

'I want more of it too, but it isn't just casual bondage or BDSM play. Your ordeal with Cory was something you had to go through so that I could be sure you could take all that; but there's more you need to know.'

'More? You mean all this isn't just a sex thing?'

'Well there's that of course, but it isn't quite that simple.'

Suddenly I have a sense of apprehension. If not sex, then I want to know what is this all about. Drawing back a little to look up at him I let myself be reassured by his continued embrace and the lifetime of trust between us.

'It's OK Anna, nothing to be alarmed about I promise.'

'But where are we? You've never mentioned anywhere like this.'

'This is my house Anna.'

'Your house? But I don't understand, you haven't told me about this place.' Suddenly there are so many questions to ask, I almost forget the circumstances by which I was brought here.

'Will you be quiet for a minute and I'll explain, or I'll have to gag you till I've finished.'

'OK tell me, tell me, then you can gag me.'

'Stop that, there is a great deal to talk about Anna.' He smiles and kisses my nose, but he cannot suppress my bouncing excitement.

'Fitz, would you mind very much if I did something I've been wanting to do for a long time?'

'What's that Anna?'

I reach an arm up around his neck, and pull his head down to mine. 'I would like you to kiss me properly.'

Our lips meet in a timeless embrace of the first kiss, the threshold of passion that allows us to cross eagerly into each other's insatiable libido, with a promise of future ecstasy. I hold him tight, unwilling to let go, almost fearful that this lifetime dream of fulfillment might be lost if there is not that certainty of his delicious mouth exploring my unexpected joy.

'I couldn't wait any longer for you to do that. You'd better know now that I may be a submissive masochist, but I'm not shy of asking for what I need.'

****

'That's the way I want you Anna. But you, me, the ordeal you've just been put through, this house, are all linked; it's going to involve explanations about where it all fits together, I hardly know where to start.'

'Just tell me; now that you've kissed me properly I promise to be good and listen.'

'Well, about three months ago an elderly uncle of mine died, I didn't really know him very well because we were never a close family. It seems I was his only living relative, and apart from a few bequests he left everything to me. He was obscenely wealthy, I mean we're talking serious millions here even after death duties. I had no idea he was worth so much.'

'Oh wow,' is all I can say in reply, but eventually I collect my thoughts: 'as I recall you told me about a family inheritance, but you didn't tell me much about it.'

'I didn't discuss it with you because it's rather unconventional and I had to sort out a lot of stuff, then perhaps include you when I thought you were ready for it.'

'And am I ready now Fitz?'

'I think your time at Madame Cory's confirmed that you are. Another reason I didn't say much about my inheritance was because it's rather more than just money, even though there's a lot of that. I didn't want anything to change between us, or that it should affect us in any way. But yes, it seems you are now ready.'

'Oh Fitz, I feel the same way, I valued you so much as a friend, you've always been there for me no matter how often I messed up my life. I never made a pass at you because I was scared to risk that too. And in all the years I've known you, you've never come across as dominant in any respect.'

He smiles softly. 'And just how are dominants supposed to be?'

'I guess I don't really know, until the encounter with Liam I've never known you to lose your temper or even raise your voice. You're certainly not arrogant and I've never even heard you swear.'

Fitz grimaces. 'Arrogant? Arrogance is just bad manners. And true dominants don't get angry, at least not in a BDSM context, or in any other way really. Getting angry means losing control; dominants do not lose control, ever.'

'But I seriously thought you were going to kill Liam.'

'That was different, when he threatened me I could make a joke of it because I dislike violence and there were other diners around us; threatening you was another matter entirely. And I most certainly did not lose control.'

With that thought, I shuddered to think what Fitz might do if he did lose control. 'But it was me who stopped you?'

'Yes pretty much; Liam and his friends gave me no choice but to do what was necessary, though I would only have hurt him a little more, I don't kill people.'

I accept his assurance but still cannot rid myself of the feeling that Fitz could inflict a lot of hurt if he chose to. The encounter with Liam showed a different man, someone altogether more dangerous. But I silently confirm my wanting through my tightening hold on him. 'Thank you for protecting me as you did, Liam told me he was dominant and I foolishly believed him. I soon realized that he was a domineering control freak, which isn't the same thing at all.'

'No it isn't; real dominants never behave like that in everyday life; that would be crass and boorish. A dominant will never say he is, and they are certainly not control freaks. Too bad you had to find that out the hard way.'

'I can see that now. I always froze up when he tried to put across his version of domination; eventually I just became frigid if he touched me at all.'

'That must have been so bad for you,' Fitz says.

I laugh nervously. 'He didn't like it much either. I was scared that he might do something really stupid; but I couldn't disguise my feelings, or lack of them to be more accurate.'

'I'm sorry.'

'Why? It had nothing to do with you.'

'I suppose I feel apologetic when men behave like idiots.'

'There's no need. I survived somehow.'

****

Fitz sums things up concisely: 'Liam was ultimately weak because he thought he had to control you by actual force. A dominant never forces a submissive; if he does in the sense that she is positively unwilling, then roles are reversed. Which is why you froze up. Your mind rejected him as a weak man without you realizing it. It's up to the submissive to decide that a dom is right for her, on her terms as much as his. Once she's made that decision, bondage is just window dressing along with all the other BDSM paraphernalia.'

'Yes he did use excessive force; I mean at random when I didn't expect it or want it. When he realized he couldn't give me what I needed he started to ridicule me about the whole BDSM thing.'

'That's typical of a self professed dom who doesn't realize how powerful the need to submit is. There's infinite variety in kinky sex, what suits one D/s relationship will not suit another. That's why a dom must fine tune himself to sustain the sub's constant desire. He certainly doesn't inflict it in any unwanted sense.'

'I don't quite understand.'

'I cannot dominate you in any sexual sense unless you decide that my style of domination is right for you. No matter how BDSM is expressed, the submissive has the immutable right to walk away at any time. If the dom says she can't then that makes him an abuser. You are free to say no to anything.'

'Yes I suppose that clarifies my position.'

'But by the same token, you have to want my domination of you. If I should sense that you are merely letting me do certain things just to please me, the relationship in any sexual context will be over.'

My insides lurch at such a cold statement.

'I had no idea that was so important sir. I'm still not sure I understand your thinking.'

'The word 'let' is sudden death, it's as well to be aware of that. You have to want whatever I do to you slightly more than I do, no matter how wild things get. That's why the driving force in all this has to come from you, in the sense that you have to seek it out.'

'I have never considered that aspect of domination and submission.'

Fitz holds me to him in reassurance: 'Your need is so intense, I doubt if it will ever crop up, but I had to make that point because it is very important.'

'Thank you for your confidence in me sir, I can't imagine not wanting all that you have shown me so far, and as part of whatever the future holds for us.'

'Trust me Anna, there will be days when you won't, but that's just normal.'

'I may have made that mistake in the past, through a lack of experience I suppose.'

Fitz nods. 'It's very easy to slip into that way of thinking Anna. The idea that a submissive can be wildly aroused all day and every day is nonsense. I would get bored with it too.'

'No one told me that. I'd never thought about it in that way.'

'What one submissive woman finds attractive and exciting, another may not, the same applies to doms too of course. A real dom doesn't seek to inflict himself on every woman he meets, it only shows itself when there is a mutual attraction and need. In that sense a BDSM relationship is stronger than a vanilla one; once ground rules are established, the relationship is based on perfect compatibility right from the start.'

'I wish you could have warned me about that before I got married, it would have saved a lot of trouble.'

'I would have, but if you recall I didn't meet Liam till your wedding day; my instincts were very negative about him but by then it was a bit too late. You were obviously besotted by him so I thought I would have to forever hold my peace, like the man said.'

'So all these years you've been involved in BDSM, and I really had no idea.' I continue to hold him tight, afraid that he might vanish if I let go.

'I'm going to explain that. I've always been into BDSM as a lifestyle thing, but I never tried to involve you because you seemed to need me in other ways. I felt I had to try to support you through whatever crisis you were going through.'

'Did I lean on you too much? I'm sorry.'

'No, it was OK, I could handle all that, but BDSM carries certain rules and responsibilities; a dominant may not inflict it on someone who might not be emotionally strong enough to deal with it. I didn't want you to see BDSM as some kind of emotional refuge.'

It had not crossed my mind that there were strict rules, and that dominants could be judged by how they were observed.

'I never met your wife. May I ask if she was inclined this way?'

'Yes she was, very much so. She was utterly submissive, yet very tough and not in the least docile; can you understand the difference?'

'Yes I think I can, docile just isn't part of me. I guess that was something that my ex just couldn't handle, other men I've been involved with couldn't deal with that either.'

Fitz seems to know what other men don't, that BDSM is not about forcing the submissive, it is about bringing out the need of the submissive.

'My wife needed to be dominated, but could destroy an idiot with a single look.'

'I wish I'd known her, she could have taught me a lot.'

'Why do you think I asked Cory to give you to Chloe?'

'You know Chloe?'

'Let's say I am aware of her talents.'

'So all that I was put through with her was arranged by you?

Fitz smiles. 'In general terms yes, I thought you might need a little creative input in certain respects.'

'You do think these things through don't you?'

'I try to, but if I'd thought of you as docile, I wouldn't have arranged all that. I don't like docility in a woman.'

'Thank you for being aware of that.'

'As to my wife, the power of my domination was driven by the force of her submissive needs. She matched me and demanded it of me; when she died, it left a gap too big to fill, and I wasn't prepared to play at it with just anyone, at least not in the sense of a full time relationship.'

'Knowing that makes me more comfortable with all this sir.'

'Her inclinations also took her into the sort of world you were introduced to at Madame Cory's. I wanted to be certain you had a need for that too, and the infinite variety and pleasure of it.'

'She enjoyed all of that?'

'Very much so; like you she was very needy and demanding sexually, we suited each other very well in that respect.'

'And all that went on at Madame Cory's, did you allow her to do that too?'

'Certainly, it was something that excited both of us, it didn't lessen our love for each other, and everything happened within defined parameters. She knew I was always around to look after her, no matter how wild a scene became. In any case manners and protocols are very strict in the BDSM scene.'

'So you were not possessive where she was concerned?'

'Doms have no need to be possessive; Livia belonged to me, and I to her, we both knew that, no further reinforcement of that fact was necessary. In any case, other Doms never involve themselves with an owned submissive, except by express invitation.'

'But what about conventional sex sir, if one can call it that?'

'That wasn't negotiable for either of us; she enjoyed being hung up and whipped while I watched, or being caged while seeing me torture another woman, but conventional physical sex was never part of that arrangement, and everything was under strict control.'

'I wondered why I wasn't used in that way at Madame Cory's. When she whipped me at our first meeting, I could barely hold back from begging Jon to take me, I was so turned on.'

'Yes, I put a stop on that, in deference to where you and I might find ourselves later. In any event, sex isn't always a necessary part of the BDSM deal.'

'But you must have known submissives in the years since she died sir?'

'Of course, but none with whom I could relate deeply. I have something of a reputation for being a sane and safe dom, and women seek me out.'

I smile at that thought. 'When you said that women had discussed all this with you I did think it was rather odd.'

' That was to give you a little reassurance.'

'I suppose I should be flattered that I am here.'

'I wouldn't want you to think you are my wife's replacement in any sense Anna, I'm not looking for that, because it is a part of my life that is behind me. You are a totally different person and I can promise you that there will be no comparisons.'

'I wouldn't be able to live with the thought of being compared to her.'

'That would be discourteous to you,' says Fitz.

'You have always shown me courtesy, I do appreciate that.'

'Courtesy precludes infliction of BDSM in any unwanted sense, which is why you had to come to me through your own need; at the wrong moment it could have wrecked you emotionally. I had no way of knowing if the crazy fantasies you told me about would turn out to be just that, and would evaporate when things got real.'

'Thank you for making it happen.'

'You can only involve yourself in BDSM from a position of strength. I had to be sure you were strong enough for it; I wouldn't want to involve us in that at half measure, it has to be full on or nothing. If you choose to join with me in all this, I will not treat you in the same laid back easy going manner as before.'

'I've suffered a lot of pain to get here, sir, I wouldn't expect or want you to.'

'At Madame Cory's you refused a safeword, I will release you from that if you want to have one with me now.'

'Thank you but I still don't want a safeword sir.'

'You are very courageous Anna. May I ask why you refuse a safeword?'

'If I can speak freely?'

'Of course.'

Chapter Fourteen

Promises

"A Dom never takes away. He only builds."
— Delaine Moore, The Secret Sex Life of a Single Mom

'The skill of a dominant should be in reading his submissive; I am going to be putting my life in your hands, so if I have to constantly worry that you might do something stupid, you shouldn't be doing this. I would be very surprised if I needed words to communicate my feelings to you.'

'I know you won't need a safeword Anna, but as with everything else in this, it's a decision that only you can take.'

The episode with Liam had showed me just how dangerous Fitz could be, but also how he could control it in an instant. That made me feel safe, while the danger about him created an irresistible aura of excitement.

'Maybe I want the fear that you could cause me harm, but also that certainty that you will not.

Safewords would mean that I wasn't quite sure, I would hate that.'

'Now it's my turn to be flattered Anna, thank you.'

I hold Fitz tight, knowing that I have found what I have been looking for. There is a wonderful certainty that my desire for his discipline will not diminish. Not having a safeword makes my commitment absolute, I want nothing less.

'That's good, it's important to be certain you want that and can take it. My discipline is going to be painful.'

'I want that pain sir, the way I know you can give it to me.'

'Any suffering can only go on if I see constant desire for it in your eyes. It's critical that your need of all that is going to happen to you is fractionally greater than mine. If that fades I can guarantee I will fade with it.'

'It won't, I know that now. I have an insatiable need for the things you have shown me.'

'I'm glad we've resolved that, but there's more that I must tell you Anna, before we allow all this to go any further.'

'More?'

'Yes.'

Suddenly I have a fear that what I have found with Fitz is transient. I want there to be no more fleeting encounters, this time ownership must be nothing less than permanent.

'It's not something that is going to affect us is it, not now we've come this far?'

'No, but it will explain a little more about me I think.'

'Please go on.'

'You remember that I was with your father when he died, when you were working abroad and couldn't get home in time because Heathrow was shut down due to that heavy snowstorm?'

'Yes it broke my heart not being able to get there, I really pulled out all the stops to reach the hospital, but it was no use. I was thankful that you were with him Fitz, it meant a lot to me.'

'It was the least I could do to be there, he had always been a good and caring friend to me.

'I was glad that you two became close friends. It was good to have you around, I always thought of you as an honorary older brother.'

'Well, a little while before he died, he made me promise to take care of you as best I could. He'd always been aware that you were inclined to get yourself into awkward emotional entanglements.'

'He didn't say he was so concerned about me.'

'Well no, and I didn't tell you about it in case it skewed the way you thought of me, in any case there was no need to. I hope you understand that he only had your best interests at heart Anna?'

'So when I married that prize idiot?'

'When you asked me to give you away I was flattered of course, if sad and a little apprehensive but I couldn't do anything else for you. All I could do was wish you the best of luck and hope you'd be OK. It wasn't my place to try to influence your decision and you would have resented it if I had, no matter what your dad expected me to do. It was your choice so I had to let you go.'

'One of my bigger mistakes I guess. Maybe you should have kidnapped me then, I certainly had those kind of fantasies and it would have saved me a lot of hassle.'

He responds with a gentle laugh. 'Nice idea, you always had a gift for calamity I think; I was always concerned about you but my promise to your father was paramount. But once you were married there was nothing I could do about it, irrespective of any promises I had made. I had no option but to kiss you goodbye, after that we lost touch.'

'Yes Liam was so petty minded and jealous he made sure I lost contact with all my old friends, it wasn't just you. I tried to suggest that you and he might be friends, but his childish insecurity wouldn't allow that.'

'I often wondered if that was what had happened, after I realized Christmas and birthday cards were not being reciprocated. It's often the way with men who see themselves as some kind of master, thinking that possessiveness and petty control are an essential part of being dominant.'

'That part of it was maybe the worst, the isolation, my every move questioned and scrutinised. When we were first married, I thought it was an erotic game until I discovered he meant it, and not in a sexy manner. Would you believe he used to check the mileage on the car on the rare occasions when I went out on my own?'

'At least I was able to help you get back into focus when we met up at that party a couple of years ago.'

'When I was at rock bottom again.' I take his hand and kiss it softly. 'Thank you so much for picking me up and giving me something to hold on to.'

'I try not to give up on people.'

'And all this, the BDSM and stuff?'

'That's always been a part of my life that didn't involve you, it's really not for the faint hearted.'

'Did you see me as faint hearted Fitz?'

'I was never quite sure how you'd react to it, we were just too close. In any case it conflicted with my promise to your dad. Doms have a duty of care first and kink second; it may not appear that way, but that's the way it works in a genuine relationship. I just left it out of our friendship altogether, I thought it best.'

'I seem to have led you a rather complicated dance to get to where we are at this moment.'

'That's putting it mildly girl, but I suppose I've always been in love with you, and I wasn't going to risk that by mixing BDSM into our relationship. I would have wanted you as a true submissive, not someone playacting to please me; it was important that you wanted it too.'

'And now you have shown me how beautiful it can be.' I tighten my hold on Fitz, reassuring myself that this time it's for real.

'BDSM only works when the submissive actually seeks it out for herself, which is why I sent you to Cory and Jon; you could have stopped what they did to you in an instant, but you did not. That told me the depth of your need of it.'

'No, I guess I didn't need persuading once I realized what Madame Cory's place was all about. I hardly know what came over me while I was there. It was as if I was free for the first time in my life.'

'Glad you found it that way; freedom is what BDSM is all about; force is just an illusion. A dominant does not choose his submissive, neither does he need to use actual force to control her. She must make the conscious decision that she wants to be owned by her chosen dominant, in full awareness of what that will mean.'

'You have made that choice easy now....sir.'

****

'Thank you; everything clicked into place when you told me about wanting to be kidnapped. I had inherited this house, and knew all about Cory's little venture. After you blurted out your kidnap fantasy, I explained to her what I wanted to set up, and she was only too happy to help me out.'

'Yes that was an amazing coincidence.'

'Sounds silly maybe, but I didn't want my inheritance getting in the way of us. I realized that I could find out if things would really work out between us before I needed to tell you about this place.

I put my arms around him. 'Fitz my love, I've always wanted you too and the inheritance wouldn't have made the slightest difference. But I do understand your thinking. I realize now that I want to be your personal property for life, if you'll have me. What you arranged for me at Madame Cory's has made me certain of that.'

'Your saying that makes me very happy Anna.'

'I know I can't do without you and what you've shown me.'

'Thank you Anna, but BDSM takes emotions to such a fine pitch, I had to be sure that nothing could come between us as it developed.'

'Jon, Madame Cory and her girls showed me what I need, and now I can never be satisfied with anything less.'

'Yes you were really put through the mill weren't you?'

'Did I come through it all to your satisfaction sir?'

'Being able to watch you submit yourself to the BDSM lifestyle was wonderful.'

'You watched me sir?'

'Certainly.' I look up questioningly, Fitz smiles and hands me an iPad. 'You and Chloe seemed to hit it off very well together.'

My blushes cannot be prevented as I begin to replay my encounter with Chloe. 'My God, was that really me?'

Fitz laughs. 'If it wasn't, you have an amazing stunt double.'

'I didn't know we were being recorded sir.'

'Chloe did. It's OK, it hasn't been copied elsewhere, and I will allow you to delete it if you wish, just for this first time.'

I look at the screen and relive my frenzied passion, begging to be used, screaming and writhing in ecstasy under such intimate attention. It is part of what I am and I don't want it deleted. I know that Fitz will ensure that the video remains in our private world. 'Thank you, I'd rather keep it.'

Fitz laughs knowingly. 'You liked Chloe then?

It is a question that needs no answer, Chloe had opened me to something new, the soft feel and taste of a woman's body against my own, a fresh and exquisite pleasure that can only demand more. 'It's odd, I sometimes had an odd lezzy fantasy, but dismissed it with the thought that I wouldn't really like it. The other girls in the van, and then Chloe changed my mind about that.' Chloe had invaded my mind in ways that I had not thought possible, and I watch myself being brought to climax again and again under her subtle touch.

'Will everything be videoed sir?'

'Not necessarily, but it will if I feel the occasion demands it. You will not be consulted, but you might be told, or not. But nothing will leave the privacy of our personal environment.' I look a little apprehensive. 'No limits, remember?'

'I..I'm sorry sir, of course; I just wasn't thinking. There is just so much to take in.'

'I understand; it will take you a little while to adjust to my ways. And I think I shall owe Madame Cory a lot of favours for helping to make all this happen.'

'Mmmmmmm...I can think of lots of ways for you to repay her sir, maybe a return visit soon?'

'You are incorrigible, now It's very late Anna, shall we shower and get to bed and talk more in the morning?'

'I think we should, but I would like sir to grant me one pleasure.'

Fitz laughs. 'Just the one?'

'Yes sir.'

'What is it?'

'Just for this first night, can I be tied to the bed close to you while you are sleeping? In case you wake and need me in the night. Please......Master?'

Fitz's expression hardens a little at that word and he draws back from me; I sense that I might have misinterpreted our relationship. I feel a cold flutter in my heart, because I want to please this man who has claimed me, and brought me out of the emotional wilderness. I pull away from him slightly.

****

'Sir.' I ask anxiously, 'I have said something wrong, please tell me what it is?'

Fitz's expression is gentle but his words are firm. 'You addressed me as master. I am not that, not yet. You have more training to undergo before we reach that stage.

'I..I'm sorry, sir?'

'Sir is correct for the moment, you were not to know the depth of commitment necessary before I become your master in a formal sense.'

'It seems I still have much to learn sir, about you, and all this.'

'Yes you do. Madame Cory's was my way of being certain that you wished to go on learning and training, which would be more to the point.'

'When will I be able to address you as master?'

'I promise that you will know when the moment is right to do that.'

'But you will not tell me?'

'No; a dominant does not tell his submissive when to address him as that.'

'Why not sir?'

'Because it would be from inside my head; it must come from within yours, now is not the time.'

'It is very confusing, how will I know sir?'

'You have trusted me this far?'

'Implicitly.'

'Then trust me that bit further - you will know. Your ongoing training will lead you to that time.'

'There is more training to come sir?'

'Much more Anna. Your time at Madame Cory's was just the start of it. In some respects the submissive's training never ceases, but by the same token, my learning about you will also never end.'

He pulls me close again, and I feel the strength of him. 'But it will be a training through love as well as suffering and cruelty. You will also be trained to know the freedom that is within yourself, if you can understand that?'

'I am glad that you want to train me, I cannot imagine anyone else doing it, not now. And I do want to be trained; I have already tasted the freedom you speak of and I don't intend to give that up.'

'There is much more to it than being submissive, it is an attitude of mind that will grow within you, if you want it to.'

'I can see I have much to learn….sir.'

'You do, but I will teach you; your mind has been messed up by bad encounters in BDSM, I intend to straighten that out, then we can go on from there.'

He takes me in his arms and holds me tight. I feel myself to be Fitz's captive, and although I may not yet speak the word, I think of him as my master and know that there can be no other who will receive that title from me, not now. I press myself against him as a woman who has discovered a new kind of liberty, feeling his erect arousal forcing itself against me as I look up at him softly, aware of its insistence.

'Sir, may I offer my mouth to pleasure you?'

'You are very eager.'

'Yes I am just that, but sir has given me so much. You seem to have awakened an appetite for more.'

'Are you always going to be like this?'

'I fear that such is the case sir, and I expect to be punished for my temerity.'

'I have no doubt that you will be, but you have my permission to take me into your mouth.'

His words bring a shiver of anticipation as I slip to my knees, and my fingers find his zip.

'And it pleases me that you know to ask for what we both desire.'

'Thank you sir, I intend to match your needs with my own if you will allow me to.' The words that grant access to his body add a new dimension to his owning me.

His rising hardness springs into my searching hands as my lips part to take him. I look up, and my eyes lock onto his with a boldness I sense he does not wish to suppress. I am aware that he wants to watch my violation and see the effect he has on me and I on him, as my mouth encircles his throbbing flesh with a mixture of tender mischief and rampant desire.

My lips and tongue work softly, tenderly to bring him to full erection, taking his entirety into my mouth. I breathe in the hot musk of him, sensing his body stiffen, trying to hold himself back while I drives myself onto him still deeper. I caress the length of his hard desire to focus the need I have, wanting to be in possession of all of him in whatever way he chooses to use me. I take his right hand gently into mine, and form his fingers around his thrusting violation to increase my sensation of being used; wanting my mouth to be merely a hole that can be filled as he chooses, when he chooses.

His left hand caresses my hair, fingers twisting into it, forcing my head forward to gain full penetration of my offered mouth. Almost involuntarily wrists are crossed behind my back, and though unbound, it accentuates my emotional posture of submissiveness. There is a need to feel restrained, a necessary show of belonging.

After sweet minutes of dalliance with my tongue, there is a slow withdrawal and a gentle caress that commands a rising to my feet. With insistent bodies thrust together, fingers softly part willing thighs, a hard desire seeking release slips between them to find the moist and eager welcome that is there for him. I rise onto my toes and lock my arms around his neck to ride onto him, the juices that betray a desperate need stimulating an increased fervor with their incessant flow. The lightest touch makes me ready and wanting, no words being necessary as open lips find his so that he can fully savour the manscent that is still on them.

But he pulls himself from me, and his left arm slips under my back, and his right slides behind my thighs. My arms are still around his neck as he lifts me effortlessly, allowing our long sweet kiss to stay unbroken; there is a strength in him that doesn't break step or alter his breathing as we cross the hallway and climb a broad staircase.

Carried with such power and tenderness towards a destiny that did not exist a day ago; there is now a soft melding, a warmth transferred one to the other until the heat of wanting fuses, and we become as one. A bedroom door is kicked open, reinforcing the all-enveloping sensation of being protected and safe with a man I know will look after me.

There is a holding tight, almost a fear that this precious moment might be lost, aware only of the need to be taken in this fashion and to remain free in utter subjection, cradled in his powerful arms.

Chapter Fifteen

Chained

The eye of the master will do more work than both his hands. –

Benjamin Franklin

The bedroom is vast; oak linenfold panels darkened with age cover the walls, tall mullioned windows allow the soft fading light and warm air of the summer evening to fill the room with romantic welcome. Arms tighten around my yielding body for a moment, then Fitz draws back a little to allow our eyes to meet. He smiles without speaking, then leans over to place me in the centre of a large antique fourposter bed, I pull his head down to renew his kiss, wanting to devour him with my mouth and entire body.

I feel owned now, and as Fitz had said, it is because there is an unspoken freedom to choose to be so; this is the first man I have encountered who I know will reciprocate my every desire. Wanting to be taken like this is confirmation that only he may possess me.

Disengaged from my tight embrace, and standing back to appraise me, there is an awareness of silent admiration and I am glad that I have a body that pleases him. The marks that are still there from the attentions of Madame Cory serve only to accentuate what I am.

Our eyes meet in mutual need and intensity as he peels off his clothes to allow me an equal moment of appreciation of sharply defined muscle and masculine desire for me. This moment of quiet space between us has become an emotional timeshift that has taken us from being lifetime friends to the immediacy of lovers. For the first time in my life I can look longingly at the power of his naked body with unashamed desire, knowing that the hardness of his need is focused on me.

'You look adorable and you have a body to be proud of, I shall expect you to flaunt your beauty like this as part of what you are.'

'It will be a privilege to show myself to you; I want you to look at me and use me because I am owned by you now.'

Fitz reaches down and lightly caresses my breasts, lifting my nipple rings appreciatively. I stiffen in anticipation and my body rises, unable to deny the need of him. My hand closes over his, pressing it tight to increase the sensation of his touch as fingers close softly around my right nipple, then the left until my eyes widen in wordless begging.

I feel the moist welcome already waiting for the moment when he chooses to take me. Inside I am screaming for him to do just that as the fire of desire is blown into full flame again.

'And I had no idea that you had been so prettily ringed, they do suit you Anna. When did you have them done?'

'Some time ago sir; I didn't know it then, but now I realise I had myself ringed for you, ready for when you wanted to own me and use me. It just took a while for you to find them.'

'The time had to be right Anna.' Fitz grins in response to my pointed remark.

'Yes it had to be right.' I reply, knowing that now is right.

'It was getting difficult to ignore you in certain respects too you know.'

'Yes.' I put my arms around his neck and kiss him again. 'We need to make up for lost time.'

'I intend to use you, will it please you to be owned?' I find it chokingly difficult to respond to such a concept, unable to tell him that I have spent a lifetime searching for this moment, without knowing what it really meant or where to find it. 'You know something now of what being owned will mean?'

'I am beginning to sir, and you have promised to teach me anything more I need to learn, and I can't tell you how it will please me to be owned by you.'

'No doubt I shall learn from you too Anna.'

'But what can I teach you sir?'

'Things you are as yet unaware of; every submissive is different, a dominant's mind must be open to those differences. We can only learn the subtleties of our art from submissives, we are not born with the knowledge of such intimacies you know.'

'I'd never thought of it quite like that sir.'

'Your mind and body are new to me, and I can only learn from being close to you; despite appearances to the contrary, involvement with a submissive can only be at her invitation.'

He releases my breast and his mouth comes to mine, to take possession of what is already his; I am spread open for him and our bodies become one, and my fingers softly reach down to guide him in. I know that my life with Fitz is going to be one of ultimate bondage but on this first night I can draw his body freely into mine, wanting our loving to be soft and tender. It is a captivity so complete that no bonds are necessary.

'But I must tell you about....' I put a finger to his lips.

'Tomorrow sir, tomorrow is soon enough my love to tell me all that needs to be told. I don't want to lose the magic of this special first night of possession by you. I've been waiting a lifetime for this moment, I can't wait any longer for the sensation of being taken and owned.'

As the words of submission are spoken, the effect of them reflects in the hardness that begins to open me, confirming the deep moist acceptance of what I have become: the property of another through the abdication of self. Yet he does not fully take the open welcome that is offered; instead he poises himself at my entrance, asserting the authority he has to take me at the moment of his choosing.

My needs are on a razor edge, yet still there is his denial. There is barely a touch of him, his entire body braced on toes and fingertips above me, hard, tense, every muscle forcing an intensity of response. No other part of him except the power of his demand touches me, focusing my attention on what I most desire at this moment, commanding me to recognize that. His eyes hold mine with a power that is greater than physical strength; they draw my entire being to him, his insistent hardness against me is bringing my mind and body under his control.

It is hypnotic, and arouses emotions from depths that I am unaware of; they build from within until my orgasm erupts. It is as if a pent up rage against previous encounters with inept lovers is somehow being expunged by this man who is now taking me as his own, remaking my sexuality in a way that will transform me into the woman I want to be.

The explosion convulses my entire body, the scream that comes from my throat is beyond human. It is pure animal, a violent ecstasy that makes me lock my arms tight around him and drag him into me at the very pinnacle of it. Mine is a bondage that now transcends the physical and consumes all emotions. I force myself up onto his waiting length and use it; wildly and obscenely demanding everything from him despite knowing that I am his submissive.

He remains deep, unmoving, hard, allowing me the freedom to take what I want of him; his lean muscular body so powerful yet so gentle in forcing this new kind of submission from me.

Fitz is making me aware of the meaning of being loved in a new way as I pivot my entire being on him, effectively raping myself on the focus of a hard and relentless desire. There is no desperate thrusting, only the stillness of him that invites me to writhe in a mindless frenzy to extract the most from this first encounter. It has become my eternal moment, allowing joy to pivot around a pleasure that takes me into infinity. It is as if I am being made love to for the very first time, instead of being used. Fitz is showing me that there is a world of difference; that domination is also about tenderness and suggestion, revealing what is within the submissive rather than concentrating on the exclusive needs of the dominant.

We close together and become as one, and the tears of happiness that come from my sea of sensations cannot be held back. Fitz has given them freely, as part of his ownership of my being. He tastes yet another part of me as he kisses the tears from my eyes while his body is being drawn down onto mine to feed the fires of an unquenchable need.

****

'You know that you are the first man to make love to me?'

He laughs softly.

'I mean make love, as opposed to just having sex or merely being used sir. You barely touched me, yet that first orgasm practically blew my head off, I don't understand how you did that.'

'You told me you couldn't climax with a man unless you did it yourself, I had to clear up that bit of nonsense.'

'Yes but how Fitz?'

'I made you want it enough.'

'You mean all these years I couldn't climax because I didn't want sex?'

'I didn't say that, I said you didn't want it enough.'

'But I climaxed in a way that didn't seem real sir. But yes I have never wanted it so much; what you just showed me was extraordinary.'

' It was the power of your need Anna, I'm glad that I have been able to show you our future.'

'You sir, are very unusual.'

Fitz laughs: 'I know.'

'And modest with it?'

'I'm still having a problem with modesty.'

'I think I can live with that,' I whisper softly. 'Anyone who can make love like you do doesn't need modesty.'

I draw his head down, and kiss him hard again. His passion responds to mine, as he holds himself inside me. I become aware of his phenomenal willpower, and realise that it is more controlling than ropes or whips can ever be. 'Does sir never lose his driving force?'

'Not as long as my pretty slave shows her need of it.'

'Somehow I believe you.'

He eases from me and silently holds my eyes with his. I feel myself becoming lost in the power of him again, and with that loss of self my body starts to pulsate almost of its own accord in a way that is beyond my control or understanding.

By deliberately allowing no physical contact between us, there is only the relentless sensation of my mind becoming fused with his in the common purpose of mutual ecstasy. Without knowing how, he is controlling me. Yet I choose to surrender to the joy of that control, giving myself up to it in an absolute sense, wanting no freedom from the feeling that throbs throughout my body as I lie enthralled only inches from him. Inviting Fitz into my mind has allowed him to run riot, forcing me to silently beg for his thrust. I cannot hold back another shuddering explosion as his mind reaches out to claim me and I submit willingly to it. It is a kind of loving I have never heard of, let alone experienced. The effect is frightening yet it is a fear that I want to be consumed by.

'Fitz, sir, please; I must have you in me, this is too much, now you are making love to me without touching me, that shouldn't be possible. I don't know what's happening inside my head.' I reach out for physical contact with him.

'Your mind is becoming mine, if you choose to gift it to me. It is important that you know what my ownership of you will mean.'

'No one can do what you are doing with just eye contact alone.'

Fitz smiles softly: 'No one?'

I have been used to men being nervously inept, or loud and boorish, or convinced that possessive aggression is domination, all leaving me angry and frustrated. Fitz is none of these; nothing has prepared me for what he is.

'You just brought me to orgasm simply by looking at me. I reacted as though you were inside me, though I knew you were not.' The turmoil in my head refuses to let me believe what he just did to me, yet I have to accept it. 'What are you?'

'I'm just me Anna, all I did was release you to be what you are. It was your wanting that drove you to do that.'

I cling tighter, almost frightened of his words. No longer sure of who I really am, there is an apprehension of where Fitz is taking me, counterbalanced by a trust that is being tested to its limit. After my ordeal at Madame Cory's I expected the same. Or more. That changed me; here Fitz is changing me yet again.

'I still don't understand Fitz, what you just did to me isn't in any way normal.

'So what is normal Anna?

'I..I don't think I know any more; perhaps I have never known. Whatever normal is, you are certainly not it.'

'I showed you the power of your mind Anna. Remember I told you women have a far greater sex drive than men once it is set free.'

'But it was your mind that did that.'

'No, I released you; that freed you of all the crap of previous encounters.'

'But it's not free sir; it belongs to you now.'

'That is because you have made the free choice to become mine, as I hoped you would. I will choose when and how you climax, and when you may not. I need you to know that, my way of making love to you makes sure you do.'

I sense that he is leading my mind into bondage, so that every sexual thought that I have becomes his. I do not know how he is doing it, only that I am following willingly. For the moment, physical restraints seem irrelevant, though I know I will be put into bondage later. Now I feel my climax rising again as we are drawn together once more. He enters slowly, making me wait as the tip of him teases me to a frenzy before sliding in by deeper and deeper stages, each moment forming an eternity around itself. The slow gentleness of every inch of him becomes a torture that seems to take minutes to reach full penetration. He has the skill to make each thrust into me a form of divine suffering, each slow withdrawal a confirmation of the need to beg for his return.

The eagerness in my eyes tells him I want nothing more than to receive that endless torture from him. Each long slow thrust becomes an assertion of his total control of me and of himself. He offers a promise to satisfy an eternity of wanting, then uses sadistic skill to hold back for long moments, keeping me on an edge of orgasmic insanity.

There is a craving for every violation, it forces my body to drive itself upwards to find him; no words are necessary to confirm that he is a master of sex itself and that I am now consumed by a desperation that threatens to devour my entire being.

****

Time and again he withdraws himself to stop my emotions from careering out of control, then as I subside a little, the next penetration is made to seem fresh and new and more intense than the last. He holds me there wordlessly using eye contact alone, and does not let me fall, despite my desperate need to.

It becomes the ultimate subjection of my will to his, an enthrallment of all that I am or could ever hope to be; it is a way of loving beyond anything I thought possible.

I do not know how he does it, how he can have such knowledge of what I need or the willpower to control himself.

He withholds what I need so that my suffering becomes an exquisite hell, not of his infinite demand, but of my own. I am past caring as my body becomes consumed by fires that he has lit; no restraint is necessary to tell me that I am already his slave in bondage, while at the same time having the freedom to pull him close and never let go.

I feel myself grasping his taut body, fingernails raking his flesh in a painful ecstasy that seems to fight against his control while desperately needing it.

There is the sound of the wetness of my need flooding around him and the feel of his thrusting intensity in response to it.

I hear myself begging in desperation: 'Sir, please, may I come? I did not know such torture could be, this is too much to hold back.'

I know that I can make myself explode in an instant, but also know that now I may not do so without his permission.

Somehow that makes it all the sweeter because it is part of my subjugation to him. He does not respond immediately, but instead watches the fire of desperate frenzy that burns in my eyes turn to frantic pleading. The torture is sublime; my inner self forces such restraint on me while a rampant libido fights for the release it must have. The conflict is explosive, and reduces me to a form of begging which barely masks a rage.

'Sir please?' With a suffering so intense, I am on the verge of tears. The more my need grows, the more the torture forces bonds to close around me as my body awaits his command. Emotions tighten, needing his soft words of release.

After a seeming eternity where my eyes offer only a silent pleading, he whispers that I may climax.

My need releases itself like a tensioned spring, hitting him with pent up feelings that become an anguished scream as my raging passion rises to meet his, revealing the urgency that forces him to reflect my desire with his own.

Dragging him down, arms tight around his neck, legs are locked around his body; the bond between us is now stronger than any rope or chain.

I will not release him until he has become mine in the fullest sense and filled me as I need to be filled. Consumed by the muted sounds of desire, my passion triggers the climax that meets his with equal force. I have surrendered myself as his submissive, yet for these moments Fitz has turned me into a raging animal that is anything but that, and released the power of the woman I know he wants me to be.

We cling tight, holding each other in mutual exhaustion, not wanting to divide our bodies and lose such a precious moment.

Chapter Sixteen

Enthralled

> *"He towered over her, as intense and savage as only he could be,*
> *making her feel small and delicate in comparison, surrounded by his utter maleness.*
> *She felt trapped and she wanted to stay in his cage forever."*
> — Cristiane Serruya, Trust: Pandora's Box

'Sir, you have shown me what bondage means; it needs no physical restraint because you make every penetration of me become an assertion of your ownership.' My mind is in a turmoil, wanting our loving always to be like this, tender yet powerful where I feel that I am being taken forcefully but able to meet his urge in equal measure with my own.

'It was necessary to show you how it could be, that bondage must be more than just physical.'

'I couldn't be bound tighter to you than I am now, no matter what you used to hold me.'

I know now that I am controlled by this man, but in a way that until now I have been unaware of. I do not know how every thrust into me is made to feel new and different to the last, or how it can cause his hold over me to tighten. He has brought me into a different form of bondage, now I realize that there can never be an escape from it.

'We must always go on this way Anna, meeting one another with such intensity and force.'

So many years of knowing Fitz, and only now is he beginning to reveal himself. 'We will, I know we will now that we have found each other sir, and you have shown me how.'

We lie as one for long minutes, breathing in the hot scent of our entwined bodies, saying nothing, lost in the tender embrace that binds us. Our lips are together, not through frenzied passion, but as part of an unwillingness to let go. His body seems to mould itself to mine; neither of us wants there to be any separation. A silent stillness covers us. We are locked into one another, still held together even though hard intensity has been subdued by his climax. He has the awareness to stay there, not pull away as other lovers have always done. It is something to be savoured as our frenzied loving was savoured, but in a different way.

We are in a mutual haze, each knowing the exhaustion of the other. I cannot bear the thought of being physically parted from him, and hold his eyes with mine as I disengage my arms from around his neck.

Extending them over my head, I put my wrists together in silent invitation; recognising my needs, he draws down two lengths of thin chain that are already fixed to the bedhead. Instead of the anticipated rope, there is now a different excitement in feeling the chill of steel, as it had been on the first night at Madame Cory's. There is the thrilling sensation at the closing of a circlet of links around each wrist, the little snicks as tiny padlocks snap shut. He eases away a little, sensuously passing the chains down my prostrate body so that the coldness of them contrasts sharply with the throbbing heat of arousal. An insistent parting of my legs allows a chain to be carefully threaded through each labial ring; feeling and hearing each link being drawn slowly down through them brings a frisson of new pleasure as my ankles are encircled tightly with steel, locked, and fastened to the foot of the bed.

Any movement causes the chain to slide gently through the rings but without pulling on them; the caress of steel on my most tender flesh brings a fresh dimension to arousal, and is likely to keep me so all night, whether asleep or awake. Testing the restraints is irresistible, the sensation of the sliding chain is so soft, so subtle where they touch, yet so unyielding. The slightest pull on them makes their hold change to a relentless bite, but by contrast relaxation leaves me almost unaware of being restrained. But it is beyond any power of will to resist a self infliction of suffering, and to intensify self torment. The emotions it drives cannot be prevented from welling up to find an outlet at the hands of such a creative tormentor.

'Sir, I can't hold on to my sanity restrained like this with chains through my rings. Hold me sir, please don't let me go.' My voice carries a different note of desperation, there is a need for Fitz to stay close now as he puts his arms around me while my chained ankles tension my body into a shattering orgasm again as it thrusts against the close heat of him. The convulsions will not stop, and with my mind and body aroused to such a fine pitch, a climax hits yet again within seconds of the last. The steel I deliberately force to bite into flexing wrists and ankles relays flashes of torment as instant arousal burns through me. Nothing can stop it and screams can only be muted by burying my mouth against his chest. I feel my teeth uncontrollably sink into his flesh: He flinches slightly at the pain I inflict on him, and his hold tightens around my tortured body. It is the only way I can relay the intensity of erotic suffering he is causing. 'Sir, is this what your bondage will mean, in our future?'

'Yes it will Anna, now that I am certain your need for it is in tune with my own.'

My words are uttered in short gasps, muted against his skin: 'It is a torture that I cannot contain sir, unless you are here to hold me. Why won't my orgasms stop?' His loving hold triggers a fresh wave of wanting as my body thrusts itself against his in a torment of infinite ecstasy, engulfing me in response to his need.

Orgasms go beyond counting, hitting again and again with an increasing ferocity until there is scarcely a pause between them, only an uncontrollable surge of emotion that continues to demand as they fuse into one another. His awareness of what I am going through makes him keep me in a tight embrace until my rage of ecstasy subsides and passion has run itself into sexual oblivion and I can take no more.

Attempts at speech result in incoherent noises, half moans, half sobs as Fitz holds my shaking body and softly strokes my hair as subspace claims me. He lets me drift into a warm sweet time while I remain limp and helpless in his arms.

There comes a time of unawareness, floating into that black solitude that takes me to another time and place. There is the certainty of Fitz holding me as I go, and the certainty of knowing he will be there when I return to some degree of normality.

****

He is smiling down at me when I open one eye and look at him; it takes a few moments to regain a degree of coherence. 'I can see why you've terrified men in the past Anna.'

'Surely you don't think that has happened before Fitz? You are the first; I don't really understand what you did to me, but somehow I know it is what I have been seeking in a lover.'

'Shhh - just teasing you a little, I know that's never happened before my love. If it had, you would be with the man who gave it to you.' I strain against my chains to kick him, giggling at the tender humour that all this allows us to exchange, while still excited by the bite of steel on my body. 'it pleases me to have been able to give you what you wanted.'

'If I terrified men it would have been because I knew I wanted something like this and they couldn't give it to me. I'm afraid it's not a very submissive trait.'

'That is the kind of submission I want. I told you I can't handle docility or mindless obedience. Without that need I cannot dominate you, neither would I wish to; the intensity of your desire is what drives me.'

'I'm glad it does sir, because there's going to be a lot of it if you use me like that. Am I normal, to react as I do?'

I flex my chained body against him to make the point and he reaches round and gives my bottom a hard slap. 'I was using you?'

I can't repress a mischievous giggle. 'Sorry sir, I deserved that, I will try to behave in future.'

'It's OK, I deliberately made you react in the way I wanted you to.'

'You made me do all that sir?'

'Let's say I pushed all the right buttons and you did all the hard work.'

'I didn't know the buttons were there.'

'Well now you do Anna.'

'I think their whereabouts will remain your secret sir.'

'Very possibly.'

Such a disarming description of ecstatic hell makes me smile. 'But I think I shall need them pushed quite often now you've found them.'

'Reacting as you did, you can be pretty sure of that.'

'I know you own me now sir, but it felt like I was raping you. Submissives aren't supposed to do that are they?'

'My submissive is; I intend to give you the kind of power that will frighten most men, that will make you exclusively mine.'

'Your thinking is very odd sir.'

'It's a popular fallacy that the sub is reluctant and must somehow be forced, only reacting to the dom's initiative and orders. I don't do things that way, I want a power to grow inside you from now on, and I expect you to use it. I will find that intensely arousing.'

'Mmmmm it was incredible, it drove my wanting beyond any imagination. My fingers never did that to me.'

'I should hope not indeed.'

My tongue caresses the bitemark on his chest, 'You made me do that too sir, so I can't apologise for it; maybe just kiss it better?'

'Remind me to punish you for that tomorrow.'

I laugh softly, moving my thighs a little, to feel cool of the chains as they run between them. It is a refined form of torture that gives a choice of subtle self-infliction: my body cannot endure it, yet it is impossible not to test that endurance.

'Sleep now pretty one, your rings are very beautiful; these chains will hold you through the night, and make sure you wake aroused in the morning in the way I want you to be.'

'I expected you to tie me with rope.'

'If I had used rope to tie you it would cut off circulation and eventually cause you the kind of pain your mind would reject. You wouldn't want that and neither would I.'

There is a delicious thrill in his care for me as the chains run the length of my body and embrace me without constriction, leaving a only light suggestiveness where they touch. Knowing that I will be restrained all night makes me feel safe and owned and happy. It is a fantasy brought to reality, to be tied, in bed next to the one who I belong to. I am where I have wanted to be all my life. Fitz leans across, places the softest of kisses on my lips and pulls the covers over both of us. I am glad we haven't showered; I want the hot scent of my man on me for the night and the intimate closeness of him sleeping close.

'Goodnight now, no more orgasms until I give you permission; you must sleep.'

'Yes sir.'

He has put my body into a new state of torment, because chained in this way I could climax myself over and over. But it has been forbidden; instead I try to take myself to a level of calm obedience.

'When you slept in my spare room the other night, I cried myself to sleep, wanting you so badly.'

'You now know why I couldn't come to you Anna, even though I wanted to?'

'Yes I do sir, that was the wrong time; thank you for making me wait until now; goodnight.' I whisper softly.

'Goodnight.'

He turns and flicks off the light, and I pull on my chains to reassure myself that I cannot get loose, while forming myself around his body within the limits that my bonds allow. I am comforted by a hand that reaches back to caress me into that position, and kiss the back of his neck. For that I receive another light slap on my bottom, but my mouth stays where it is, to taste the salt heat of our lovemaking. I need to be close to him, my body softly moulded to his to make us as one. We both know that if he turned and flogged me, it would serve only to awaken an even more rapacious need.

As I hear his breathing change into a deep sleep I move my ankles a little, to feel the effect of the chains that Fitz has put on me. They are an extension of him, and I wear them with a possessive pride as they move across my body; the sound they make is intensely arousing, as is the lightness of their caress.

Sleep is going to be difficult. They trail down close to my mouth, and I suck in a few links as if to hold onto those ongoing promises that I want fulfilled. I have to use all my willpower not to bring myself off lying there next to him; there is a need within me that will not be stilled, I know that I will be wet and wanting him long before he wakes in the morning.

Chapter Seventeen

Entwined

A Master has to master the mind of His slave and not to torment her body – only then He's worth the most precious gift that was given to Him - the slave herself! –
Sir Peter Mclaughlin

I wake with a start, for the moment unaware of where I am.

Fitz is leaning up on one elbow, looking at me. His left hand has strayed between my legs, and is toying lightly with my rings, and the chains that pass through them. I think my fading dream had involved itself in that. My wet arousal seems to confirm it. The painful tug on my wrists gives me a sharp reminder that I had asked Fitz to chain me to his bed the night before. There is a thrumming sound on the oak headboard as I pull on them, they dig into my skin, hurting, but it is a hurt I want and I cannot resist testing the restraints that still hold me. My sleeping had been full of dreams that are now fast deserting me, just as dreams always do. I don't want to lose them.

'Sir...y..you let me sleep on, I should be up to serve you.'

'I prefer to have you wake up this way Anna. I wanted you to sleep on for a little while longer'

I enjoy his fingers for a few moments before replying. 'Why not sir?'

'Because you looked so content, chained to my bed like this. You seemed to be under a silent spell, and had become my own sleeping beauty. It gave me an intensity of pleasure that I didn't want to lose.'

I jerk on my chains, and his right hand strokes my wrists where the steel cuts in. His left hand stays between my legs, aware of my reawakening arousal. 'I am content, I wanted to be restrained next to you, the chains were an unexpected surprise.' The sound of my chains as I move is almost musical, somehow in tune with the rustle of the curtains as they are disturbed by the soft morning breeze through the open window. 'Things got a bit wild last night, I must look a mess sir.'

Leaving his hand between my legs, he leans over and kisses my nose, my half-open eyes, then softly brushes my lips with his as I drift into full wakefulness.

'You have an inner loveliness that means you can never look anything but beautiful, and wanting to sleep in chains next to me was such an exquisite gift.'

'I wanted to give myself like that sir, it seemed the natural thing to do.'

He kisses me on the mouth, his fingers sliding deeper, my aroused welcome reflecting a need of their probing.

'How long had you been playing with me, before I woke up sir?'

'Oh, hours and hours.'

I make to kick him, but the chains around my ankles hold me back to the bed to remind me how tightly held I am.

'Stop teasing me.'

He laughs, in that gentle way of his. 'You were wet before I touched you. Your dreams must have been very interesting.'

He kisses me again and my body surrenders itself to him. His touch is so light, so delicate I can barely feel him, yet it re-ignites the fires he left smouldering last night. 'I just wanted to share in those dreams I guessed you must be having, but not to cut them short.' My body reacts to the warmth of his touch, our nakedness allowing for no inhibition of intimate closeness; I feel that wonderful certainty that we are where we need to be: swinging on the same pendulum of domination and submission, complete in our mutual desire for one another.

I look up at him and whisper the word that now comes naturally to my lips: 'Sir?'

'Welcome to your new life.'

'Yes, my first night in the kind of bondage I've been seeking. I think I was destined to spend it with you.'

'Yes, strange how destiny has a way of unfolding. I like your new awareness of yourself.'

'Please, I need to come...urgently sir? Being chained all night, I cannot describe what that has done to me. Dreams fade so fast, please help me to hold onto them.'

He draws back a little to watch my body begin to pulsate to the rhythm of my need; I can see that he is torn between torturing me with denial and the exquisite sensation of taking me to an ecstatic explosion.

'You have my permission.'

'Kiss me sir.'

On the instant of my emotions being granted their freedom, my mouth is pressed against his to form itself into a muffled scream that devours us both. My climax is violent, and will not be denied, I tug hard on chains that I know will hold me fast. Making that unyielding thrumming sound again against the oak headboard, they dig deeper furrows in imprisoned flesh as spasms take my body into rigidity at his touch. I hold there for long moments, before I collapse into a blissful softness against him. My nipple rings press hard against his chest as he holds me tight in mutual silence and tenderness, while the fingers of his imprisoned hand feel the fluttering aftershocks of my explosion.

Our lips break away, but only momentarily, as my open mouth thrusts itself at him again to silence another long shuddering inner scream that mounts from deep within my throat. I devour his tongue as the restrained and hungry rigidity of my body clamps his hand tightly again and defines what I am. I scream my climax at him like the wanton slut I know he wants me to be and with my freedom granted, I take flight with it. My orgasms stimulated from his physical closeness, I am riding on his hand and fingers, picking up the thread of delirious pleasure from where I left off last night.

Fitz knows he has awakened something that has drawn me from more than mere sleep. It is an exquisite sensuality, an intense desire that I am fulfilling both from within myself and drawing out of him.

''What have I done to you?' He whispers in mock concern.

'Sir, you only have to touch me, or even look at me, and I explode, it is almost impossible to control. Nothing like this has happened to me before; I know you've explained something of what is happening but it's still very difficult to understand.'

'I have only released what was already within you Anna, I haven't changed what you are.'

'It is still very strange sir, you have a power that would frighten me if my trust in you wasn't absolute.'

'You have no need to be scared of it, I will take good care of you.'

****

The incident with Liam had revealed a dangerous part of Fitz that I had never seen before, but that encounter had also shown me that he could control it. I find myself being irresistibly attracted to that powerful part of him that would protect me no matter what.

'Thank you sir, if we hadn't known each other for so long I think I would run from all this. When I said I was putting my life in your hands, it didn't occur to me to mention my sanity. Last night you reduced me to a gibbering wreck.'

He laughs lightly at that.

'I am going to enjoy our awakenings Anna, they are all going to be like this.'

'Somehow I believe you, two days ago I wouldn't have thought it possible.'

His right hand tenderly caresses the thin chains that are locked around wrists held above my head; my violent reactions have embedded them deeply into my skin but the wildness in my eyes tells him that the bite of it is something that I must have, so he does not release them. He draws his touch away, then retreats again and looks at me. My body strains itself towards him, chains creaking with a desperate frenzy.

My words form themselves with a deep and pleading desperation: 'Please sir, may I again? My orgasms will not stop, they are overwhelming me. And somehow I can't do it now without your permission.'

'Wait.' He holds my eyes to delay my climax for a fleeting eternity; but he does not touch me. Instead he reaches back to a bedside drawer and pulls out a ballgag, dangling it provocatively by its strap. 'I think you need something to keep the screams in.'

I look at the gag, then into Fitz's eyes as I lick my lips then perversely clamp them shut. Fitz responds with a look of mock surprise, as the ball is brushed lightly against a closed mouth.

'No?'

Shaking my head, eyes holding his with determined and mischievous provocation I refuse his gag.

'No matter.' He kisses my closed lips by brushing his own across them. Those lightest of kisses make me melt, but I still hold my mouth shut.

Fitz's tongue slowly trails down my neck and shoulder, leaving a shuddering wake of anticipation as it finds a hard ringed nipple, while a teasing hand moves further down to discover more undisguised wet need.

'Your denial is unconvincing Anna.'

My closed lips let out a gasp as his teeth bite softly, while the ball dangles in front of my mouth as a suggestive bargain, to trade silence for suffering. Slowly the bite gets harder, more insistent, nipple rolled between tongue and teeth to gradually increase a torture level to where it cannot be endured. Tighter, harder, teeth take a soft bite beyond endurance by infinitesimal degrees as the ballgag waits for the scream that must come.

My mounting agony tells me that the pain will cease when the ball is accepted. Yet that is Fitz's torture, I do not want it to cease. I need that pain, and he knows it can only come from him, and cannot get enough of it. His inflicted hurt is now my ecstasy, need that cannot be hidden from Fitz's fingers as they probe lightly while he discovers new thresholds of suffering. My world of normality is being distorted to make pain and pleasure indistinguishable.

Fitz looks up at me, but still the fight continues, the refusal to submit even though suffering mounts. What had been a soft bite is now a blazing flame, one that provides its own quenching flood that is there to be used when my mouth opens for the scream that must be released in acceptance of the inevitable. The sound that eventually comes rends my soul.

'That's what you wanted isn't it my love?'

In response, my lips part wide to devour the offered ball. I thrust my head forward to snatch it from him with a screaming demand that it should be forced deeper than I can take it, shoved in with a hard careless brutality to silence even the slightest protest at what is being done to me. By expressing my need to fight, to resist, I have revealed the truth that submission is the inevitable result no matter what resistance is offered. By belonging there can never be another outcome, nor do I want there to be. Only to know that my need will generate a force in him that cannot be resisted.

The gag is another symbol of the freedom I want to gift to him, another part of me that Fitz must control, that I may speak only when he allows it. The ball is forced between my teeth, and my aroused welcome of it transcends any cruelty as I hear the rasp of the buckle tightening on the leather strap at the back of my neck as it closes to the last notch, excited as the straps distend my cheeks and reduces any words to mewling incoherence.

Fitz pauses for a moment and meets my gaze; I can hold him only with pleading eyes and we both know that it is a test of wills: that he could keep me like this for hours but ultimately he must give me what I want.

'Yes my perfect slave, now you have my permission to come.'

My entire body instantly convulses on itself, muscles straining tautly between the wrist and ankle chains that form part of a glittering line of bondage that chills where it touches to heat my desire still more. My legs flex to maximize the tension of the chains that pass through my rings, using them to pivot my emotions into an inward surge of pure joy and suffering. I bite down hard on the gag, my screams of release turned inward to a pitiful mewling.

He brushes a soft kiss over my distended lips, and whispers: 'And again.' His barely audible command triggers mindshocks through my already inflamed senses. I can do no other than obey him, climaxing under his double edged control: my eyes raging at him while adoring him for his creative use of me, that certainty that he can order me to orgasm, and I can only submit.

I become aware that this is a loving like no other, that I am being taken to places I have never been. All that I have known, after a lifetime of faking it, is telling me that I cannot be made to orgasm merely by being told to. Yet I am chained to a bed, losing control of my mind and body to a lover who can control my most fundamental femininity without touching me. I lie there, trying to get closer to him, shuddering and mewling in torment, losing contact with reality.

In me Fitz now has a true submissive, one whose sexual responses are under his exclusive command. I now want it to be a timeless gift: the surrender of my sexuality into an enthrallment where I can be made to explode just by a look or a word. He has raised me to that pitch of excitement and desperation where the sensation of being in emotional bondage makes me climax; yet another bond that I do not want to break. It is the ultimate expression of domination to be able to bring me to orgasm repeatedly despite knowing that he is turning them into my torture.

I feel his fingers teasing the strap from its buckle at the back of my neck, but I shake my head away.

'You want to stay gagged?'

With eyes closed I nod, and instead welcome his arm slipped around me; being chained and gagged and held tight gives me that feeling of being safe and cared for. It is as if breaking this spell might destroy the aura with which he has surrounded me. I do not want to lose that exquisite inner sensation of tranquility that only those who have given themselves into bondage can know. We lie for long minutes as subspace claims my senses again; the gag enforces the silence that I have chosen for myself.

I know he will be waiting for me when I come back.

****

I have a vague sensation of the ball being removed from my mouth, though no awareness of how long it had been there. Only that Fitz holds me close. It is difficult to string words together, tied and pleasured as I am.

'Fitz, sir, how do you know to use me in the way you do? Such bondage is almost unreal in its sensuality and torture. With you I came in five seconds flat, maybe less, and you didn't touch me; that just isn't possible.'

'But you did.'

'You made me do it, what are you, where did you learn stuff like that?'

'Submissives are wonderful teachers, when a man allows them to be.'

'But what have I taught you?'

'I know only what your mind and body tell me, words are not always a necessary part of that telling, just as physical restraints and whips are not always a necessary part of bondage and discipline.'

'Until you took control of me sir, I didn't know that.'

'There is much you have to learn my love, about bondage and discipline, and about me, but most of it you know already; think of me as just turning the pages for you.'

'You have the Irish gift with words Fitz.'

He puts on the Irish brogue to tease me a little: 'Ah to be sure now, and aren't you me little English nymphomaniac?'

'I am what you have made me Fitz, I belong to you now, don't try teasing me out of it.' I thrust my body at him within the limits that the chains allow, to make my point.

'I could never do that Anna.'

'We have much to discuss my love, before we really start on our new future together.' He unchains my wrists, and kisses the deep red marks that the metal has left when I deliberately embedded them in my skin. 'The chains hurt you Anna.'

'They did, and I liked it; is that so terrible?'

His fingers gently and slowly tease the glittering chains out through my rings so that my ankles can be unlocked, as he reaches down to do that I embrace him with my freed arms and draw him tighter to me with renewed insistence. 'Must I tie you down again so that we can talk?'

I look down and smile softly: 'As sir desires, but as sir is rather hard right now, and I am rather wet, perhaps sir might like to use his slave while we talk?

'You are insatiable. I shall punish you for being so forward.'

'You released me to be like this sir, no one else knew how.'

'Did I?'

I look at him with a raised eyebrow. 'You know perfectly well you did.....sir. You knew exactly what you were doing, which is a revelation in itself.'

Fitz laughs at my pointed sarcasm. 'It won't absolve you from my intended punishment of you.'

'Thank you sir, I would expect nothing less now. But sir's erection is just so beautiful this morning, and sleeping in chains gave rise to such unusual dreams, especially being chained in that fashion; they seemed to allow me to relive the past couple of days.'

'I can imagine! Later you shall tell me what you dreamed of.' He brings my hands to the front, and re-chains them, giving me about eighteen inches of slack between my wrists. 'That is just to let you make a bathroom visit slave, your bondage will normally be much stricter than that. Through that door over there.'

'Oh—er, yes of course, thank you sir. Things are a bit—well, urgent.'

I get up, then plant a quick kiss on him as I scramble across the bed.

'Just a little something to keep that hard for me till I get back sir.'

Fitz gives my bottom a swat as I bound away to get to the bathroom.

'Cheeky.' He laughs.

'Ouch! I was only keeping my place sir.'

'You are very presumptuous, bottoms as pretty as yours invite constant chastisement. And one of us has to remain sane.'

'Oh, thank you sir. I think you are better at that than I am.'

I wiggle my bottom in his direction, then see him pick up the ballgag, and quickly shut the bathroom door as I hear the ball bouncing off it.

One minute he has me climaxing myself into oblivion, the next I'm in fits of laughter. I run the shower, and revel in the hot water and soap on my body; I towel my body hard, wanting to rejuvenate myself.

Returning from the bathroom, I pick up the ballgag and walk to the side of the bed, where he is lounging back. I sink to my knees, thighs spread wider than my shoulders; my head is bowed in submission with chained wrists resting on my knees, palms upwards. I want nothing to be secret from Fitz's gaze.

'You dropped your ballgag sir.'

'Did I now? You'd better keep it handy, I have a feeling I'm going to need it.'

He leans down and lifts my chin to look up at him.

'Presenting yourself in this manner is what I expect of you Anna, you look perfect. But come and sit beside me, we have a few things to discuss.'

'Yes sir.'

I jump up and snuggle my chained nakedness against him on the bed, fully aware that my submissiveness has become blatant provocation. It is something that we both know will result in much chastisement in our future; not that Fitz expects punishments to change what I am, neither would he want them to other than to increase my need of him.

'Control yourself, last night we both got carried away, today we really do have things to talk about.'

I find control difficult, my body is telling me that I have a lifetime of missed pleasure to catch up on. 'Yes sir.'

'I mean it, or I shall put you in a straitjacket and chastity belt, stuff like that must be around here somewhere.'

I think back to my first encounter with Chloe, locked into a chastity belt, and can't resist using my new found confidence: 'Now sir?'

'I can't win can I?'

I hold him tighter. 'You set me free to be like this sir. I'm not going back in my cage ever again, unless it's one you lock me in.'

Fitz lifts her face up, and smiles: 'You and I are going to talk, OK?'

I nod with as much meekness as I can muster. 'Sorry sir.'

'You know I told you about my rich uncle last night, and how I inherited all this, and his millions?'

'Yes sir, but it needn't get in the way of...well ...us need it? I really don't care about the money.'

'It's not quite that simple Anna, I want you to be fully aware of everything, and to be part of it. Like it or not, my inheritance is part of that too. I can't pretend it doesn't exist unless I donate it all to a cats home.'

'As far as I am concerned, the money doesn't exist sir, I just want to be here with you.'

'I want us to be together too, but we still have to talk and I'm afraid the money does exist.'

'Sir?'

'I think we established last night that we might have a future together?'

'Oh yes sir it's what I want more than anything, I just didn't realize it, even though we've known each other for so long.'

'Yes I know, I held back on my feelings for you too.'

'Why sir?'

'That is also something we have to talk about Anna, I've always been involved in BDSM, but I wasn't sure if you had the emotional strength to deal with it, at not at my level. We've both had screw-ups in our lives, but our friendship has remained rock solid no matter what. I didn't want to risk that; you've always been so special to me you see, much more important than kinky sex play. I can get that anywhere, but there's been no one in my life quite like you.'

'So when I said I wanted to be kidnapped and stuff, couldn't you have told me then sir?'

'Well no, I had to be certain it was the real thing, not another of your flights of fancy that you might not have enjoyed when you were exposed to all that BDSM involves. Many people think BDSM is just playing tie up games in bed, when in fact it is far more than that. I couldn't risk your pretending to want it just to please me, then getting bored; it has to go much deeper.'

Chapter Eighteen

Inheritance

A mediocre Master tells,
A good Master teaches,
An excellent Master explains,
But a True Master inspires
-Anonymous

'I'd guessed that Madame Cory's was something of an initiation test, and I didn't know exactly what. But now you're telling me it was more than that?'

'Yes, I knew you would be safe with her and Jon, but if you backed out, I knew there would be no harm done and we could go on just being close friends. On the other hand, if you survived their tender mercies and wanted more, then I could be pretty sure we would work out together in a dominant and submissive relationship.'

'Madame doesn't spare the rod does she sir?'

'No she doesn't, I could only throw you in at the deep end so to speak, but I knew she would look after you, and not let things get out of hand. You could have stopped it all after the first cut from her whip. She really is a sweetie at heart, but don't tell her I told you that.'

'From the way her maids are devoted to her sir, that is pretty obvious, and thank you for taking care of me, just like you always have.'

'That's important Anna, for both of us, if things had gone wrong, it would have destroyed our friendship and I wasn't prepared to take a chance on that. With Madame Cory, the only thing that was at risk was you actually calling a halt to it all. If you had done that, then you wouldn't have known that it was me who set it up.'

'You make me feel very special and cherished sir.'

'You are.'

I snuggle in closer into him. 'Thank you.'

'Now I want to tell you about my uncle. I barely knew him, he became a recluse as he got older, and didn't welcome visitors, even though I was his only living relative. Anyway, it seems he had a housekeeper who had looked after him for many years; it was she who found him dead in bed. To be fair to the old boy, he left her very well provided for as a thank you; I got the rest of his fortune, along with this mansion.'

'It does seem rather large sir.'

'Would you believe twenty bedrooms and a hundred acres of parkland? Most of it is sixteenth century but I understand some parts of it date back to the twelfth century. Back then it was a monastery, in fact an old chapel from those days is still part of the building though it's no longer consecrated of course. And there's much more to it than an inheritance, big though that is.'

'What do you mean sir?'

'That is all part of what I have to discuss with you.'

Fitz unchains my wrists and hands me a bathrobe, picks one up for himself and starts to explain as they wrap themselves in fluffy softness.

'When I inherited this place, it was stipulated in the will that I should keep it as it is. He left ample funds to do that, so I have no problems there, but once I took over and realized what was here, I really didn't know what to do about it. Being into pervy sex is one thing, but inheriting an international kink emporium like this is something else entirely.'

'Can you tell me about it sir?'

'Well it seems that in addition to being a wealthy entrepreneur with global business interests, dear old uncle Leo had also been a world class perv in his heyday. Almost every part of the house is themed for sexual kink of one kind or another, forty years ago it must have been party night every night here.'

'So the housekeeper must have known about it all sir?'

'There can be no doubt about that, she was very much a part of it. Uncle Leo was about eighty five, his housekeeper is about seventy—so you can imagine the age gap being just right when they were both much younger.'

'Much like we are now?'

'Yes, just about the same age I suppose. I met her, Laura, at the funeral, and again at the lawyer's office when the will was read out. She just smiled sweetly but all she told me was that she'd left everything in order and hoped I'd find it all to my liking.'

'She didn't go into any details?'

'No, but I did notice she was wearing the committment collar around her neck that one sees on true submissives.

'A committment collar sir?'

'A collar that denotes a committed submissive.'

'Oh I see.'

'I thought it was odd at the time, because of course I had seen the same thing before, but on women more my own age; I suppose my mind was too occupied with other things to form the connection. Somehow you don't expect to see senior citizens wearing slave collars, but as I found out later, that's what it was.'

'Was she aware that you'd seen it sir?'

'Oh yes, she just gave me a knowing grin when our eyes met, after she had noticed me looking at it. She was quite open about wearing it, because only another master or slave would know what it meant. From what I've learned since I came here, the collar was as I thought, permanent, and could only be cut off. She obviously had no intention of doing that.'

'Cut off sir?'

'Certainly. Submissives entering into full time slavery tend to want a collar that demonstrates their commitment to their master. A fixed collar is the ultimate expression of that. The submissive cannot remove it, nor does she want to.'

Looking up at him, my fingers involuntarily touch my throat. I cannot deny the excitement of such a concept, to be permanently collared and be unafraid to show myself as such.

'That's why it's called a commitment or an eternity collar. The submissive is not expected to hide it, anymore than she would hide a wedding ring.'

"Yes I think I can understand that sir, but she didn't actually tell you what was here?'

'No she didn't, it was something of a shock when I took over. I haven't had time to explore it all yet, most of the stuff here is still under dust sheets.'

'How did your uncle know you were inclined this way sir?'

'I think Doms just have an inner awareness of people of like mind somehow, they just know. Or maybe he had me checked out, that wouldn't have been difficult. Doms and subs always seem to be able to find each other, like you and me.'

Involuntarily I move closer to him. 'Oh yes.'

'He certainly guessed right about me, even though we never exchanged so much as a word about all this. In any case, he had retired from the scene long before I got involved in it and his will stipulated that the housekeeper should hand over the keys to his safe when I took over the house.'

'So you think the housekeeper was his slave sir?'

'Certain of it, and a very willing one; she obviously stayed on here to look after him when his health began to decline and the party scene faded. There's no doubt she genuinely loved him, and he her of course.'

'Yes I can see how that would be so sir, if she became his property she would want to keep all the memories of happy times alive here, but wouldn't want to stay here after he died. It's very sad, yet beautiful in its way.'

'It seems that Uncle Leo set up a generous trust fund for her many years ago, because of their age gap and the inevitability that that put on their future.'

'That was very thoughtful sir.'

'The trust was invested wisely, which meant that his slave Laura became an independently wealthy woman long before he died.'

'It shows how truly caring he was sir.'

'That trust made sure she remained uncle Leo's property willingly, and from the documents I've read here, that was the only condition he stipulated in their relationship.'

'That she should be willing?'

'Yes, though much more than willing.'

'They never married?'

'Not in the conventional sense; uncle Leo wanted her freedom to be absolute, the trust made sure of that.'

'I am a little confused sir. You said they were not married in the conventional sense?'

'No, they had a collaring ceremony a long time ago; in a BDSM relationship and within that community it means much more than conventional marriage.'

'Yes sir, that begins to make sense, with the fixed collar that she had.'

'I will try to explain further Anna.'

'Please do sir, I want to know what I'm getting into.'

'You see, entering into a committed dominant and submissive relationship can only function if the dominant knows that the submissive is there of her own free will, and her captivity is drawn from a need within herself despite the cruelty of her owner.'

'The thought of cruelty and suffering excites me sir, I'm afraid I can't help it.'

'I know that Anna, but never lose sight of the fact that you can walk away from it, that puts you in control of everything that happens. A lot of people tend to ignore that part.'

'But I feel that you own me now sir, I wouldn't want that to change.'

'I don't want things to change, but you must be aware that I wouldn't raise a hand to stop you if you felt otherwise at any time.'

'Please, I don't even want to think about that, it will upset me.' I reply, pulling myself tighter to Fitz.

'It's OK, just something that had to be said, it needn't be mentioned again.'

'Everything feels so right here, even though I've only known you in this context for less than twenty four hours sir. But I do understand why you had to say that.'

'I'm glad you've come to understand so quickly Anna, that a real dominant doesn't need to use real force to hold his submissive, no matter how brutal it might appear to an outsider.'

'So the trust fund gave her a way out if she chose to take it?'

'Exactly. That was uncle John's way of making sure she was where she wanted to be, simply through her implicit freedom not to be. He made no conditions, other than she should be the sole beneficiary and be in full control of her own finances.'

'A subtle form of bondage sir.'

'It pleases me that you see it that way Anna. This place has bondage equipment even I have never heard of, and her need for it was obviously insatiable. I have no doubt uncle John fed her desire for incarceration to its limits and beyond when they were both active in the scene.'

Fitz recognizes the light of excitement in my eyes at his suggestion of what is here and all that this place means.

'The trust will allow her to live in comfort for the rest of her life. He realised that continuing to live here by herself would be painfully lonely so he also bought a lovely house for her on the south coast overlooking the sea, just outside Brighton.'

'Brighton is famous for its pervy scene sir.' I laugh.

'Yes I know, she has a lot of friends from the old days living in that area, so after uncle Leo died and everything was taken care of, she moved there and hasn't set foot in this house since.'

The thought of uncle Leo and his loving slave and the sexual ambience of this house somehow moves both of us, and I find myself held tighter in his arms. Our kisses meet with a deep passion, and he reacts to my intense response with a hardness thrust against me. Our robes fall open and our bodies make sensual contact. My fingers slip down to caress him softly, and he reacts again under my touch.

'I'm so glad your feelings about that are the same as mine Anna, and you recognize the beauty of their relationship.'

'It would be hard not to sir, and thinking of everything that's happened here over the years makes me so needy again.' My whisper to him carries a pleading desperation, and he becomes aware that putting me into bondage has unleashed an animal of an unknown wildness. The thought that this house has known something of what we know is in itself exciting.

'Your uncle would want you to keep this house alive in his memory, that is why he arranged his affairs so carefully, so that the chain would remain unbroken. He wanted to link the generations with a new dominant and his submissive.'

Trying to discuss the immediate matters of the house cannot suppress an arousal of need as I know it must; it carries the question of what I should do next to please him. The thought that I have fallen into a condition of immediate subjection to his will is arousing in itself, and he pulls me close, forcing my head down while spreading his thighs wide.

'I want to watch that pretty mouth take me again.'

I sink slowly down in immediate obedience, but look up and hold his eyes with mine for a brief moment before my lips seek out his rampant desire. I submit eagerly as he leans forward, takes one of my hands and forces it behind my back. I immediately bring the other one round to meet it so that he can rechain my wrists and twist the loose end of it in his fingers, jerking my hands high up towards my shoulders. He hears my yelp of pain before I bury him in my mouth. The hurt that he causes me is immediately reflected in teeth that he feels closing on him. It is the kind of love pain I want to give him, so that he can lose himself in the thrill of it.

While making me suffer I want him to feel my tongue and use my mouth. There is a need to feel his control in infinite ways, I cannot function without it now. The intensity of his passion is making him twist the chain that holds me even tighter, making my mouth work even harder on him to earn the hurt that he is inflicting.

Suffering and being made to give pleasure has become my driving force. His suffocating embrace seems to fold me into him and his hand tightens in my hair as he forces himself in to the hilt. I want to feel myself drowning in the love I have for him, to keep him where he is right now so that every part of my body will always be open to him. His thrusting depth within my mouth acts as a gag; I cannot ask for release so I shudder to another climax punctuated by muted screams driven by the excitement of his choking violation of me.

With my head forced back against his hand, my eyes hold his with provocative boldness; my mouth extracts itself, and trails slowly up his body with a line of intense kisses that eventually exchange with his own. The intensity is softer now as we rejoice in such sudden spontaneity, with hot bodies lying in such tender closeness. He holds me tight, to savour the taste of himself on the lips that I press to his, as I enclose him within myself and use my body to push him back onto the bed with a gentle yet forceful insistence.

Fitz has a rising hardness that is a reaction to the sight of me straddling him, and he reaches round to free the chains that hold my wrists behind my back.

Immediately my released fingers encircle him so that he is brought to probe the moist depth that is waiting.

'Please sir?' My eyes reinforce my pleading words, the need I have to feel him thrust deep, to feel myself being used forcefully.

'You may pleasure yourself.' He whispers softly. But as he grants me permission he takes me on an unexpected path. Still deep within me, his legs slowly part until my hips sink between them. Going still wider, I feel myself being embraced tightly, gripped and pulled to him by embracing thighs. It is so new, so different, making me reverse our sensation focus, where it feels as if I am taking him despite knowing that it is he who is thrusting into me. My legs are held tight together, the sensation between them is of just Fitz, driving himself harder in. I want to hold him tighter now that he has shown me how.

'Now you may come.'

Those words drive me to a frenzy again, as he knows they must. Only this time, I focus the tension of my thighs to crush him into me, and my need grips him deep and tight. It is something I have never done before but instinctively it feels right; that part of my submission that is there to create new pleasures for him. It brings a fresh intensity to our loving as he finds himself shuddering and gasping at the way my thighs tighten. I put my hands on his shoulders and force myself down on him, our positions reversed as my legs clamp tightly together while his are spread apart. It feels impossible, yet it is so beautiful. This is the first time I have taken the lead in our lovemaking, he has given me the freedom to do it as I take him deeper and deeper in. The power of each thrust brings him closer to the climax that I seek as his legs open wider and lock together behind my back to drag me harder to him. I feel his urgency rising to meet mine but hold him on my own crest for long minutes. We are locked in a tight stillness once more, each delaying and provoking the other through subtle mischief as muscles contract at the mounting of each other's pinnacles of ecstasy; his shuddering, gasping explosion becomes an instant trigger for my own, his urgent pulsing causing us to fuse again into a single entity and the bliss of mutual fulfillment.

His spasms fill my immediate need, yet with barely a pause drive me on to more; I ride him on to my next wave, my next exploding climax, and the next. My open mouth devours his as orgasms follow one another in rapid succession, crushing my body down on him as each comes closer to the one before it until we cannot tell when one ends and the next starts. But now there is no end, no beginning; having found that infinite source of pleasure the riding of it is timeless until I scream myself into a tsunami of unendurable ecstasy that crashes on top of him.

His immediate power is spent, yet my tightly closed thighs refuse to let go and neither do his. Locked tight around me there is an intensity in our physical contact that drains him completely, and I drive myself on into subspace until I know nothing but the forces that have transformed our union into an endless bondage. It is a restraint that has gone beyond physical; I cannot be bound closer to him than I am at this moment.

With a mind that has vacated normality and removed itself to another place, he can only hold me.

My entire being has been wracked with uncontrollable convulsions that forced my deepest self to transcend climax. There is no awareness other than what we are at this time. There had been an expectation of control through harsh physical restraints and mindless torture, yet what has been unleashed is his control of my emotions, removing my ability to think or speak beyond the immediacy of now and my focus on him. It allows nothing more than a soft sigh of exhalation saying that I can neither give nor take more.

My stillness is broken by a sudden shivering, brought on by the heat of our passion; Fitz reaches out for a cover and draws it over both of us, and I mumble a barely coherent thanks, and gather it around myself. Such a tiny gesture of care reveals the man.

He knows that I will not return to him until my consciousness allows me to recover a degree of sanity.

He stays inside, unmoving beneath me; we both lie locked in that mutual harmony of spent lovers, aware only of what each has given the other. A haze of quiet time passes until we refocus unwillingly on reality.

'I am now your prisoner in the fullest sense, and will never seek release from that; thank you for allowing me to pleasure you sir.'

'Oh, was that what happened? I think I lost track of who was doing what to whom.' He bites my ear playfully. 'You may be my prisoner, but you seem to have collapsed on top of me my pretty slave.'

I am still between his thighs and my arms are locked around his neck, a drowsy response tells him that I am unable to fully waken: 'I know sir, but since you set all this in motion I have been able to express my need in so many different ways.'

Fitz whispers softly: 'It was very beautiful for me too. I want you as my submissive but I don't want to have to give you orders all the time. I adore your free mind, and would never seek to subdue it.'

'But how did I get into this position? It feels strange and different, but wonderful, you are so tight in me sir.'

'A little gift I thought you might enjoy.' He says.

'Is there no end to your creativity Fitz?'

'I hope not.'

'So do I, the last two days seem to have been spent catching up after a lifetime of crap sex, I think my brains are no longer where they should be sir.'

'I hoped you would find it so, now you've discovered what I intend to do to you Anna.'

I expected to be punished severely for coming so hard and often and making such demands on him, yet I am only responding to his need of me.

'I didn't know that a woman could make love in that way sir, it just sort of happened that positions became reversed, it was very odd.' I don't attempt to move, I doubt if I can. His limp self is still locked between tightly closed thighs, and my head rests on his shoulder with long wisps of my blonde hair falling across his face. The fury of sexuality that has been released is precisely what I have been seeking for so many years. He seems to know so many ways to blow my mind.

'I'm sure I shall chastise you more than adequately later.'

'Thank you sir, that is something I badly need and deserve. Forgive me, I lost count of the number of times I exploded on you while you were tight inside like that with my legs together. I couldn't help myself, next time I promise to be better behaved.'

He merely smiles and strokes my hair, and with my conscious mind submerging again, we lie entwined and drowse into the advancing morning.

Chapter Nineteen

Awakening

"My Dominant nature is always at work, a carnal orchestra of desires and bliss, a perpetual readiness to accept your submission and take us to the deepest and darkest places of our minds."
Joseph McNamara

I find myself swirling up from the blackness again, the place where I go after Fitz has driven me with the intensity of his loving. I see now that Fitz knows this; he allows me to recover in my own time, knowing that I will want more of what only he can give me.

With closed eyes I realise that there are no restraints on my body, so reach out for Fitz. Still half asleep my hand pats around expecting him to be there, but I find that I am alone, sprawled across the bed where we had made love with such endless passion. Have I been asleep for minutes? Hours? Hard to tell. There doesn't seem to be a clock anywhere, and I haven't seen my watch since I was abducted. No doubt that will turn up sometime.

Fitz is not by my side with the reassuring voice and boyish grin that supplies the certainty of all this.

Such a post orgasmic oblivion has somehow altered the concept of time but as my eyes open with reluctant admission of reality I know at least that it is still daylight. I can only assume that it is still the same day.

The rows of red marks left on my skin by his chains are still there, reawakening the delicious memory of spending my first night with Fitz. How can it be that this man can make every fantasy somehow become real, as if he has access to thoughts that until now had been my private and exclusive domain? I didn't have to explain what I wanted, he made it happen as part of the bondage he created for me through the night. Reaching down to touch the rings that Fitz had used so creatively, there is still the wet excitement in reliving the intense ecstasy that came from him.

Self teasing fingers softly explore to confirm the delights of our night of sublime loving, that it was not a dream, or a fantasy, but something that had been done to give precisely the pleasure that was wanted, to stay bound and sweetly helpless, pressed against the man who had taken me into his subtle world of erotic restraint. Being restrained is my normality now, I seek nothing other than that, whether it is to be outwardly severe or subtly unobtrusive. There must be the sensation of being under his control, of being owned in a physical sense.

I sit up and look around; when Fitz had carried me into this room last night I was too consumed by him to take stock of my surroundings. It is a room that invites sensuality: the soft glow of oak paneled walls that blend into darkened corners, a multi faceted chandelier hanging from a high beamed ceiling, tall mullioned windows allowing morning sunlight to stream in where the curtains don't quite meet. The enormous four poster bed that I had been chained to is the ultimate symbol of my incarceration, the chains that had held me for Fitz still lie where he had left them, trailing across the bed in glittering contrast to the rumpled black of satin sheets. I pick up the chain, letting the links slide through fingers to rekindle memories of past hours here, feeling a delicious chill as I use it to touch places that Fitz had touched in such exquisite ways.

Why hasn't Fitz left me bound? Then I could lie here and relax back into a private time in bondage just thinking about him, and await his return.

A vast stone fireplace at the far end of the room with armchairs on either side of it makes me aware that this is a master bedroom in the fullest sense of the word. I visualize Fitz sitting there in front of the fire, and myself kneeling at his feet; it gives me a sense of privilege having being brought here.

The ballgag that Fitz used to silence my screams is still lying on the bed where he left it; I pick it up it up and toy with it, swinging it a little on its strap. In the cold light of day it looks almost innocuous. But I bring it to my mouth and lick my tongue around it as if to taste the ecstasy it brought me, wanting to relive the sensuality of being gagged for a man's pleasure. Then denying it to myself as I had denied Fitz last night until he tortured me into acceptance of it. I wonder if I can take it again, as deep as Fitz pressed it in. Or perhaps deeper.

My lips part with excited anticipation and my tongue flicks out to moisten it. There is a full-length mirror across the room, I get off the bed, and walk to it with the strap of the ballgag carelessly dangling in my fingers. The mirror invites an appraisal of my new status: that of a dedicated submissive, looking at the bold nakedness I used to hide from. Now that reticence has been removed, and there is a self assurance in seeing a complete woman in control of her destiny, even though that destiny has been freely given into the hands of another.

I part my lips, tracing their pouting outline with a finger as if I am applying lipstick. Instead I am thinking of how the ball will distend them into an inviting O. Then that such an invitation can only be for him. There is a certainty about where the ball must go, but there is still that tremor of delight in teasing myself, the delay of putting it in, the sense that it must be self enforced.

As all of this is.

****

There is a silent wish that Fitz was standing behind me, doing it, that he could be teased again by a refusal and overpower me by using my desire for him. Or is this a quiet time he has left me to discover myself, alone?

But ultimately the hard ball is irresistible, and as if to reinforce my certainty of need, I lubricate it with juices brought up on self arousing fingers. With Fitz I have become used to enjoying the taste of myself; I see the ball wet and shiny, my tongue licking my own sweetness as the gag seems to find its natural place behind my teeth. I use the heel of my hand to force it in, wanting to convince myself that I can take it deeper than Fitz had done it. The straps meet at the back of my neck, and I lift my unruly hair to find the buckle, rasping it tight, making sure the buckle is closed to the last hole, so that I can watch the leather making deep furrows in my bulging cheeks. Fingers lightly caress the ball that now distends my mouth, while the mirror reflects eyes that widen in disbelief at such a self violation. The feel of it is exciting and it is impossible to deny the sensations it ignites. I look at myself, certain of myself. It is a wonderful new feeling, to be doing this to please my lover, not something just to fulfill a private fantasy.

Because the gag is such a signature of ownership, it carries with it an unspoken command that it may not now be removed other by he who commands my submission. I turn to left and right, blatantly admiring myself from every angle, while carefully rearranging my hair back into place, not wanting it tangled in the strap. It looks so right to be like that, to be available to Fitz, unable to protest even if I wanted to. The naked woman who looks back at me is someone I scarcely know yet. This is not the woman who used to put herself in bondage, here there is a purpose, a need to give, a pride in being gagged into silence as someone owned.

Fingers stray to my rings to renew an intensity of need and know the hardness of my nipples, thinking of what Fitz's teeth might do to them. Then feeling a peak approaching, I slip my hands behind my back as if by instinct, to stop myself and complete the image I desire to see. A combination of stimulation and denial. The self arousal is so intense, it would be easy to drive myself to climax, but now I belong to Fitz, my sexual release is his to control or withhold.

I go back to the bed and open the bedside drawer from which Fitz had produced my ballgag. I find a pair of open handcuffs, and a set of slightly larger cuffs with a longer chain between them. Neither set of cuffs has a key. They are clearly intended to accommodate wrists and ankles, and the glittering steel of them offers me the same sensation that my chains did last night, something I want to feel on my body again. I toy with them and an open cuff on the larger set offers an irresistible invitation to reach down to my left ankle and lock it on.

Again that touch of cold steel on warm skin, the scary certainty of having no means of release. Watching the first closing of the metal circle, then hearing a satisfying series of clicks as the steel ratchet tightens smoothly. Such an innocent sound, yet so imbued with sensuality. I look down at it for lingering moments before snicking it one last notch. The metal bites with a gentle hurting, but I want it tight as a symbol of what Fitz means to me. I tighten the other shackle until my legs are constricted by about eighteen inches of chain. I sit on the edge of the bed and look down proudly, twisting my ankles from side to side. The sheer sexiness of it seems to form a constriction of excitement in my chest. Picking up the open handcuffs, I fit one around my left wrist. Again the sound of steel closing on steel creates the kind of wet excitement I want to fan into full flame, but dare not. Instead as an act of self will I put my cuffed wrist behind my back and bring my free right hand round to meet it.

Slipping my right wrist into the open cuff, the fingers of my left hand twist around to close it, then through the simple expedient of rolling on my back on the bed, use my body weight to close it tighter to complete the restraint that I feel to be rightfully mine.

That I have no key also feels right. I want no keys. I have done this many times before, to fulfill my private fantasies, but then a key had to be within reach. That was the frustrating part. I hated being able to free myself. Keys must belong to Fitz now; I need that sensation of vulnerability and his power over me. I am my own gift to him, bound to him; only he may release me.

****

I stand, give a light tug on my restraints to test their tightness and take short hobbled steps back to the mirror. Much better. I find it difficult to believe how right it looks, to be bound in this way. Fitz has told me I am beautiful. Naked like this, mouth distended by a tight ball and my hands secured behind my back I remember his words: that until I see myself as beautiful, no one else will. I see the truth in that, and have the confidence to be certain of it.

Turning proudly to look back at my shackled wrists and ankles I see what I am, someone I didn't know existed until Fitz created me. The change he has wrought in me is profound, that I can put myself in bondage for the pleasure of becoming a gift to another. Such physical restraint shows off my body to perfection, arms pulled behind my back serve to thrust my breasts forward into a provocative sensuality I had been unaware of. Without self-consciousness I admire them, something unthinkable only a couple of days ago. Ringed nipples set them off to perfection, as does the slight soreness still on them from Fitz's biting torment. That too is a residual part of him. Moving sensually around the room, I try to absorb all that is there. Such a room conjures limitless possibilities of a slave being available to her master. I move to the open window and brushing the curtain aside with my shoulder, I find that it leads onto a small balcony.

Taking time to admire the view, I make no attempt to hide myself as the movements of the warm morning air allow the curtains to caress my body. The well kept private grounds unfold towards the Thames fifty yards away, and somehow reflect my serenity at being held in bondage. Being bound, gagged, naked and on view, should they care to look, to the occasional pleasure cruiser passing on the river only adds to my bold self assurance.

My predicament would certainly be obvious to anyone using binoculars but I do not want to hide what I am, because of the pride in being myself. Were I able to, I would scream that I am owned now and in my natural element; I have no desire to be other than what I have become. There is a delight in the confidence that my self imposed captivity brings, and the undeniable heat that is beginning to re-ignite the increasingly moist desire for my new found love.

I have put myself into a position where I can neither ask for what I want nor prevent my lover from doing what he wants. With my wrists cuffed behind my back, I cannot pleasure myself; a frustration that serves to accentuate my thoughts of loving to come. I could lie across the bed and gyrate myself to a climax as I have done in the past, or even just think myself to orgasm, but denial carries its own masochistic pleasure now that that is in Fitz's gift. Self pleasure is no longer an option, my time with Madame Cory has taken that away. But I cannot deny my growing need, and know that I must either wait here for Fitz's return or go and find him and beg for release in whatever way he might see fit to grant it.

Taking tiny steps across the bedroom to reach the heavy oak door, I wince as steel bites into my wrists as I twist my hands behind my back to grasp the iron door handle. Luckily Fitz has not locked me in.

The hinges creak as I open it, allowing me out onto the galleried landing. The house is silent except for the soft sound of my bare feet padding on the polished oak floor and the chains providing their own tinkling accompaniment to my movements as they give a biting pull between my ankles at every step. Only days ago, being naked and helpless in a strange house would have scared me witless, but here I know I am under Fitz's care, he will not let me come to harm. There is an excited pride in such instinctive awareness of that protection as I carefully make my way downstairs, step by careful step.

Chapter Twenty

Freedom

Ordinary life does not interest me. I seek only the high moments.
I am in accord with the surrealists, searching for the marvelous.

~ *Anais Nin*

I open the door softly, twisting my wrists behind my back as I did on the bedroom door. Fitz is working quietly at his desk with his back to me. If he hears me he gives no indication of it, so I walk softly across the room to him, and sink to my knees at his side.

I let my head rest on his thigh as a gesture of quiet supplication. As he continues with his work, he says nothing, an exchange of words would break the spell of such a sublime moment. Right now I want to be like this, sensing myself as his possession, an object that I hope he will cherish. I do not want more just yet, despite my need of him. Being ignored is another way of reinforcing what I am. I cannot speak to him or reach for him. I must await his pleasure.

We allow ourselves such sweet closeness for minutes, until there is a soft stroke of my hair, it is light yet it sends tremors coursing through my already tensed body.

He smiles down at my bowed head. 'You came to find me?'

Without looking up, I can only nod, excited by the depth of such abject submission to him.

He strokes my cheek gently to feel the tightness of the strap that holds my gag in place, then lifts my face up to look at him. We exchange looks that express a wonderful depth of feeling. He runs a finger around my distended lips and smiles at my wrists cuffed behind my back. My posture tells him I am content to be there, a silent expression of the power of need that makes a woman present herself, unbidden, in this fashion. He returns to his paperwork and occasionally lets a hand stray to me as a reassurance that I am where I belong. That I am his property.

Every touch increases my ache for him, but there is also a deep sense of contentment in being close, silent and submissive as part of his private world. It is different to the demands of physical sex, but no less exciting. No words are necessary, for the moment the lightest touch of a hand has become just as arousing as the deepest thrust into my body. I close my eyes in the bliss of being where I am, and let time drift silently between us for as long as he will allow me to kneel at his feet.

****

I feel fingers opening the buckle at the back of my neck, and the ball being eased from between distended lips. He lifts my chin so that our eyes can meet.

'You have presented yourself to me so exquisitely Anna.' He says.

His words of approval send a new frisson of excitement through me. I want to melt against him.

I lick my lips before speaking. 'I'm glad you approve sir, I wanted to show you how I felt, how beautiful you have made me.'

'I'm glad you know it now.'

'Sir, now that you own me, being without some form of restraint feels unnatural, so I took the liberty of looking for some means to present myself as the slave I am; I wanted my mouth gagged, and these cuffs were in a bedside drawer.'

I look up imploringly, my eyes wanting to show him my need. 'Forgive me sir for restraining myself, and for my wild needs on your body in bed. The way you made love to me created such a storm of wanting, I was unable to hold back, the orgasms just wouldn't stop.' I lean forward in supplication: 'It is all so new to me, I didn't know sex could be like that, I couldn't prevent the orgasms, I kept coming until there was nothing but blackness.'

Fitz softly strokes my hair in reassurance.

'Yes I know, your body just shut itself down for a while.'

'You know about what happened to me, while we were making love just now?'

'Of course, you can only take so many orgasms, think of it as your safety valve.'

'I mean, you actually knew what was happening in my head?'

247

Fitz chuckles softly: 'Certainly; orgasmically speaking, women function differently to men. A woman can come fifty, even a hundred times for every once a man can, most unfair, but there it is. But it also means you black out afterwards because your body just can't take any more.'

'That's really weird, I've never met a man who was aware of anything like that, still less able to concern himself with it.'

'Well I know about stuff like that, and it's part of what makes you so adorable.'

'I still don't understand how you made me like that sir.'

'I didn't, I just released what was already in you, and freed the real woman that you are.'

'Thank you again for looking after me sir.'

He points across to a corner of the room where a thin whippy cane is lying a across a chair. His command to 'fetch' drives home what I am. I shuffle across the room on my knees, and pick up the cane in my teeth and return with it. Fitz has returned to his paperwork; I have no choice but to sit at his feet like the horny bitch I am, the cane held in my mouth, waiting obediently for his attentions when he decides to take it from me. There is a flooding wetness growing as I kneel in submission; yet there is a joy in such abject humiliation.

He ignores my eagerness, making me wait on him, driving home the point that I belong to him, knowing that when he takes the cane from me I am going to be thrashed with it. The waiting serves only to heighten my need to feel the pain I know he is going to inflict on me. He finally accepts the cane I am offering him when my whimpering tells him what he has reduced me to.

'Now you may kiss my feet.'

On the instant, my head goes down, my tongue slowly exploring his bare feet with a needy desperation to please. The intensity of it is exquisite, and such a posture raises my naked bottom irresistibly until I feel the tip of the long thin cane being drawn across my flesh, depressing a line of temptation for him. My ordeal at Madame Cory's has taught me to want the pain it brings.

'You know the routine.'

I lift my cuffed hands out of the way and whisper softly: 'One.'

The cutting impact marks me fully with a red welt as my backside bounces under his cane. The pain it causes reflects itself in the repressed sound that comes from my throat and gags itself within my busy mouth. The frantic licking of my submissive tongue becomes more intense.

'Thank you sir.'

"It pleases me that lessons learned at Madame Cory's have not been forgotten.'

'No those lessons will never be forgotten sir..... Two.'

Again his cane cuts through the air and makes its mark across my offered flesh as he hears my intake of breath with the pain of it.

'Thank you sir.'

The downward sound of the cane reveals my excitement at being beaten in this way, presenting myself to receive his punishment, knowing that I cannot get enough of anything he chooses to give me.

I neither want nor expect any mercy in the cuts administered as his caning follows my counting to the full six he intends me to have. Then as if to drive him further, I add one to make it seven, to reinforce the message that I am insatiable and intend to tax his dominance to the limit. My breathing is short and labored under the pain, yet I do not break in my task of using my tongue on his feet as each lash falls across my offered backside; if anything it makes me more desperate to please.

For demanding one extra I get five more cuts, in rapid succession, rounding the total to a dozen.

He leans down and grasps my hair, pulling my head up. 'You know why you were beaten?'

'I was thrashed for putting myself in bondage without your permission, and for using your body so blatantly last night and this morning.'

'Yes, but more than that my pretty slut, I gave you five extra to make you aware that you will not control what I do to you.'

'I'm sorry sir, asking for one extra was cheeky of me, but I can't describe what it does to me, being thrashed by you.

'And the next time?'

'I will try not to do it again, but it felt divine sir, and last night I was desperate to have you inside me. Being punished for being unable to resist it is a price that will perhaps have to be paid.'

'I think your bottom is going to be permanently striped.'

'It feels as though it might sir, I will be honoured to receive your attentions, in whatever form they come. I want you to control me, even though I know I can be difficult.'

He catches my knowing smile as I give my attention back to foot worship. As with all submissives, a dominant can only feed her desires no matter what he does.

'You are a painslut.'

I reply without breaking off from foot worship: 'Yes sir, I am most definitely a painslut.'

He lets me continue with my tongue on his feet, then drags my head up again. 'And all our activity has left me hungry, you must be starving too.'

'Yes sir, I am really hungry from so much exertion.'

'There's a well stocked kitchen, we must have breakfast.'

'I would like that sir, to serve you in every way, not just sex.'

'Very well, in the closet over there you will find a selection of outfits in various sizes, choose something appropriate; I will be down the hallway in the kitchen getting the breakfast things ready, I can't expect you to know where everything is on your first day here.'

'Yes sir, thank you.' I stand and turn around, laughing and wiggling my cuffed hands and feet at Fitz.

'Oh yes, your cuffs. Difficult with those on, lucky for you I have a master key for all restraints.'

'When I put them on I sort of hoped you would have sir, otherwise we really would have a problem.'

I feel him busy behind my back releasing my shackles.

'Now go and get changed, I'm starving.'

'Me too sir, I won't be long.'

I walk across to the doorway Fitz has pointed out, while he disappears towards the kitchen. Calling it a closet is something of an understatement. Uncle Leo obviously kept himself well prepared for anyone and everyone who came here. Luckily it's all stuff that never dates, with a range of outfits very expensively tailored in leather, PVC, silks, all in a variety of sizes and styles and colours to suite every taste. I riffle through the racks, thinking it's more like a small department store than the closet the Fitz had described.

After making a mental note of some of the other pervy options here for the future, and knowing Fitz will be waiting for me, I go for a very short black silk kimono style wrap with red trim and a red silk tie belt; I pull it apart very slightly to make sure it stays slightly open above and below the waist. Black seamed stockings and suspender belt and a delicious pair of five inch heels complete the ensemble. I figure most of what I wear won't stay on very long anyway, not this morning.

I look in the mirror and admire myself. What a slut. I think Fitz will be pleased.

I wander back into the hall, and open a few doors before finding Fitz, already cooking breakfast.

'Is this what sir had in mind? It seems your uncle kept a comprehensive wardrobe for girls who came here; this sort of outfit never dates.'

I stand in the kitchen doorway and he makes a circling motion with his hand, and I twirl for his inspection.

'You have chosen well Anna, I am pleased with you.'

With deliberate provocation I take the hem of my silk kimono in my fingertips and make a low curtsey. Then I walk to him and kiss him on the mouth, and feel his hardening response to me.

'You are very desirable, yet we must eat or collapse because of malnutrition brought on by too much sex.'

I giggle, knowing the mischief I can set off. 'As Sir orders.' I love the undiminished desire that I see in his eyes, and have to stop myself reacting to it.

'Turn around.'

I obey, and he unties the silk belt of my kimono and ties my hands behind my back with it. While no less tight than other ways that Fitz has tied me, it carries a gentle softness. It is simple, effective, a different way of being bound.

'Oh sir.' I say in mock concern. 'I thought I was going to have breakfast too.' Without the belt, my kimono falls open, and Fitz tries to scold me while looking at me with undisguised appreciation and desire.

'You are, but I think I need to keep you out of mischief while I actually cook it. Now go and kneel by the table and behave yourself.'

'Yes sir.' I walk across the kitchen and kneel submissively as instructed, watching Fitz prepare our food. Bacon eggs, sausage, tomatoes, mushrooms, all on one big plate which he brings to the table, together with orange juice in two glasses, one with a straw. He sits down and I can only look up at him eagerly from my kneeling posture. It is a delicious reinforcement of my status.

He begins to eat, then offers me a morsel which I take from him. Bound, naked, kneeling and being fed this way adds yet another dimension to his control of me. He offers me the glass of orange juice with the straw and I suck my drink gratefully. I find myself wanting every aspect of my life to be under this level of control. Eating with Fitz, like this, somehow seems so natural and satisfying. I revel in being fed like a pet as we continue to eat.

Our meal finished he orders me to stand, and he unties my hands, handing me the red silk belt.

'Now cover yourself up girl, we have to talk about that which concerns us here, and everything to do with this place. Which is what I began to discuss last night, before I was interrupted.'

He pulls me onto his knee and I settle warmly against him.

'Last night was just so special sir, I couldn't help myself.'

'I shall have to put more stringent controls on you.'

I respond with a knowing smile. 'I want them sir, being here makes me feel free for the first time in my life, your controls can only add to that.'

I have fallen into the mindset of the true submissive, where an infinity of torment can only bring an infinity of ecstasy, we are already becoming the prisoner of each other's needs.

'As I was trying to tell you, when I opened the safe, some of the papers in there referred to an exclusive network of establishments dedicated to

BDSM all over the world. In the past uncle Leo's trips abroad on business had always included visits to places like this, mainly in the USA and Europe and the Far East. He always reciprocated their hospitality here of course.'

'It hadn't occurred to me that there could be a world wide group dedicated to this kind of thing sir.'

'It is a very exclusive network of people with the means to indulge themselves discreetly in whatever pleasures they are inclined to. Uncle Leo's name is sufficient to introduce me to them should I so wish.'

'And Madame Cory's was one of the places on his list?'

'Yes. She was closest to here and knew all about this house but had respected uncle Leo's wish for a reclusive retirement. She and Jon came over with a couple of their servant girls to check everything; she was very kind and helped me sort myself out and decide what to do with it all. We agreed that everything here is too beautiful to be kept as some kind of museum, or broken up and sold off; it demands to be used.'

'Surely a place of this size needed servants too sir, just as Madame Cory's does?'

'Certainly it did, and on the same basis. But a place like this, with all that it has on offer, will never have staff shortage problems. It is one of the more interesting quirks of the female mind: the need to be kept under subjection, provided it is done with grace, understanding and good taste, and without crude brutality.'

'So women came here voluntarily?'

'Eagerly would be more accurate.'

'Like me?'

'Very much so; once establishments of this kind become known, and there are no issues with safety, then they become a kind of refuge. It is a huge boost to a woman's self esteem, to be used in creative ways such as uncle Leo could offer.'

'Yes sir, I have learned that already.'

'Of course, just like Madame Cory, uncle Leo was a sadist of the highest refinement, but anyone who came here knew they were 100% safe, which was more important than anything else. Women came and went, dropping into role, then getting back to reality when they felt ready. There was never any coercion involved.'

'One of the other girls kidnapped at Madame Cory's said it was therapeutic.'

'Women seem to find it so, when all the niceties are observed. And the cruelties too of course.'

I laugh at the concept. 'So when I said I wanted to be kidnapped, it fitted neatly into what was happening in your life here?'

'Yes that was an amazing coincidence; Madame Cory had already told me about her little abduction venture, I immediately saw it as a way of including you in all this, to find out if you really shared my own inclinations and it wasn't merely a passing phase that would ultimately scare you or just fizzle out.'

'Yes sir I can understand that and very much want to be part of it now.'

'Do you understand now why I had to remain in the background?'

'Of course sir, I had to come into all this because I needed to.'

'It has to be real and inside your head, not forced on you. I didn't want you doing all this just to please me. I want you to be my submissive, and to enjoy all this with me but your desires must match my own, or even fractionally exceed them.'

'Exceed them sir?'

'Maybe difficult to understand, but no matter what I'm doing to you, it has to be desired by you.'

'I rather thought I'd demonstrated that part sir.'

'You did, but my meaning goes deeper than that.'

'I just want to be yours sir.'

'Then you must understand how uncle Leo's relationship will affect us.'

'How can that be sir?'

'Well, we've agreed that you can only be here because you need to be, but your desire for it must always stay fresh and strong. Being uncle Leo's slave was a lifetime commitment on her part, and he was similarly devoted to her.'

'But sir, I have already....'

He raises a hand to cut me short, and I stop talking.

'No, listen to what I have to say on this, it is very important to me, and ultimately to you.'

'Very well sir.'

'Right now, we have an intensity of passion and need, and seem to match one another's desires perfectly.'

'We do sir.'

I snuggle in closer, and he finds it difficult to concentrate.

'Now we've found each other in this way, I want it to be for always; but whether we like it or not, real life has a nasty habit of getting in the way, this isn't romantic fiction.'

'Sir?' I look at him quizzically.

'I want you to move in here, with me. But it has to be a decision taken by you without my persuasion. I really want you to think about what it would mean, being here.'

'You mean I would become your submissive, twenty four seven?'

'That would be the ultimate intention, but only in the sense that you would want that; no dominant can hold a submissive who does not wish it so. As I told you last night, a submissive must decide to be owned; you have the ultimate freedom to walk away should you so choose.'

'But sir, I have my career to think of, my personal future. You said yourself that real life can get in the way of what we both want.'

'I've already thought of that Anna; as you know, I've developed a fair sized civil engineering company, but frankly I'm getting tired of the business because I'm just bogged down with all the hassle of running it.'

'But you built it into the international business it is now sir.'

'Yes I know that, but the time has come for new ideas in the company, I don't want to spend the rest of my life wading through the mud on building sites, then having to deal with all the red tape associated with keeping several thousand people employed. And now there's all this to cope with too.'

'How does that affect us sir?'

'I'm coming to that. Now that I have this inheritance, I intend to make my construction business a workers co-operative, turn it over to my employees and let them run it for their own benefit. Several of my staff can run the company as well as I can, and I really don't need any more money. Doing that frees me to get back to what I really enjoy doing.'

'If that is what you think will work best for you sir.'

'It will. My intention is to remain as a freelance consultant to the firm, I will still be involved but essentially working to develop new projects. It will obviously be necessary to travel abroad to promote them, and that's where you come in Anna.

'Sir?'

'Well, I can't do it without a p.a., and you have all the social and business skills to help me in that respect, and in any case I don't think we would want to be apart for long periods.'

'You are offering me a job sir?'

'In a sense yes, I want us to be together, but at the same time I want you to feel independently secure in yourself, you have to know that I need you for much more than kinky sex.'

'Would we be trying to repeat the history of this place sir, your uncle and his slave?'

'No not exactly, though there are bound to be some similarities; you would be living here, attending to my needs, and I to yours of course. It's a two way thing but I wouldn't try to relive the past, that's never a sensible idea.'

'It would be a big step sir, moving into all this full time.'

'Don't worry about it Anna, take your time, there's no pressure on you for a decision. Let's enjoy this time together, and everything here. I want to show you around to see the collection of stuff that uncle Leo built up over the years.'

'I would love a tour of all the rooms here sir, to see everything.'

'I want you to see them all, particularly the cellars, which have all been converted to dungeons and torture chambers.'

'Now sir?'

I cannot repress my eagerness.

'In the drawer over there you will find a collar and leash, get it and put it on.'

I jump to my feet eagerly to obey, and he watches me take out the collar to fit it around my neck. I walk back across the room and hand him the leash.

'Thank you Anna, a collar and leash completes your ensemble.'

'Thank you sir, I like it.'

'Do you know why I told you to put it on yourself, and I didn't do it?'

'Not exactly sir.'

'Because if this relationship progresses to where we both want it to, then I will ask you if you wish to accept my collar in a formal sense, if you do then I will put one around your neck permanently as part of a collaring ceremony. But that is for another time, not now.'

'The sensation of this collar is exciting sir, but you mean the collar like your uncle's submissive wore, the kind that can't be taken off?'

'Yes, a commitment collar; I will show you.'

Fitz opens a drawer and takes out a small flat box, beautifully made in polished mahogany. On the lid is a gold nameplate, engraved with the initials JF. He takes a tiny key, inserts it into a lock and opens it. Inside is a circlet finely wrought with strands of gold interwoven to suggest the pattern of a rope.

'The gold rope is woven as it is to disguise a core of hardened steel.' Says Fitz. 'it is both beautiful and practical.' The size and curved contour of it gives a clear intention that it should fit around a neck. It is laid in a cushion of soft blue velvet and has the look of a tiara, but with a much deeper meaning. There is a smaller ring also wrought in gold attached to it at the front with a small clasp, holding a gold nameplate fashioned in the same style as on the box lid, and having the same engraved letters on it. I recognize it as a nametag. The initials are clearly not intended to be those of the wearer, but of the owner. At the opposite side, the circlet lies open but with its ends close together.

Laid in the centre of the circlet, is a small gold padlock, with two keys. Each of the keys is threaded onto a long gold chain. The intention of that is not immediately clear to me but no doubt Fitz will explain that in due course. The gold on blue velvet suggests its own invitation, and I touch it tentatively, knowing that wearing of such a collar carrying Fitz's initials would be a sublime statement and acceptance of his ownership. With that around my neck I would be unequivocally his. There is an ache in me that says how much I want that.

'Should you so decide that you wish to become my property, this is the collar I shall ask you to accept from me, not the leather one you have just put upon yourself.'

Fitz picks the gold collar and hands it to me, so that I can hold it and absorb its intent. He shows me the open ends, and that there is no lock, only a male to female socket joint which he explains: 'When the collar is put around the neck, one end is pushed into the other and a little spring inside releases a tiny steel catch. Once closed, it cannot be opened and the collar forms an unbroken ring around the neck of whoever wears it.'

It becomes impossible to speak immediately, lost as I am in the thought of it around my neck, knowing that it will be Fitz's prerogative to place it there. 'It is just so lovely sir.'

'And be aware that you will be expected to wear it openly. You will not have the option of being my secret submissive. The design is such that others in the lifestyle will recognize it, but otherwise it looks like a gold necklace.'

'I can think of nothing more beautiful to wear as a symbol of being owned sir.'

'I'm glad you like it, but bear in mind that when I ask you to accept this from me, I will ask only once. I will not ask a second time, because that would be persuasion. You will be free to refuse it, and I will think none the less of you if you do.'

Sensing that this is not for now, but some future time I caress it lightly with my fingers, imagining the weight of gold and steel around my neck, aware of it as the perfect symbol of submission. The pride in wearing such a beautiful object would be the ultimate expression of my being. When the time comes I will need no second thoughts about it.

'I'm sure I shall be ready for this collar when you decide the time is right sir, and I would want to wear it openly as a declaration of what I would be.'

Carefully replacing the commitment collar on its velvet cushion, I close the lid of the box and hand it back to Fitz.

'I do hope so Anna, because should you change your mind, getting it off would mean destroying it; I don't think either of us would like that.' The meaning of the collar causes a lurch of emotion and reassurance of a need of all this. Fitz gives a tug on the leash, and it brings us close. Our lips brush together lightly. 'Keep that need to be collared, your ongoing desire for it is vital.'

I know I will be eager for it, whenever Fitz should decide the time is right for such a commitment. 'That need will always be there now sir, that much is certain. Thank you so much for showing it to me. I wish only to serve you and be worthy to wear your commitment collar when the time comes.'

Chapter Twenty-one

Exploration

The body is both a pleasure palace and a torture chamber. -- Charles Levin

'Come girl, we must begin our tour of what is to be your future. Your collar is sufficient to hold you for the time being, I want your hands free to examine all that is here.'

'Thank you sir.'

Fitz tugs on my leash, and picks up the recently used thin whippy cane. I look at it and after a moment of apprehension, follow obediently, my heels making a pretty sound on the oak floor of the great hall.

'Now, where shall we start? Do you have any preference?

'I'm sure you will make the tour interesting sir.'

'Parts of this place are around eight hundred years old, I think the cellars date from that period.'

I smile up at him: 'Very suitable for certain activities sir?' Then I flinch slightly as the cane is lightly caressed across my backside.

'That kind of eagerness will get you in trouble.'

A cheeky suggestion of more need is irresistible: 'I do hope so sir.'

'Behave yourself.'

'I'll try sir, but there's so much to take in here.'

'There's the medieval torture suite, which interconnects with the inquisition chamber. There are some lovely dungeons below there too, where prisoners can be kept in chains until they are required. Or we can try a spot of Victorian discipline when I'm in a Dickensian mood. Or what about a Roman theme? You would look delicious on an auction block and I do a sadistic Roman emperor rather well.'

'You spoil me for choice sir.' I laugh.

'What about the Roaring Twenties suite? Or maybe we should try the wild west, although that might be better outside on a nice day. Out in the stable block there's several ponycarts and sets of harness, I shall definitely want to put you in harness soon, maybe bring some girls over from Madame Cory's for races.'

'It seems your uncle Leo was a man of varied tastes sir.'

'Oh he was.'

I think Fitz knows that there will be little to faze me in all this.

Various rooms are opened up in turn, and my eagerness increases as dust covers are pulled off, turning back to look at him with knowing anticipation as I discover the range of implements that are intended to make a woman suffer endlessly. Fitz flicks spotlights on in succession, and the torture palace comes to life as it is filled with light and the desires of a needy submissive. There is an atmosphere about the place that seems to echo the screams of previous occupants, and Fitz knows there will be more screams now that I want such torment to go on.

The medieval suite catches my attention: 'Sir, some old video tapes have been left in this cupboard.'

Fitz gestures that they should be brought to him. 'I would like to see them.' I bring them to him, and kneel. It is a posture that somehow feels natural with him. It is not affected, but something I choose to do. He accepts them from me. 'As they have been kept in here, I guess they can only have one theme. There are just initials on the labels, only uncle Leo would have known who or what they showed. I wonder if there's a tape player around here somewhere?'

'There must be sir.'

I search for the VCR, and pull dust sheets off various torture devices. A St Andrew's cross, and a perfect replica rack are revealed, together with an iron suspension cage which is held upright by a heavy chain that links to an overhead pulley system. It is tall and very narrow, steel glinting in the low lighting of the dungeon. I cannot resist a light almost apprehensive touch of it. 'Can a girl really be put into a cage like this sir? It seems very small and confining.'

'It's meant to be tight Anna, once inside, the door is forced shut against your body, any parts of you that don't fit into it protrude out through the bars; thus you become available for intimate attention by anyone who might feel so inclined. Or not, as the case may be.'

'You mean I would be unable to move no matter what was being done to me?'

'That would be the general idea.'

Fitz recognises the effect that thought has on me, aware that the cage has an irresistible allure as I touch it again with an undisguised need. The thought of steel pressing tight on my body generates a fresh excitement. There is a catch in my throat that reflects the emotion that has embraced the cage's significance. 'It would be hell in there sir.'

He watches as I continue to stroke the bars, knowing full well that it would be just the opposite. 'You can be made to suffer, while your suffering is enjoyed by everyone else. The door is in three sections, each can be opened independently for access to whoever is caged.' Tentatively swinging open each of its beckoning doors in turn, there is a light of challenge in my eyes that invites him to cage me, to subdue me, but always with the certainty that it could never be in an absolute sense.

I know now that he would always want that spark of resistance against the enforcement of his will. There is a moment of silence between us, we are both aware that I want to give myself, yet with the tight compression of cold unyielding steel between us to form a barrier that would serve to enhance our mutual desire. Then by unspoken consent it becomes a thought set aside for future pleasuring.

More drawers and cupboards are opened, to reveal rope and whips and chains to my squeals of delight at each new find. Now that the room is fully lit, rings in the floor, walls and ceiling make their purpose obvious as they are lifted and lightly tugged with an eye to future use. Full length mirrors have been strategically placed around the room to reflect any suffering. Opening another drawer and finding a soft leather hood, I hold it up and look at Fitz, draping it over open hands, knowing fingers suggestively caressing the large penis gag hanging loosely to the side of its mouth opening.

'There's a fabulous collection of toys here sir. Madame Cory's girls wore hoods like this.'

'Did they indeed; best put that away girl, you're giving me ideas.'

'Oh sir, surely not.' I put the hood down with a mischievous laugh. 'Here's the tape player sir.' An ornate cabinet is opened to reveal an old CRT television set and player, covered in dust. 'And there's a remote, and an unopened pack of batteries, it's likely the old ones in the remote will be dead by now sir.'

'Yes they will, change them.'

'Yes sir.'

I turn away from Fitz to fiddle with the new batteries and the remote, bending in such a way that I know will display myself to him, and the marks he put on me.

'I hope everything still works, that thing looks as though it came out of the ark. I have a feeling that some of these tapes might make interesting viewing though.'

'I am sure they will sir.'

'When uncle Leo had all this installed I guess it was state of the art.'

'Yes sir, years ago it would have been.'

Something big is set against one wall, opposite the screen. I drag the covers off, to reveal a large chair upholstered in red leather set on a red carpeted dais. It was obviously installed there to accommodate whoever was intended to control the activity in this room; it is also ideally placed to watch the TV. Recognizing its significance I fall to my knees beside it, head bowed. 'This is master's chair sir.' Though such immediate supplication needs no words. It is a place for me to be, and I want Fitz to be there to complete that wish.

Fitz walks to it and sits, and I reposition myself at his feet, picking the leash up and handing to him. 'Thank you Anna, your instinct in all this pleases me.'

I feel a shiver at his words of praise.

'Being on a leash feels so right sir, here with you like this. I love the sensation of you controlling me, the way we are right now makes me want to submit to you more deeply.'

'I want you to do that, so it's important that you are content.'

'I am sir; more than content now.'

'Pick a tape at random and see what's on there.'

'Yes sir.'

****

Fitz leans back and watches me get up and walk across to the tape player. I revel in the fact that he wants to look at me. I want him to, enjoying the confidence I have in flaunting myself, knowing now that eventually he will snap and punish me. Bending forward to find the mains socket, the hem of my

269

kimono lifts to show my desire for him. The screen flickers on and I return to sit at his feet, handing him the remote and my leash again. He gives a slight pull on it so that as my head rests softly against his thigh, my arms instinctively slip around his leg. After so many years of searching it is still hard to believe I am here, and I want to hold him in any way I can.

The video flickers into focus. 'This looks like the room we are in right now sir.'

'Yes it is, but the picture quality isn't very good.' Observes Fitz.

The camera is focused on the St Andrews cross, and a beautiful blonde is stretched out on it: naked and bound so that her skin is drum tight. Not merely wrists and ankles, but criss-crossed with thin cord that bites deeply and prevents the slightest movement. With a tanned body glistening with sweat, the torture is real and obvious, made more so by a prominent line of red weals that betray a recent flogging.

Every muscle is straining in taut outline under the ropes that hold her down. Although helpless, the camera reflects a direct look of defiance. And she is not alone. Three girls are in attendance, one is standing on either side while the third is kneeling between parted legs, with arms tightly lashed together behind her back. The girl on the cross has a ball gag strapped into her mouth that is intended to render her screams into near silence. But they are screams that will not be held in, the sounds that are forced from behind it are somehow made more powerful by the gag that tries to control them.

They are screams of desperate ecstasy, from a body that is thrusting itself against the cords that hold her because each of the standing girls has one of her nipples in her mouth, and a hand twisted into the hair of the kneeling girl who's head is being forced forward rhythmically, obviously being made to use her tongue on the blonde spread-eagled on the cross.

'The woman tied on the cross, that's Laura, uncle Leo's submissive.'

'Are you sure sir?'

'Certain of it, though in this movie she looks about twenty-five. But I still recognize her. Even at seventy, there is still the same elegant confident manner about her that is there in this movie. In a woman like that, supreme confidence is a lifestyle thing and can never be lost at any age.'

'So if this was shot maybe fifty years ago, the video must have been transferred from an old cine film; that accounts for the fuzzy quality and bad sound.'

'Yes of course.'

'Laura is reacting to all this just like I do sir, it's like seeing myself.'

There is an excitement in recognising a kindred spirit; even under torture she has an expression of pride in a lifetime of submission that makes her want to be seen, not as the elderly lady she is now, but as the young voracious beauty she used to be.

'And because all this stuff has been left here, she obviously wasn't concerned about you finding it sir.'

'No, she obviously intended it to be found.' Says Fitz.

****

The sound of each orgasm hitting Laura on the cross forces a rising crescendo of ecstatic agony from her throat as her tormentors bring her to repeated climax. It is a sweet suffering that is unendurable, yet her master's pleasure demands that it must be endured. No doubt it is Leo off camera, her defiant look is directed at him, and the orgasm itself has become the torture and he is making her endure it. The ropes that hold her down simultaneously add to her suffering and increase her pleasure. I want to be there on the cross, being tortured like she is with Fitz directing my suffering.

The picture quality on the old videotape system isn't great, but uncle Leo has to be admired for creating such a scene of raw sensuality.

'I shall update all this Anna, with the latest cameras, lighting and recording system. A sixty inch flat screen with surround sound at the very least.'

'That will be wonderful sir, this is so exciting to watch.'

'And you shall have a starring role.'

'Thank you sir, I would like that.'

My head is resting against his knee, watching the screen. But I cannot prevent my fingers tightening on his thigh, and my breathing shortening as I watch the on screen action getting more intense between the girls. I feel his hand softly stroking my hair before twisting his fingers in it and tugging on my leash to turn my head to look at him. 'Behave yourself girl, or you will be punished again.'

I look at him imploringly. 'Sir, it is so difficult, watching all this. It keeps me on a razor edge of climax all the time. This whole situation is driving me crazy, especially after my time at Madame's where Chloe used me. I get wet no matter how much I try to prevent it.'

'Then you must be taught to control yourself.'

'Yes sir.' I murmur submissively, in the full knowledge that whatever Fitz does to can only feed the need for more. He has lit the fires of my sexual furnace, and now they are all consuming. I cannot control myself, I belong to Fitz now, I am his to control and to do with as he pleases.

'Remove your kimono.'

'Yes sir.'

Fitz sits back and watches as I shrug it clear of my shoulders, folding it neatly over the back of a chair. I stand facing him wearing nothing except a black suspender belt, stockings and shoes.

'You may leave your stockings and shoes on.'

'Yes sir.'

'Now go and fetch that leather hood you were fondling earlier.'

'Yes sir.'

I bring it back to him obediently, and as I kneel Fitz leans forward and unbuckles my collar.

'Put it on.'

Opening the hood wide with both hands I look up at Fitz before slipping it over my head. Turning to one of the mirrors I tuck in my hair and smooth the soft leather over the contours of my face and down around my throat, then reach behind my head to methodically tighten the laces.

Fitz is looking at me, silently. I want him to take pleasure in seeing what I have become. I recognize the pleasure he takes in watching me put myself in bondage.

There are holes below my nose for breathing, and openings for my eyes and mouth. Each of those has press-studs at the sides to allow a gag to be inserted and fixed and a blindfold added when needed. Running fingers over it, I can feel that my facial contours have now been subverted into a sculpted shape of black leather. Looking at myself in the mirror, I recognize a different kind of beauty.

The time spent at Madame Cory's has not only taught me the anticipation of such things, it has brought an eager desire for all the ecstasy they can bring.

The cock gag and blindfold hang to one side, each fixed on a pair of press studs. Fitz makes a hand movement towards me, I know what he wants me to do: I flick my tongue provocatively around parted lips and then over the waiting gag. I give him a questioning look; he nods in approval as I hold the cock delicately in my fingers before easing it into my mouth with a slow deep thrust, pushing it in until its leather pad closes against the hood. With my mouth filled to his satisfaction, fingers find the little studs; I click them into place and I have silenced myself. In doing it my eyes have not left his, and now they flash him a dancing laughter in response to what he has made me do, an unflinching gaze that offers a muted challenge to create more torments.

Words are unnecessary; there is a muted space between us that demands to be filled. By taking the pleasure of having me gagged, he denies himself any other delights my mouth might bring. I sense that for the moment he does not want the contact of my eyes closed off, the interplay they allow is too beautiful to deny. Wordlessly they ask and beg of him to use me for his pleasure.

Chapter Twenty-two

Isolation

Go confidently in the direction of your dreams. Live the life you've imagined. --
Henry David Thoreau

While I sense that he derives a powerful eroticism in forcing me into subjection, there is an equal pleasure in having such a gift of awareness that I can put myself in bondage through need. He had punished me for that earlier, but at the same time I recognized his pleasure in it. I wanted his punishment of me, we both knew that. Perhaps uncle Leo had had some sort of premonition that his dungeon complex would one day come alive again to welcome a woman such as I seek to be.

Fitz points to a coil of rough hemp rope hanging on a wall hook. I fetch it obediently, then eagerly anticipate the next command by turning and placing my wrists together behind my back. The strength of his right arm cannot be resisted as he pulls me back against him. We stand under a soft light where falling shadows seem to accentuate every curve reflected in the full length mirror across the room. I see my image being drawn into his sublime bondage yet my head encased in black leather creates an almost surreal vision, of someone unknown.

Our eyes meet via the mirror.

'You need to feel my ropes.'

It is a statement of fact, not a question. I cannot speak, but my look in response tells of my aching need to be bound by him, to feel his cords on my waiting flesh. I know they are going to hurt me, but it is a hurt I cannot live without, not now.

There is a sharp intake of breath as Fitz slips a strong arm behind my elbows. My body submits to him as they are drawn together. Then outraged muscles reflex to try to overcome the sudden biting tension of the forced acceptance of the doubled loop of cord that he slips around them.

I can feel loop following doubled loop, the rope being carefully and precisely turned a dozen times, leaving no slack, each becoming tighter than the last. Then a cinching loop forced between my elbows so that the harsh restraint forms my bound arms into a living column of rope. I watch his concentration on placing each line of cord as if the symmetry of them has become as important as their sexual torment.

Knots are drawn tight as they close, my searching fingers brush lightly against the reflected arousal in him as my body moves back to meet his, welcoming the suffering that such restraint brings.

I can only watch in the mirror as the pull on my elbows thrusts my breasts forward, forcing me to accept that every tightening cord changes me into the woman I seek to become. The pull back is agony, it would be unendurable if I had not sought it from him. The muted sounds from behind my gag are not silent screams for release but for the torture to continue. My body pushes hard back against him as my wrists are securely tied with palms facing; the close scent of the leather mixes with the wet desire that his fingers reach around to find, bringing it to his own lips to taste my urgent need of him.

The gag in my mouth allows no more than a muted moan in response as I watch him draw the moistness around my mouth panel and under my nose to let me absorb the aroma of my own arousal. My thighs open wider in moist welcome, watching in the mirror as his fingers return to probe deeper into my flood of wanting.

Once within me, thighs close tight to keep them there, driving myself down to create more ecstatic intensity. He pauses, and our eyes meet in exchange of smiles as he allows me to appreciate the bound beauty that he has turned me into. I can only look at myself, almost in disbelief at what he has done to me.

My leather encased head forces itself back against his shoulder, gasping as he takes my body weight with one hand around my throat and the other between my legs. Bound hands reach back and invitingly caress a growing hardness with a boldness that stimulates my rising excitement.

Silenced within the leather hood, I cannot ask permission to come; instead I take it by gyrating on his fingers to make them give the explosion that I need, screams muted by biting down on the gag that fills my mouth and his choking hand around my neck. It is part of his tender sadism that he makes me watch my own climax in the mirror, driving home the reality of what I am.

We hang there in a delicious haze of mutual stimulation, each driving the other to fresh expressions of urgent need as I again force myself back so that my fingers can find his hard insistence. I cannot help but look at myself, hooded and bound, scarcely recognizing the woman Fitz has made me.

'Is there no stopping you, my beautiful one?'

Unable to speak, I shake my head and push back harder against him, my fingers closing tight around his hard need of me. Wanting only to have Fitz find new ways of using me, the sensation of need grows again as a doubled cord is carefully passed around and above my breasts causing them to become engorged as the circles of tightening rope close tightly, making them thrust out in anticipation of more attention.

The deep furrowing of my skin reflects that of my arms, as it is looped around again to form itself below them in a harsh torture of caressing that forces them forward in response to the knots being jerked tight behind my back.

On a body that is becoming a subtle web of rope they are lifted tightly outwards and reformed into erotic globes, cruelly yet beautifully outlined as more rope is laced over my shoulders. Fingers tenderly lift tight cord to find space where there should be none so that more can be looped through and tightened yet again. Seeing my cleavage being reshaped and lifted to separate two drum tight orbs of provocation, I know that I am silently offering them for yet more cruel attention.

I can only watch my reflection as hands softly explore my arousal again, to draw up yet more moist excitement to make teasing circles around each outthrust nipple. They too glisten with hard desire, their rings now wet and shining with an excess of wanting. Breasts engorged by circles of cruel rope are left moist by tracing fingers, and I see powerful hands give tightening squeezes on both nipples.

The pain that shoots through me forces gasps from behind my gag as soft kisses and gentle bites are placed on my neck to counterbalance it. The mirror lets me see Fitz's knowing smile over my left shoulder, while his fingernails rake white lines on reddening skin to find new ways to inflict subtle pain, as my bound hands come together to hold the focus of his need of me.

Sadistic cruelty competes with loving tenderness as Fitz weaves me into the magic of his corded embrace; every twist and pull and slow drawn knot serving to stimulate the need I have for more of it. There is a futile forcing of muscles outward against the biting cord that draws my elbows together, inflaming the reality of the bondage that has become my pattern of living fire; a reflection of a need that seeks the pain of rope burning into skin.

At each closing of a knot, Fitz feels the thrust of my body forcing itself against him in silent wanting of more, to tell him that ropes can never be tight enough. In the mirror his hands become almost disembodied, moving over me with a touch now so delicate that it overrides my suffering, pausing randomly to find fresh pleasure spots that I am unaware of. Every part of me awaits his stimulation as a line of lightest touch is drawn along every cord. The torment that it brings transmits the sensation of his hand through the rope to imprisoned flesh beneath it. I respond almost involuntarily, as if to test the need he has to give me what I want.

It is a wordless telling that the imprint of his rope belongs on my body, as the mark of my owner. I want the deep marks that I know the ropes are going to leave on me.

In the mirror, I now recognize the power that Fitz promised me as the gift of his bondage. My bonds are now part of him. I am free to be his because I choose to be.

Disengaging a little, he turns me to face him, to see the bold pride in my eyes at being bound so lovingly, the ecstasy that can only come from within. I respond with a tremor as fingers run behind my back to test each cutting rope.

He twists them for more tightened suffering; I wince, but I want him to know how much I want his pain. It is almost as if he is playing a stringed instrument, so finely tuned has he made me, awaiting the next sonata to be drawn from my finely tuned body.

Our eyes lock and I refuse to let him go; there is a power in me that draws him closer and closer until only the rope laced onto my body divides us. With breasts obscenely distorted by cord and crushed hard against him, an endless craving drives me on into whatever excess his mind can devise. He places a soft kiss on the leather pad that holds my gag, then brushes another across each of my eyes. The torture of it lies between the suffering and gentleness.

On the other side of the room there is a polished steel bar, about four feet long and two inches wide, held three feet off the ground by an upright support at each end. On one of the upright supports is a sliding switch with a fiendishly obvious function: in the middle of the bar is a large upward pointing perfectly moulded eight inch phallus. Underneath it is a low step stool.

The meaning of such an arrangement requires no words. Fitz grasps my shoulders and turns me to face it then points silently. I want to be taken by Fitz, but with him I must be obedient and ready for the unexpected.

I need no second bidding; immediately disengaging myself from him, I walk to the switch and twisting my bound hands behind my back, slide it up and down then turn to watch a corresponding reaction in the erect dildo. It does not move, instead there is a mechanism within it that gives a slow visible pulsation that moves from its base to tip.

Using only eyes to throw a mischievous grin at Fitz, I set the switch to maximum, so that the pulse moves rapidly up and down, then walk to the vibrator and bend my head to it in a kiss of supplication through the gag that keeps me silent. I step up onto the stool and stand with one leg either side of the bar, elegantly poised over the now throbbing upright cock. Again I want him to see my need, and holding his eyes with mine I very slowly let my body sink down.

Fitz watches as my wet desire offers no resistance to the acceptance of self violation. The pulsing continues, and I accept its insistent welcome. I have given myself to Fitz to use for as long as he pleases, knowing that it has been designed to offer sensual accommodation for many hours.

Once fully settled on the vibrator I kick the stool dismissively away; with feet that cannot reach the floor or the stool, and with arms tightly bound there is no choice but to stay impaled on the throbbing monstrosity until Fitz chooses my time of release. With eyes half closed in acceptance of this new form of penetration, it has become yet another demonstration of a need that is being constantly revealed. It is made willingly through anticipation of every desire my lover might have, and as an invitation to create yet more suffering.

Fitz watches me express this need for all he has to give, knowing now that no matter what he does, it can only increase my wanting. Disconnected bliss is exchanged for brief moments, I cannot speak and he finds words superfluous.

He moves to my side, the hands that had fought to protect me now appreciating every curve of my body with a caring softness. He strokes my body tenderly, lightly moving fingers to the point where I am being penetrated, then traces the length of my legs, splaying out first the right, then the left. He ties each ankle to a floor ring, and jerks tight until my body is held rigidly on the bar in an inverted Y, unable now even to gyrate myself on the invading phallus. It remains driven in, responding relentlessly to legs splayed apart with such obscene invitation.

As Fitz reaches up to stroke my face, my eyes draw him silently in until he can take no more and the leather eyepad invites closure, to shut me off entirely. I know that he is torturing himself by leaving me nothing but inner sensations and the caress of knowing hands.

'It is time my lovely Anna.' Clicking the press studs shut, there is suddenly nothing but a dark sensuality. Head tightly encased in black leather, now I can feel only fingers that use tantalising touch to drive the violation of my body against the cruel ropes. Mounting excitement is now the only way I have to respond to words that carry yet another promise of torments to come. But what promise? I know that Fitz uses words with measured care, they always have meaning even if that meaning is not immediately obvious. I scream silently from within: time for what? Another level of torture that will enforce more self abasement?

The future Fitz has planned is beyond knowing, but the need of it is all consuming.

****

I squirm under his hands as within my dark isolation I feel myself gently touched. Aware of a flooding need, I want that knowing caress, but instead it is withdrawn. With a position so rigidly enforced, and impaled as I am, I cannot thrust myself at him; I must wait upon whatever suffering he has in mind. The violating phallus is a sweet torture, but is no substitute for Fitz.

My inner thoughts keep repeating: no limits, no limits. Yet Fitz has the sadistic skill to take me so close what might be a limit, but never past it; he gives no orders, yet somehow there is a compulsion to obey commands that seem to come from within myself. It is I who must beg to be taken further than my mind knew was possible. His tongue flicks lightly over one nipple, then the other, drawing them to erect hardness as he pulls on my rings. My impaled body anticipates pain yet now there is none, only a flooding pleasure as his gift.

'To feel the intensity of your wanting is very beautiful Anna.' He whispers.

I feel something hard and thin drawn across my exposed breasts, while at the same time fingers tease me into renewed frenzy.

A tensed awareness recognizes the touch of a whip, but at the same time I sense that it is an invitation not an infliction. That is the essence of his cruelty: he forces me into a state of constant wanting, then denies me.

My stretched body begins to pulse under Fitz's fine control, breasts inflamed with that line of sensation, telling of the pain it can bring. It is masterly control, forcing my body forward as best I can to offer myself for torment. He could use the lash indiscriminately, but this way suffering will be made more exquisite. Unable to count the strokes or back away from them, my flooding excitement cannot deny an intensity of need.

His touch is light, fleeting, yet extracts desire from the very depths of my being. I am willing to pay for such pleasure, and in response to the whip that tantalizes my breasts, I try to offer them in supplication, knowing that pain will be his and his alone to inflict. Sensing that Fitz wants such eagerness, the gasping rhythm of my arousal moving in tune with his control means that it cannot be disguised. Forcing myself down on the violation that he has created, climax builds and explodes as it meets the flash of the whipstroke placed with sadistic precision across erect nipples at that exact moment.

The gag cannot suppress my screams at the twin torments of agony and ecstasy as they meld into a single instant of suffering. I know he is making short whipstrokes because his other hand does not stop its insistent pleasuring—he is mixing pain and pleasure in such a way that I can no longer distinguish the two. There is a demand for both. The blinding pain of every stroke of the whip delivers an orgasm of equal intensity.

He is training me to seek out the whip and trade its pain for pleasure.

Inwardly I repeat my mantra: no limits, no limits, no limits. Saying it over and over confirms the reason for all this, to be owned and dominated completely. Fitz is inflicting nothing, instead he is remaking me so that I am in control of myself, taking the pain he gives because I know only that will bring fulfillment. I barely subside before his touch forces me to rise to meet him again, knowing now that as I ride to the inevitable climax, his lash will explode only when willing flesh is offered.

I want both, for as long as Fitz chooses to give them. He is like a drug, where each hit brings with it the climax that fuels the craving for the next. The muted sound of my orgasm tunes itself perfectly to the sound of the whip as it leaves another line of suffering across exposed nipples.

Blind, mute and bound, held on the pulsating dildo that I had eagerly mounted; now wholly under his control, wanting only to be held like that into infinity. The fire of the whip and the rage of each orgasm are telling me of more to come: His hand brings me up to meet his lash again, to crash against it with a scream that cannot deny an ultimate pleasure, leaving no option but to welcome it.

Questions whirl in the dark isolation of my torment: If I have no limits, does he? So where will this possibly end? What kind of man is this, who can hold the endless edge of climax, forcing me to a peak, then denying that final plunge into a personal abyss until I accept the tender enforcement of his pain?

Again and again the offer is brought forward, each time met with the lash of exquisite flame in precisely the way I know he intends. Enough to elicit a muted scream, but never enough to prevent the desperate wanting of the next one. Breasts on fire, I do not want the flogging to stop, yet this utter subjection decrees that it must, because I sense that he is taking me beyond this.

With breasts on fire, and certain that they are covered in red weals, I become aware that the whipstrokes have ceased and fingers no longer drive me to arousal. Instead there comes a soft stroking against my hooded face, and a sensation of physical closeness. Muted words come through the all enclosing leather: 'Yes it is definitely time my love.'

Those words repeated again, and because my brain is such a tangle of emotion I neither know nor care what he intends to do. Only that a quiet subsidence is happening. The vibrator has obviously been powered down; it remains inside me but now on a subdued almost comforting slow pulsation.

I feel his care for me, something that transcends all this suffering as I sag forward in exhaustion, within the limits that my bonds will allow. I want him to hold me, but he does not.

Instead, knowing hands move across my body, this time infusing a gentle calm until I cease to quiver under his touch. Then there comes an awareness that all is silent, no hands, no whip, no sound except that of my own pounding heart and laboured breathing around the mouth filling gag and ropes that creak as they bite into straining muscles. After endless torment under Fitz's hand, it is a contrasting sense of unexpected peace and solitude.

Although still cruelly bound, this can only be a time of waiting while the pulsing phallus continues its work. It is relentless, a movement that denies any rest. Every rise to meet it results in ropes cutting deeper as muscles fight against them. I try to kick, but Fitz has tied my ankles too rigidly for that. Kicking serves only to drive myself down even harder. But of course I want it harder. Any movement causes suffering, but my penetration forces movement from a body that simultaneously fights against and demands this violation.

Yet nothing is what it seems here, am I being videoed again? Watched? Aware that such a posture presents the ultimate image of obscene availability, could Fitz be sitting quietly only feet away, saying and doing nothing, amused by the spectacle of such degradation, ready for another session of sexual depravity when the mood takes him? With no limits, he is free to do as he pleases. Leave me to suffer, maybe pass me on to others. Who knows? There must be acceptance of everything that such a mind can devise. With such implicit trust of him, there can only be a constant unknown. Left splayed open in such obscenity all choice has been removed until I am taken off this hellish device.

Imprisoned in solitary silence, there is now no way of measuring time. Any attempt to move invites ropes to tighten with a relentless cruelty, while the gag silences anything but the soft moans of supplication that I cannot suppress. My breathing comes in short gasps but such sadistic bondage contrives to force an eventual acceptance. To reach this point has meant a series of ordeals, and instinctively I know there are more to come. It is a time of waiting, but for what? I know only that every ordeal demands submission to all that Fitz has devised.

There is a drifting into a silent void where time and space and emotion fuse into a single entity, through which an imprisoned soul might lose itself in a warm serenity of being. I seem to have known only endless penetration, orgasms driving themselves into a single torment of timeless suffering, where I have known nothing other than a rage of consuming ecstasy. After such intense attentions from Fitz, this is a different form of torture that once again allows me to fall into subspace where bonds lose their biting cruelty and allow me to enjoy a sublime timelessness.

Chapter Twenty-three

Commitment

When you have bid your servant once adieu;
Nor dare I question with my jealous thought
Where you may be, or your affairs suppose,
William Shakespeare Sonnet 57

Returning from my private time in subspace, there is an awareness that my vibrator has been switched off. Now different fingers are touching; lighter, softer, and from both sides. Feminine fingers, untying ropes that have cut so deep that they have almost become part of my yielding body, allowing a reawakened blood supply to rush through constricted elbows and wrists to tingling fingers. No words, only an unthreatening sensation of nearness, taking care of me in a new way.

Is Fitz close by, silently commanding someone else to wreak havoc on already overwrought senses? Perhaps we had not been alone together in his mansion. These are certainly not Fitz's hands that untie my stretched legs and guide the stool to my feet below the bar. They steady me to stand up as I ease off the vibrator, so that I can be helped down to the floor.

The hood and gag are not removed, so no questions or protests are possible. Neither do my captors speak. Only firm yet gentle hands grasp each arm to act in steadying guidance towards whatever is to come next in this unbroken litany of torment.

In this silent darkness, trust in Fitz is stretched to its limit, but remains a certainty. There is now no way that it could be broken.

A sensation of rope tied around each wrist, then arms drawn out and upwards to each side and tightly bound outstretched. Is this the precursor to another flogging? It is the perfect position in which to receive one. But there is no sound of a whip slicing through the air to impact on my tensed body, or any words of explanation offered. Instead I feel my suspender belt being undone, stockings being rolled down and removed, and as my five inch heels are taken off, I cannot contain a moan as the upward tension on my overstretched arms takes my body weight.

My bare feet sink to the stone floor and I feel its chill, now there is only tense and naked vulnerability, hanging, bound in such a way as to invite every excess. An undeniable desire for that excess is confirmed by a hand that lightly teases the source of it, and draws out another shuddering reaction. Muted moans come from behind my gag, unbound legs twist and writhe on unseen fingers while stretched arms pull against ropes in an uncontrollable response.

Instead of pain there comes an unexpected sensation of a soft material falling across skin, hands busily draping it over my shoulders, allowing it to brush sensually down and around in a way that creates a new feeling, a different sensuality. Encased in unknowing darkness, there is a certainty that it is a garment, but for what purpose cannot be known. It has a silken lightness, barely there at all, flowing almost carelessly over breasts and thighs then down to ankles, falling gracefully to my feet before being gathered and adjusted into place by unseen hands. It is certainly too flimsy to hide nakedness, so it must be part of the continued display of what I am in this place.

Left only with the sense of touch, I can only guess at its purpose. I feel a cord looped around my waist to form a sash with the obvious intent of holding it together in some way; when tightened and knotted it leaves loose ends trailing provocatively between my thighs.

My wrists are released from suspending cords, but not rebound as I expected.

Instead there is a creak of a heavy door opening, and the sound of the high heels of my captors on the stone floor that chills my bare feet. My arms are held gently but firmly again but not in restraint, only to enforce direction. The walk is a long one, with twists and turns that pass through more doors. I am carefully taken down a flight of stone steps. To another dungeon awaiting me with yet more torments? It would be possible to resist, the hands that hold me still offer only sufficient insistence to guide, no more than that.

There is a strange, wordless rapport between myself and those who lead me; I become aware that if I hesitated, so would they. I am unbound, so have an unspoken freedom. It is all unknown now, a growing awareness that this is something altogether different, perhaps a destiny that can only be of my own choosing.

Fitz had said that it was time. Now there is only a questioning of the unknown ordeal to which I am being led.

The sound of another door opening, then perhaps another twenty paces, and a gentle but forceful downward pressure that is an obvious insistence to adopt a kneeling position. I am guided, not to sit back on my heels, but in an upright attentive posture, as if at prayer. My knees are not on a stone floor, but a thick fur, and I feel the soft folds of my garment falling gently around me.

Then controlling hands are released, there is no further restraint or any enforcement other than the leather hood that holds me in blindfolded silence; my hands are free, I could unlace my hood and remove my gag if I chose to. I do not. I sense that I must remain kneeling as an act of free will, an unsaid acceptance of what is to come. Throughout my ordeals, nothing has been forced upon me; which tells me that I not being forced now.

Nothing now but to await either the cruelty or tenderness of the next moment.

It could be either. Over the last couple of days my mind has been switched relentlessly from one to the other.

Fingers are at the panel that holds my gag in place. It is withdrawn slowly. I pass my tongue around dry lips. The laces at the back of my hood are being undone and I feel it being loosened and drawn up over my head.

It takes a few moments to get used to the light.

****

'Anna Kelhorn.' At the sound of my name I look up, recognising a familiar voice. It is Jon, standing in front of me, in formal black tie evening dress. Cory is standing to his left, and I recognize Chloe standing beside her even though she is unmasked. Both are dressed in flowing diaphanous full length white linen robes, which I recognize as similar to the one that was put upon me earlier. Chloe is holding a large burning candle with both hands, but does not acknowledge me. A growing awareness of my surroundings tells me that I am in a chapel of some kind, kneeling before an altar. The stonework is ancient, and it is lit only with flickering candles set in iron sconces on the walls; I realise it can only be the medieval chapel that Fitz had spoken of.

Without turning my head I sense that there are other people in the room behind me. Jon's voice jerks me back into focus: 'do you kneel here of your own free will?'

My mind races; the whirlwind of the last two days has taught me to accept what comes, to respond instinctively but not to be afraid. I am not restrained or under any duress, so even without knowing what might happen I can only answer truthfully: 'This girl kneels willingly sir.' Eyes cast down again, I become aware of someone standing close, to my left.

'Jason Fitzhearne, Anna Kelhorn kneels at your side, is it your wish that she so kneels there?'

My heart pounds and my stomach knots up as I recognise Fitz's's voice, although I have not looked up at him.

'It is my wish that she so kneels, if it is of her own volition.'

'Anna Kelhorn, do you so kneel?'

'This girl kneels willingly sir.' I reply again, risking a glance up at Fitz, who is also in evening dress and looking towards Jon impassively. There is a certainty now that I could not kneel beside anyone else, there is a glow in the growing awareness of why I have been brought to this place.

Jon gestures with his right hand, and Cory picks up a wooden box and unlocks it, and offers it to Jon on her open hands. Jon lifts the lid of the box, and I look up again and immediately recognize the mahogany box and the gold collar resting on its velvet cushion that Fitz had shown me earlier, with the padlock and key resting in the middle of it. Jon looks down at me.

'Anna Kelhorn, do you know what this is?'

'It is a commitment collar sir.'

'Are you aware of the meaning behind this collar?'

'This girl is fully aware of that meaning sir.'

'Knowing that, are you ready to accept it around your neck from Jason Fitzhearne?'

'This girl is ready to commit herself fully and to be collared by him sir.' I can barely remain in my kneeling posture, having been brought to collaring by Fitz who has given me so much already.

'And you know that this collar cannot be removed once it has been fixed, other than by destroying it?'

'This girl is fully aware of that sir, and would have no desire for it to be removed.'

'In accepting this collar, it becomes a symbol of your absolute submission, or to go to the next stage, your enslavement. You are free to choose acceptance of submission or full enslavement. With submission you retain your individual identity. By accepting enslavement you become property.'

'This girl freely chooses enslavement and desires to become property sir.'

'Jason Fitzhearne, do you accept supplicant Anna Kelhorn as your slave and property?'

'It will be my privilege to so accept her.'

'And do you Jason Fitzhearne vow to love honour and protect Anna Kelhorn, and to treat her with all due respect and care now that she has chosen to accept your collar and become your slave and property?'

'I, Jason Fitzhearne do so vow to love honour and protect Anna Kelhorn and promise that she shall receive all due respect and love and protection from me.'

'And do you Anna Kelhorn, in exercise of free will, having expressed your desire to become enslaved to and property of Jason Fitzhearne, vow to love honour and obey him in all things, by accepting his collar around your neck by witness of all here?'

I take my response from Fitz's words: 'This girl desires to become so enslaved and owned, and will love honour and obey him in all things.'

'All present here have witnessed and heard your vows. All may now speak in common assent to that. If there is dissent, that too must now be heard.' There is a pause and then a soft murmuring of assent from the unseen assembly ranged behind me. 'your vows have been witnessed by all present, do you understand that hereafter they may not be broken?'

'This girl understands Sir.'

'Then the collaring ceremony shall commence' Says Jon. He turns and offers the box to Cory, who takes the collar from its velvet cushion. She lifts it, obviously to show to all here, then turns to Chloe who offers the burning candle.

'Let the gold of this collar be further purified by flame.' Cory passes it three times through the flame of the candle held by Chloe. 'Anna Kelhorn will now bow her head in submission to he who is to become her owner.'

I dutifully bow my head as Chloe moves to my side, and feel her parting and lifting my hair. She gathers it and pins it up so that my neck is bare in readiness for the collar, then moves aside.

Fitz steps forward, I sense he is taking the collar from Cory, though with my eyes cast down I cannot see that. He returns to my side, and I become aware of the metal encircling my neck after he springs the open ends apart. He leaves it resting on my skin, not yet closed.

'Jason Fitzhearne, the collar rests on the neck of your supplicant, is it your wish that the collar is sealed around her neck?'

'It is my wish.' I hear Fitz say.

'Anna Kelhorn, the collar rests upon your neck, is it your wish that the collar is sealed upon you?'

Recognising the significance of what I have to say next I hesitate, then make my ultimate commitment:

'It is this girl's wish that the collar should be sealed sir.'

'Jason Fitzhearne, Anna Kelhorn has stated her wish to be sealed into your collar and thus your bondage, you may now close it around her neck.'

I feel Fitz's hands delay slightly as they caress my skin. Sensing his momentary hesitation at this fateful step, I reach up and touch both his hands, giving them the lightest inward pressure to confirm my wish as he takes hold of the collar more firmly. There is a shiver of ecstasy laced with a little fear as I feel it on my skin and hear the collar snick shut; there is a scary finality in knowing that it will never come off.

'Anna Kelhorn, you may now stand.' I get off my knees and face Cory and Jon. 'you will now part your legs.' I do as instructed, and Cory takes the gold padlock and keys out of the box and comes to me, and bends down. I sense her fingers parting the folds of my linen robe and teasing out my labia rings. I feel a tremor of excitement as the lock is threaded through them and snapped shut. Cory steps back a pace, and Jon hands the keys on their long gold chains to me.

'Anna Kelhorn, your collar is permanently locked and your person is now sealed. You have one final freedom; you may keep these keys, or give them to whoever you wish.'

Without hesitation I turn to Chloe, and after getting a nod of assent from Madame, I hang one key around her neck at which she mouths a silent 'thank you'. Then I turn to Fitz knowing that at last I have arrived at my life's destination. My eyes are wet with emotion and I can see that his are too as he looks at me as I hang the final key around his neck. I then kneel unbidden, take both his hands in mine, kiss them then look up and utter the word I know I can now say to him: 'Master.'

Epilogue

Avoid any Dom with a large ego. Do not mistake arrogance for confidence."
— *Red Phoenix, Socrates Inspires Cherry to Blossom*

Having read my story, I hope you enjoyed sharing the journey that brought me to the fulfillment of submission and being owned. The account of my adventures will not dovetail exactly into your way of thinking, because no two minds are alike. But you might take something from it.

It is a lifestyle that cannot suit everyone, though of course you may want to sample some parts that I have described. Neither is it for the foolhardy, as I openly admit I was until I found Fitz, or rather he found me.

You can get hurt, emotionally and physically; there are self professed dominants out there I wouldn't trust with a Barbie doll, let alone a full blooded female. I hope that my musings in this book will help to avoid people like that, and recognize the one who is right for you. If you are drawn to the lifestyle, then please be careful.

Doms are not mindreaders, they have to read signals, which can be misunderstood. As you become emotionally closer, the easier the signals will be to read. I don't have a safeword, because my Master knows what I want almost before I do. Remember safe sane and consensual, -always.

Despite appearances, and porn-fiction, all that happens must be what you want, because you are the one likely to get hurt more than you're asking for. Pain is for your sake first, his second, even though it's dressed up to look otherwise. Remember, as a submissive, you get to choose your dominant. As to finding a good dominant, (one who cares about you more than he does about himself) I'd say there's a dozen or more submissives out there for every one of those, no matter what popular opinion suggests to the contrary.

Coming clean about the nature of the relationship with my new man was something of a revelation, when good friends no longer believed my casual explanations about why I couldn't take my collar off. But now it's accepted as normal, and my radiance and happiness are obvious. I rather suspect there is a little envy there too.

These are my own experiences. They are not a definitive guide, other than that a master must be someone who is recognized as such by his submissive, and gives her the freedom to come to him without persuasion.

If he asks you to 'let' him do whatever, then the roles in your Dominant/submissive relationship have been reversed. Never a good idea. The submissive does not 'let' her Master do anything, neither does he 'ask'.

He takes, but only what is being freely offered. And head for the door, fast, if a man orders you to call him master and demands your immediate submission just because he says he's dominant. Finding out that no real dominant will do that was a painful lesson in what BDSM is not. When you meet your Master, he will not find it necessary to tell you he is, you will know. Trust me (and more importantly trust yourself) on that one. My Master rarely orders me to do anything, he has the skill to somehow plant ideas in my head that seem to be my own, so natural have they become to me. He has been my mentor in all this.

If on the other hand you are an aspiring dominant, do not attempt to persuade your submissive. Let her come to you. She will, if you can forget yourself and concentrate on making her feel safe and cared for. To me, being tied up lying next to my Master is the safest place in the world. You cannot be a dominant unless you can create that safe place in the submissive's head.

Much has been written on the BDSM lifestyle, and a great deal of criticism raised over it, and a lot of nonsense too. But it has to be a freely taken choice. It has not changed me, instead it has brought out the woman I was meant to be: submissive yes, but only to Him.

In all other respects I am now far more powerful and self confident, and I know He wants me that way. Avoid the so called 'master' who wants you cowering and docile and tells you it is submission; it is nothing of the kind. He is an abuser. Avoid the 'master' who chases you and tries to persuade, he is weak.

Now that I have found my true Master I accept no bullying or abuse from anyone. My floggings (and they are real) are not domestic violence, casual brutality or abuse; they are expressions of loving tenderness, though no outsider would see it that way. I am flogged because I need it, he does not exceed those needs, and I desire him to administer it. We meet on mutual ground. I carry his marks for days, and look at them with pride. I always seek out more because I am a masochist. Under no circumstances would he inflict punishment on me in any unwanted sense.

The risks I took on my journey were all my own, my choices. I was not forced or coerced into anything I did not desire. I am not a victim, or a doormat. There is a constant awareness that His restraint is absolute simply because I have the freedom to walk away from it and the certainty that He would not lift a finger to stop me.

His power lies in being the sole source of all the suffering and discipline I crave. I need it and we both know that; it lies unsaid as our mutual bond and is stronger than any rope or chain or written contract.

Of course, this book has been a somewhat lurid description of our pervy sex life, and though it is essentially factual, it has been time-condensed to help with the flow of narrative. Just like everybody else, our life together is mostly what passes for normal. Way more normal than kink I can assure you.

Popular fiction might have all concerned in a state of permanent arousal, as an interplay between

Master and slave; that really is just fiction and would eventually become very tiresome. Ordinary life has to be lived, and while I might carry a few weals on my backside while I'm pushing a supermarket trolley, usually that is our secret. My openly worn collar gets more than a second glance sometimes, as do red marks on my bare arms and wrists and ankles in summertime. Then there might be an exchange of looks and a knowing smile of recognition from a kindred spirit. They mean nothing to anyone else.

Fitz and I spend far more time talking, cuddling in front of the TV and putting the world to rights than He does torturing me into ecstatic oblivion. Or we might just make glorious vanilla love, for no better reason than spontaneity precludes setting up all the necessary paraphernalia of kink. Then again I might put myself in bondage for Him to 'find' as a nice surprise.

That guarantees explosive results. With Him every time is fresh and new, which of course is the way it should be with every Master. Oh, and in case you're wondering...yes He can make me orgasm a dozen times in a row.

I do hope you find the One you seek, or find new ways to love the One you have. Mine is spoken for.

My Poetry

I have written a book of one hundred and one erotic poems for kinky lovers, this is a small selection from it that I think you might enjoy.

It is available on Kindle and in paperback and might make the perfect gift for that special perv in your life.

Voices

Your control is now so absolute
that you no longer
need to touch your slave
only lie close by and
hold her eyes with yours
and rape her with the
softest words that take her mind
 to places she had not known
until she followed you.

Such powerful words
that herald all the tortures
yet to come and do things to
her mind that wakes the promise
of your wild imagination
and forces her to crave the
words of discipline that
bind so tight that she cannot
leave the embrace of them.

You my master storyteller
tell her of such things
that were beyond imagining
until her mind was taken there
through the labyrinth of words
you wove to show
all the images of torment that might
be devised to pleasure such as she
 into a state of absolute delirium

The Prisoner

Now tell me such a tale sir
while I am tightly bound
of captive maidens held sir
where evil knights abound

Then taken to be used sir
in their castles of renown
of tortured girls so sweet sir
but forced so to kneel down

Then tell me of the dungeons sir
within the castle drear
with chains upon the walls sir
where I might be held in fear

Then show me what it means sir
to be such a prisoner
where nothing else is real sir
but myself as a damsel fair

Then make me live the thought sir
that I might so lie within
and tortured all day long sir
for each imagined sin

Then secretly find pleasure sir
in all that's done to me
while my knightly captor sir
has me on my knees

Then eventually confess sir,
to all my worldly sins

while my sadistic lord sir
is making me more commit

Then tie me even tighter sir
with every knot aware
rough climax I now need sir
to think myself as there

Then make me taste your whip sir
to force me to submit
of the marks you leave sir
you care not a single whit

Then take me as you will sir
and drive me really wild
make sure I'm deeply kissed sir
where I feel it burn inside

Then hold me in your keep sir
and bend me to your will
and use my body more sir
for my needs are never still

Then stand me on the brink sir
and show me just the edge
of where I shall be pushed sir
with just the slightest nudge

Then tie me up and leave sir
to dream and squirm at will
of the ways I might be used sir
in your castle on the hill

Denial

Looking at you lying there
so exquisitely beautiful
in the ropes I have put
upon your squirming body
that you now use so knowingly
to seduce me into using you.

You know that conflict in myself
that wants to keep you bound
and torture you for hours on end
yet in doing so deny myself
the fulfillment of taking you as
you know I want to do.

You use your power so blatantly
inviting retribution for such
torment of me while knowing that
any punishment I mete out will
only serve to increase your pleasure
and my desire for you.

****

Held

What can you do
to me that you
have not already done?
yet still you find new ways
to force me to explore
the ecstatic labyrinths
of your torture garden

I scream inside
there can be no more
yet you make me want
much more till
I cry and beat my fists
against your breast
and sob against you in my passion

Are you forcing me to
demand more perhaps than you
can ultimately give?
I did not want this till you
took me as your own
my life was quiet till
you unleashed the beast within me

what are you, to do this
to turn me into a groveling
creature, who must bend the knee
through need of you

and what you are to me
knowing inside that such debasement
is my choice alone.
.

is this the meaning of my bondage
to have what only you can give
by turning pain into such sweet ecstasy
to become a drug I need more of
that holds me through my own will
with a driving urge that
will not let me be

Am I destined thus to grovel at your feet
for such crumbs of pleasure as you
choose to give me, as we swing
on life's eternal pendulum
begging your torture
in the certainty that
I can get it from no other?

The Tree

I am left
in quiet solitude
knowing nothing
of where I am
save my body pressed
against this tree
and the bite of rope

So that I know

I am his naked slut
here at his whim
bound tight with
rope cutting into
me as I squirm
in futile helplessness
bringing myself such pain

So that I know

I cannot scream
or plead for His release
however it should come
his gag has left me
silent and unknowing
with no sound of him who bound
me thus, naked, alone

So that I know

I cannot see

his blindfold gives me
only blackness and a fear
that it might not be Him
who finds me thus or
that hands that touch me
might not be His
.
So that I know

But I am his and
that I have given myself
to him to dispose
as he pleases.
forcing desires from
the very depth of me
with arousal I cannot hide

So that I know

I must listen for footsteps
softly treading on the
fallen leaves around me
and straining against his
ropes will drive me harder
to mark my skin
and make me wet with need

So that I know

I want the kiss of
his lips or his lash
to caress me, the hands of
the stranger who will come

and give me what I want
while I am here, so helpless
and so tightly bound

So that I know

After

you offer a different love
as you watch me dress
after we have spent
our night in endless loving

you see the marks
that are your gift
which I wear so proudly
now I know their meaning

you own me now
but my body is free
to be itself, delighting
in the pleasure that it brings you

you say nothing
but I can see that
certainty of a beauty
that I did not know was there until

you told me that
it was so and that I had
only to look to
see it for myself as

you smile softly
and I can see
that you want me
yet again to satisfy our infinite desire.

Heat

You offer me the whip,
To draw across my lips,
a hotly eager tongue
that makes the leather wet
with anticipation and desire
wanting it to trace the lines
of blazing pain across my flesh

There is such searing want
driven by Your touch
and incandescent need of You.
Your endless skill in finding me,
using the furnace of my body
to forge the links of chains
that hold me for eternity.

Feeling the burning cords
that hold me for Your lash
hurting in ways I want to hurt
a hurt that is my gift to You
A hurt that becomes a part
Of my heated love for You
that is now all of what we are.

You open up my mind
to make me beg for every
burning line across my body,
helpless as I wait for hot pain
that will reveal my warmly
flowing Juices to Your hand
as you explore my heated need.

I begin the count and listen as the whip
cuts through the air
to brand me with Your marks
that I will forever wear
and cause hot juices to flow
from me when I touch
Your fiery lines of torment.

My flowing juices invite your hand
To know my urgent need of more
Making me squirm and writhe
Letting the glowing embers of my pain
Subside a little to Your
Fingers as they take their
Soothing pleasure of me.

When offered to my lips
I drink my juices eagerly
wanting You to know
Your wet fingers are sucked
with the joy of where we are
a soft bite driving You
To flog me until I leave our now.

Hard and relentless
my body rises to meet all
the lashes that fall upon my count
Something I cannot contain within me
to have such searing pain
to bring me to a climax

such as you have made for me.

The cross that holds me bound
shudders as my being takes release
in ways that You have intended.
It is too much, pain and pleasure mixed into
this boiling cauldron of insanity
so that I know not where I am
or care.

Only that You are gently untying me
and carrying me to our loving bed
where I can be held by You
and lay my head across Your breast
to feel You stroke my hair
until I can return in gentle tenderness
From the place You sent me for this time of bliss.

Reflection

I love to stand and watch you tie me,
long mirror reflecting all you do
as ropes flick round your fingers
twisting, knotting, running through.
Making them bite hard in me
such cruelty I need from you.

You pass a cord across my shoulders
force it down around my breasts,
then take another just below them
till they are deliciously compressed
looking so obscenely sluttish now.
My blouse roughly jerked apart
and teasing out my nipples hard.

So another round my arms goes,
doubled now to give you grip,
relentless pulling till my gasping
tells you that my elbows touch.
Yet I do still want it harder
so I shall your torture know.

No one should take such cruel tying
but my wrists now feel your hold,
I feel more rope around them passing
more knots to seal my bondage fate.
You turn me round so I can see there
the pattern that your ropes create.

Still my mirror'd look is bolder
defying all the pain you give,

I feel a moist arousal starting
as your hands around me stray.
The wanton feeling of desiring
your instrument for creative play.

Strumming lightly, lifting, feeding
such cruelties this woman needs,
ropes so tight I'm barely breathing
speaking softly to take my mind.
There comes a frenzy of needing more
knowing just what I need from you.

Knowing well your bondage talents
not an inch of slack is felt,
rigid are the ropes around me
tightening with every move I make.
Slipping cords around my waist now
knotting hard so it bites deep.

Then to pass 'tween my legs and
jerking up to lift me off my feet,
gasping clenching of my teeth
as flooding welcomes such intrusion.
Trapping all my pleasure senses
soaking rope for inner fusion.

Why do I drive you thus my sadist
revealing all my wanton needs,
fighting 'gainst the cords that strain
to make me into all you're wanting.
Standing here to watch my pain
forcing down upon my knees now
then face down upon the floor.

Rope lashed tight around my ankles
lifting straining back and up
your pull is strict and hard now
so my feet and wrists together touch.
My body bent in graceful curve
tying tight and swiftly knotting
till I'm tensed at every nerve.

Now a ballgag you are forcing
my lips part in obedience wide,
deep and deeper in you shove it
strapping tight behind my neck.
The metal of the buckle rasping
forcing now my cheeks to bulging
till muted sound's my only speech.

Now I see myself completed
straining as each cord cuts in
seeing self in wanton squirming
helpless in reflecting glass.
A pretty victim tightly bound
there is nothing I can do here
but enjoy the sight of what I am.

Is it me that lies there gasping
or another tortured creature here,
someone else who is so aroused.
The ropes that cruelly crease my body
reflect in her why I'm so excited
as a climax starts to build
welling up from deep inside.

Then my wild explosion hits me
screaming out behind my gag,
the ropes that you have tightened
now close around me like a vice
and do not in the slightest give.
The woman in the glass exploding
She too an ecstasy is meeting.

I cannot now tell pain from pleasure
you have put me twixt the two,
my bonds are cutting me so deeply
is it she who is still suffering
while I lie here in pleasure spent?
Such things perhaps are not for telling
until you have been here too.

****